SILVER RAIN

RAIN

JAN RUTH

SILVER RAIN
Copyright Jan Ruth

SECOND EDITION 2016

Published by Celtic Connections.

My son; for his patience with all matters technical.

John Hudspith Editing Services;
for super sharp crossing and dotting.

JD Smith Design; for beautiful insides and outs.

FOR MUM AND DAD

Chapter One

Al

Why couldn't he have kept his big mouth shut?

His wife wanted nothing more to do with him.

It was too late now, of course. Late ... his first lucid thought of the day always began with the same mantra. The thought of being late sometimes had him leaping out of bed in a lather of anxiety. According to his watch, it was the twenty-seventh of October, and this fact alone felt significant. Or ... maybe it just *used* to be significant, and he'd been in trouble for forgetting it? Yes, it was more likely residual conditioning after living with a control freak for twenty-nine years.

Al slunk back under the quilt and searched his befuddled brain, but nothing came to mind. Through the window he could glimpse the top of the lime tree, and a vivid memory of his children hiding in its leafy canopy took him back to when they were still tiny and dependant. Happy, easy days. His life then had been simple; all he had to do was be the best daddy in the world and as far as Al was concerned, it was the best job in the world. He'd played the goon by day and the eccentric artist by night. The perfect life balance. The closest he got to it now was when his son allowed him to look after his grandchildren, but they came with a list of health and safety instructions, and usually ended with Al getting into trouble with his daughter-in-law; the head teacher from Hell. He was normally silver-tongued when it came to women, but this one was in a class of her own. She'd *still* not forgiven him for buying white rats as Christmas presents for the children. And anyway, how could he possibly have known that they'd *both* been pregnant?

Bloody women, but how he loved them! There were female forms on both sides of him. Jo was a lot younger, blonder, and with a keen sexual appetite, but she was asleep. Restless, Al turned over and met the soulful eyes of his dog, drank in the faint dogginess of her fur, the cold inquiring nose, and the stilton-like kiss of her breath. A heavy paw hit the middle of his chest. Even though she was betrothed to a male Weimaraner with exceptional presence, the dog was still jealous of his girlfriend. Al turned onto his back in what he hoped was a position of impartiality and thought about his wife, the ultimate drama queen. The woman he'd married thirty years ago and lost eleven and a half months ago, practically a year of drifting, of wondering why and what for.

Too late for a midlife crisis, so what the hell was it?

In the face of all his debts, his wife Helen had said it was just sheer complacency and blind, blind stupidity. Oh, and you could add some adolescent tendencies to the list too. Tom, their Oxford English son, a modern day Lord Fauntleroy, treated him like an overgrown child, and seemed permanently exasperated with him.

'Really, Father, if you haven't acquired any common sense now that you are fifty I think we all may as well forget it.'

'Good. That *is* a relief. Now I don't need to worry.'

Although he did worry. The marital home had been sold from under his nose and he'd done nothing about finding somewhere else to live, but Al had a desperate sort of plan. In truth, everything seemed a bit desperate; his financial status, his love life, and his family relationships, all on the brink of desperation – except maybe for his daughter, Maisie. Maisie mostly saw the funny side of everything, a girl after his own heart.

Sometimes funny was the only course of action left.

Throwing the quilt off his legs again, Al padded across the bare bedroom floor, catching his foot on an empty Moet bottle. Jo's phone was blinking and buzzing already with notifications and messages. Bloody Facebook and Twitter. It must be some kind of OCD, this need she had to constantly update her "status" to the world and be informed at all times of the day and night who had left some building in New York or who had just put their recycling out. Like trying to keep track of a million people to see if they were having a better time. He already knew the answer to that.

The shower obliged and for a moment Al caught sight of his reflection in the stainless steel screen. Not too bad, all things considered. *Fifty.* Christ, how did that happen? It seemed like the blink of an eye, all those years of hell-raising and child-raising, and then … this. The big relationship breakdown. According to *Helen*, he hadn't made an effort. According to *Helen*, life with him had been one long boy's adventure and she was *sick and tired* of his Morrissey records. Al had heard all of that before, of course, and it didn't usually rile him, but on that one fatal occasion, it had.

Why couldn't he have kept his big mouth shut?

Al soaped himself vigorously and turned his face to the jets of water. He needed to talk to Jo, persuade her to accompany him to his brother's place for the weekend. She'd turn her nose up, not only because she hated all that country stuff, but mostly because George and Fran lived in a rural location with a poor mobile signal and the slowest Internet connection known to man. Then he grinned to himself. Without her gadgets she'd have more time for him.

Later though, when the time came to explain his plans for the day, there was an argument of sorts. Not only did Jo like to plan her wardrobe before she went *anywhere,* she was puzzled at the reasoning behind his idea.

'It's silly. You told me you don't get on with your brother.'

'Time we sorted a few things out.'

'You can't just … turn up and decide to move in!'

Al chewed an unlit cigarette and continued to load the camper van with all his worldly possessions. Years of manually typed manuscripts took up the most space. Boxed up, it all looked a bit pathetic really. A few clothes, a truly massive record collection on vinyl, a book collection, and two mongrels who thought they were going on holiday.

Jo climbed in, shunted the door shut, folded her arms, and let out an audible sigh. 'You could move in with me, see how it goes?'

'We've been through this,' Al said, 'what about the dogs?'

He pulled off the drive and she continued to stare ahead.

'You'd get pissed off with me in less than a week,' he went on, then risked mimicking her voice, 'Al … switch the light off … it's gone three and I need to sleep.'

A little twist played around her mouth and she turned to look out of the passenger window. Al knew she was grinning and he almost smiled too. Then, through the rear-view mirror, he caught sight of the For Sale board in the front garden nailed to the lime tree, with a red *sold* slash across it. He wasn't normally sentimental, but this added more than it should have to his underlying anxiety.

Located in the backwaters of a Cheshire village, number thirty-two Chapel Gardens was an estate agent's dream. Substantial family home with original features. Four bedrooms, large mature gardens. Needs some attention. The latter observation was an understatement, really, but the agent seemed to think it was what everyone wanted; to "add value."

Al joined the traffic flow and drove to Jo's flat to collect a different set of co-ordinated clothes, and then headed out towards North Wales. An hour later, on a childish whim, he took an unnecessary diversion through Llandudno along the coastal road. Jo had no idea it was a diversion. October half-term meant that the seaside town was busy and progress was slow. They inched past The Orme View, a three-storey, sandstone-coloured guest house on the seafront, belonging to Helen's parents. It was more of a small hotel, really. There was a coach parked outside and lots of people on the pavement waiting for bags. He wondered what his wife was doing; preparing the lunches? Pathetic, really, the fact it still bothered him after all this time. He felt certain that Helen didn't wonder what *he* was doing at random times of the day, but then she could probably guess.

Helen had taken early retirement from the bank and Al imagined she was now sitting pretty with a reasonable pension and the promise of a small lump sum when the marital home was sold. In the meantime, she had a cosy part-time job at her parents' place, no doubt with free accommodation and meals. A fresh start, that's what she'd wanted, sixty miles away from him, and it seemed she had succeeded.

She wanted nothing more to do with him.

Their last argument had been especially nasty, of soul-destroying proportion. Somehow, he'd managed to blow his marriage to smithereens with a couple of sentences. Helen had tried for years to get the truth out of him about the strained relationship with his brother, and in any argument, this was always her trump card.

'So, tell me then! Come on, Al?' She'd folded her arms defiantly. 'Why does he hate you? What happened fifteen years ago?'

'He doesn't hate me, you're reading too much into it.'

'I don't think so; he *owes* you big time,' she'd said and pushed her face next to his. 'Fifty per cent of that *tip* of a house they live in and all that land, actually belongs to *you*! He's a bloody bank manager, can't you get him to pay you off?'

'No! They can't afford to do that, and anyway, it wouldn't be fair to Fran and Becca. What would happen to all the animals?'

'Goddammit Al, *the animals?* Are you for real? We could pay the mortgage off!'

'I know! But I can't just throw them out!'

She'd sneered, sighed, and chewed her bottom lip, eyes flashing.

'You're hiding something.'

'Rubbish,' he'd said quietly; too quietly and not nearly fast enough. He'd turned to go from the room then but she'd grabbed his arm, determined to push it to the limits of destruction.

'Leave it, Helen.'

'No.'

For less than three seconds she'd glared at his carefully guarded face, then suddenly made a lunge for his old guitar and slung it through the open bedroom window. Some of his Morrissey records followed, shimmering like black Frisbees down the garden.

That was the last straw, and she knew it.

Al had caught hold of her wrist and she'd stared at him with that mix of teary defiance. Helen had always been fiery and Al had always played the pacifist, the voice of reason, but this was deadly serious. A breakpoint. Fearing he had nothing much to lose by then, Al had hoped that telling her the bare bones of truth might just fall in his favour; after all, it had been some fourteen years ago.

It didn't.

To say it backfired was an understatement. Helen's mouth dropped open at first and then she'd gasped, shock radiating from every pore. Before Al could finish what he needed to say, she flew at him, grabbed his hair, and twisted what was left of it into a painful tourniquet.

'I *hate* you!'

The final nail was driven home.

It used to work between them but time had played a horrible trick on the perception of their relationship. Where once upon a time they had been a fun couple now it was more along the lines of 'Helen is a raving, menopausal lunatic and Al is … a waste of space?'

Al came to the end of the prom and stopped to let the dogs run on the delegated strip of sand by the cliffs. Jo wouldn't get out of the van but slid the window back and peered out. Her loose hair was a wild mess in seconds, sticking to her glossy lips.

'Al? It's freezing …'

'Look … over there, Punch and Judy. Shall we go and watch?' Al said, knowing what the answer would be. He rubbed his hands together and turned up the collar on his leather jacket. Despite the chill, the vast, open space was just what he needed. The beach was virtually colourless; a study of grey, highlighted with white where the sea foamed and a bank of sea-washed pebbles caught the dying light. Somehow, it seemed the more vibrant for its simplicity. Al felt reassured by his lift of spirits, it might even kick-start his flagging creativity.

Butter and Marge ran to explore the remains of a picnic, scattering the gulls into an angry, noisy vortex. On the promenade, crowds of pensioners and young families were huddled around the Punch and Judy tent, laughing and shouting. His eyes were drawn to the row of properties along the seafront curving in an elegant horseshoe, until he located the right facade. It had colourful window boxes and an old wrought iron bench outside with one of those fancy patio heaters and some fairy lights. That was new.

'Why are we here anyway? I thought your brother lived

in the country?'

'It's only twenty minutes away.'

'That means forty in this bus ... can we go, please?' When he didn't respond, she followed his line of sight and the penny dropped. 'Oh, I get it. This is where the hotel is, right? *She* lives here and you want to spy!'

She slammed the window shut and, unable to think of anything to say, Al called up the dogs and threw another cigarette to his lips. He never lit them these days, despite the temptation. He'd remembered the significant date, eventually. It was his 30th wedding anniversary. He was bound to feel a little nostalgic, wasn't he?

Al chose the scenic Great Orme toll road to give him time to chat to Jo before they arrived at his brother's place. It was bad enough that his wife and his brother hated him without his girlfriend of just two months wanting to knife him as well. The scenery was mostly rocks and sea, the narrow road clinging to the perimeter, but Jo stared ahead.

Al said, 'Come on, Jo, what's with the silent treatment? I was just being nosy, that's all.'

'You know what?' she said. 'Let's go to the hotel for dinner, then you can get it out of your system.'

He changed down to second gear and the camper groaned along the incline. Marge crawled into his lap and stared at him, clearly disturbed by the atmosphere. Al couldn't think of anything worse than turning up at his in-laws' place with a young blonde in tow. He doubted if Helen's parents would even let him over the threshold. He felt certain they would know the full story of his demise by now, with several shiny knobs on.

'Dinner?' he said, laughing. 'It's a three-star discount B&B. I can't see you enjoying the menu to be honest, it's not exactly refined. Even I used to baulk at the Seaside Special Pie. I never did find out what the filling was meant to be.'

She rolled her eyes at this, but shot him the beginnings

of a grin. The best thing about Jo was that she didn't sulk ... for long. He grabbed her hand and kissed it, ignoring Marge when she curled her lip and growled. If only his brother could be charmed with such ease. Al had a lot of talking and standing firm to do, something he wasn't very good at.

He took the valley road and concentrated on the twists and turns in the gathering gloom. When they eventually stopped in front of the house, Jo looked distinctly subdued. Chathill looked a lot more ramshackle than he remembered. A rambling farmhouse of sorts, it had been added to and subtracted from over the years so that it had a haphazard, unplanned sprawl to it.

When their parents had been alive, Al and George had roamed the heather-clad hills with the sure knowledge that it would all be theirs in time. It used to be a comfort; now it was a bloody mess. An emotional, financial, and physical mess.

The battered front door was unlocked, the hallway piled high with muddy boots, animal food, and saddles. Al wandered through, dragging a reluctant Jo by the hand.

'Fran?' he yelled, pushing open doors – except his brother's private sitting room-cum-office space; that was always locked. Every room looked as if it had been burgled. In the long back porch there was a huge birdcage in the way, well, it was more a small aviary. It was dominated by a bright green parrot.

'Where the bleeding hell have you been?' the parrot screeched.

Jo grimaced at the smell and held her nose. Hungry for an audience, the bird piped up again with a long list of perfectly enunciated expletives, then cocked its head to one side. Al sniggered, caught hold of Jo's cold hand, and pushed through the dirty glass back door. As always, the familiar scene made him catch his breath. It was approaching dusk, and the landscape of burnished autumn

9

when Fran flung herself at his girlfriend in her usual hands-on way, and Jo did reciprocate, but then occupied herself with brushing something off her coat. It was all a bit awkward, and after the introductions he was grateful to Becca for dragging them round the stables. She wanted a competition horse for her next birthday but George had *insisted* some of the ponies be sold first. It sounded a familiar argument to Al, but clearly she'd grown out of ponies, even to his untrained eye.

'They'd go for meat though … wouldn't they?' Becca said. 'Pumpkin Pie and Candy Floss are too old and no one would want them. Don't lie to me, I know what happens.'

'We'll *retire* them, don't worry. They deserve it.'

This all sounded like trouble to Al.

They wandered across the yard, Fran chattering and laughing about some huge old pig they'd rescued from the jaws of death, just 'found' it, apparently, on the side of the road. Jo wasn't sure what to make of it all, but Becca hung on to his arm and it all felt good. *Goddammit* Chathill was still his home, and George, Fran, and Becca, they were his family too. He really needed this, despite the tug of apprehension in the pit of his stomach.

They reached a row of looseboxes, and Al dutifully stuck his head in each one as his niece described the inmates. They were mostly all rescued animals, so Al reckoned he was in the right place on that count.

'Mum's called it Bacon,' Becca said, taking his arm again.

'Huh?'

'The pig.'

Al laughed, 'Seriously?'

'So anyway, there's a horse sale tomorrow, will you come along? We're just looking.'

'Yeah, course,' Al said. He tried to catch Jo's eye for some sort of approval, but she was busy trying to scrape manure off her boots.

Chapter Two

Kate

Guilty. Guilty for living, and then complaining about it. Guilty for continuing to wear black, and enjoying it. Black suited Kate; it set her red hair alight and contrasted well with her china blue eyes and her pale, freckled skin. An arresting combination on a slender adolescent, but positively witch-like on a mature woman who didn't give a damn. Since she was stuck with the latter, Kate dragged her hair into an elastic band and soldiered on.

Steeling herself against the guilt, she grabbed Greg's cycling shoes and shoved them into a charity bag, then stopped and looked at the calendar above the shoe rack. Saturday, the twenty-seventh of October. The photograph was of mature oak trees, aged golden trees against a cold, blue sky. Beautiful, but close to their long hibernation; a form of living death. It seemed nature just gave up and let go in late autumn, but instead of looking drab, the photograph was stunning. The analogy should have filled her with hope, but rather than lift her spirits, her heavy burden threatened to overcome even rational thought.

Moving into the dining room, she flicked the light on and her eye caught the yellowing lampshade clinging to its dusty bulb. Greg would never have tolerated that – he'd been an obsessive cleaner. She cooked and created, he'd always cleaned, ironed, and fixed. She was sloppy with exercise, clothes, and haircuts. Towards the end, Greg's streamlined head became almost as aerodynamic as his lean, Lycra-clad body, so that he became almost one with the love of his life. Kate glanced at the cycle helmet on the old sideboard and wondered why the hell it was still crouched there like a shiny, dead turtle. With no further thought, she shoved it quickly in the bag with the shoes, and to hell with the guilt. She couldn't live like this.

Greg Roberts, the man she'd married some four years ago; and lost exactly three hundred and sixty-five days ago. A year of coming to terms. She hadn't gone completely to pieces, so why couldn't she function and just get on with it? Maybe she *needed* to go completely to pieces, but somehow, it just wasn't in her.

Time healed, everyone had told her so. Kate had agreed with them all, she still did. At the time of the funeral and for a long time afterwards, she'd played a superb role as the grieving widow, accepting the well wishes and offers of support with calm dignity. Everyone had presumed she'd perhaps been sedated, or was maybe so traumatised by Greg's death that the shadow of loss had momentarily stolen her mind, but that wasn't the case.

Fran, Greg's sister, had stolen everyone's attention by properly breaking down. She'd gone through an emotional explosion and come out the other side, but that was how Fran operated. She was up and running again in a matter of weeks and Kate admired her tenacity. As people, they couldn't be more different, but maybe that was the secret to their relationship. Although she'd only known Fran for some five years, it felt like a lifetime in terms of friendship.

The sorting of Greg's stuff into bin liners was a little overdue but once done, Kate found her phone and made an equally overdue call.

'Frannie? It's me. Does that invite still stand?'

'Oh, Kate, of *course* it does! I was half expecting you. Look, I've just got to pop out to get salt licks and a sack of bran, then I'll make up one of the rooms.'

Kate almost grinned at this, knowing full well the room would be as she left it several weeks ago. Fran was not the best when it came to domestic chores; her Noah's Ark of unwanted animals always came first.

It didn't take long to pack a bag – warm, practical clothing was all that she required. No make-up, just a jar of good face cream for mature skin and some lip balm. Kate zipped up her bag, stowed it in the boot of her car, then slung in an old waterproof coat and a pair of Wellington boots for good measure. That done, she found her spirits did actually lift as she nosed the car out of town and along the valley road. Dry and bright, the low winter sun flickered through the trees, and she hunted out her tinted spectacles with one hand. Yes, she had done the right thing in phoning Fran.

George and Fran's home, Chathill, was a gloriously messy small-holding, the perfect place to consolidate and consider. Fran was always glad to have anyone's company, and Kate needed to make plans, talk them through with someone, and maybe, just maybe, this time she might feel brave enough to confide some truths to Fran about Greg. Would that be too cruel, or did she need to do it to allow herself to move on? Kate couldn't decide.

She remembered to stop for provisions. Fran would never accept financial help with the housekeeping so Kate always made sure to stock the kitchen cupboards. It was an arrangement which suited them both. Fran was no cook. If truth be told she could burn water, but Kate found it mostly therapeutic and looked forward to preparing meals for someone other than just herself; a fact which never failed to thrill George, and continued to baffle Fran.

Turning off the main road, Kate's car bumped along the narrow single-track lane, a strip of grass and moss running through the middle and bordered by overgrown hedges. She knew there was a water-filled ditch on the left too, and the pot holes were huge. She worried for the safety of her old car, but once negotiated, the vista of the house came into view and then she couldn't help smiling.

The usual cacophony of barking signalled her arrival. Other than half a dozen enthusiastic dogs, no one came to meet her, but then it was dusk and Kate knew Fran and her daughter Rebecca, or 'Becca' as she preferred to call herself, would be out feeding the animals. Once she'd parked up, next to a camper van and Fran's filthy estate car, Kate retrieved her bags from the boot and shoved open the front door with her backside. Some of the dogs barged inside and followed her expectantly into the kitchen.

'Hello? Anyone home?' she yelled, not really expecting an answer. Through the kitchen window, she could just make out Fran's shadowy figure stuffing hay-nets. She smiled to herself and made for the stairs, clambering over the baby gate George had secured there in an effort to stop animals – mostly the dogs – from diving upstairs. The same spare room she'd used on her previous visit was exactly as she'd left it some three months ago, with the blue candlewick bedspread folded across the end of the bed, this time with two cats curled in the centre. Kate always took the single room under the eaves rather than the double she used to share with Greg, although she wasn't in the least sentimental, so it was puzzling why it bothered her.

She went to glance through the window at the darkening sky, and further surprised herself when she smiled at the pinpricks of stars glinting like diamond chips, a clear silhouette of Foel-fras in the distance. Closer to home, down in the yard, a couple of grey horses moved about like ghosts, their hooves clattering on slate and stone. Fran saw her and waved cheerily, indicating with her hand she'd be five minutes. Kate knew it wouldn't be and decided she may as well get on with preparing dinner. She'd brought fresh pasta and the ingredients to make a wild mushroom sauce. Suddenly glad of something to do, Kate turned from the window and began to unpack, mentally going over the recipe and hoping Fran had at least some olive oil hidden away. The last time she'd searched for it, some of the kitchen doors had fallen off and a couple of shelves had decided to give way, only to discover that Becca had used it to oil her saddle and brush it through several manes and tails.

Deciding on a freshen up first, Kate walked purposefully along the narrow landing. The recently renovated main bathroom was something of a pleasant surprise at Chathill. Greg used to hate staying over but when the plumbing was improved a couple of years ago, he came round to the idea. The floorboards were still creaky and crooked though, a bit like a funhouse. Kate prepared to duck slightly and pushed open the wooden door.

Once inside, she was confronted by a naked man. Starkers! Well, he would be, since it seemed he'd been in the shower cubicle. She was too old to be embarrassed by nudity, but it was still a shock. The little wooden sign swinging on the handle outside had clearly said "vacant", and there was a distinct absence of any noisy, running water. He was glistening, though, and his hair was dripping. Kate kept her eyes on his, although it was difficult not to glance down – almost impossible, in fact – but he was watching her every movement, so she felt not only trapped, but compelled to keep eye contact. Despite all of this, he didn't flinch or attempt to cover himself in any way, nor did he grab a towel from the rail, presumably because they were slightly out of reach.

'Hi,' he said, and extended a hand towards her, 'I'm Al.'

Blue eyes. If she were maybe feeling whimsical, and she hardly ever was, she'd say they were like faded denim.

'Sorry ... I wasn't expecting anyone to be in here,' Kate said, leaving his hand suspended in mid-air. When he started to grin, she retreated back into the hall and struggled to pull the door shut. It didn't fully close because the wood was warped, like most of the other doors, but she made heavy weather of turning the sign round to "engaged".

When she and Greg had become engaged, they'd bought a sign like that, for fun. For a while, Kate had hung it over the bedroom door until it became a nuisance, and then eventually it went to the charity shop. The charity shop would be filled to the rafters with all the stuff she'd packed up from the house, all of Greg's cycling gear and magazines, but she'd had to do it. After some space away from the house, she could go back in there and re-decorate. Or perhaps she wouldn't, maybe it was time to sell it and move on.

Her mobile phone sprang into life, jolting her from daydreaming, and Kate fumbled in her bag. It identified the caller as her sister, but when Kate answered, she recognised Carol's voice instead.

'Is that you, Kate?'

'Oh, hello, Carol.'

'Any chance you can come and pick up Annemarie? Only she's legless in Fountains Bar again. Making a bit of a show of herself ... you know.'

Kate tried not to sigh too obviously. 'No, actually, I can't, Carol. I'm not at home, I'm at George and Fran's place.'

'Uh, blast. Well, could you not come anyway? It would only take you an hour to get to town from there.'

She was only partially listening then to Carol's long story of woe, something about happy-hour cocktails and some bastard of a man. The small lift of spirits she'd felt driving to Chathill suddenly plummeted.

'Kate, are you there? She's in a bad way this time.'

'Look, I'm sorry, I've run around after Annemarie for years, collecting her from bars and nightclubs, cleaning her up and putting her to bed, looking after her kids. No can do, not this time.'

'Well, thanks for nothing!'

'Pleasure!'

The angry voice suddenly died in her hand, but of course the stab of guilt didn't.

Her sister was forty-six and behaved like a teenager. Annemarie had gone through three supposedly serious relationships in her life so far, producing four children along the way, the youngest of which was barely out of infant school. The eldest, Jewel, had married one of her mother's boyfriends and now they didn't speak so there was no point calling *her*. Levi, her (remarkably sensible) son, was travelling around Asia, and the other two youngest were most likely farmed out somewhere, no doubt watching unsuitable DVDs.

No, enough was enough.

Her sister consistently added to an already overburdened weight in her head. Was it all guilt or was her conscience just playing tricks? Sometimes it really was difficult to tell. It mushroomed like a black cloud, sometimes following behind, at other times virtually suffocating, like a fully-exploded airbag might feel; preceded by the necessary emergency stop.

Kate retraced her steps to the bathroom. The door was swinging open this time, full of steam and a masculine scent, and the black cloud dispersed, just a little.

An hour or so later, Kate had dinner underway and Fran had opened two bottles of wine; an un-chilled supermarket white, and a red with an expensive, dusty label.

'How many should I set the table for? Only there was a man in the bathroom earlier,' Kate said, rooting through the cutlery drawer.

'Oh, yes, sorry, I should have said. George's brother, actually,' Fran said, then lowered her voice, 'with a bit of posh fluff in tow.'

'*Brother?*'

'Truth is, he's the black sheep of the family. He and George had a massive falling out years ago.'

Kate wasn't sure that explained nearly enough but continued to set the table for six, with some difficulty given that two of the better forks were stuck in tins of cat food on top of the fridge. *Brother?* Given that she'd not known Greg's family that well or for too long, Kate found it odd that she'd never met the 'other' brother-in-law. Although she could maybe recall some distant mention ... but then Greg had never talked very much about relatives, and she couldn't very well ask him now, could she?

A volley of expletives from the parrot, followed by the crashing of the back door, signalled the arrival of Becca, pink-cheeked from the cold and still sporting dirty riding gear. She kicked off her Wellingtons and collided in the doorway with a lot of hungry dogs.

'Oh, *great*, Aunt Kate is in the kitchen!' she said gratefully. 'That'll put Dad in a good mood, then he won't argue with Uncle Al.'

On cue, Uncle Al made an appearance, mercifully dressed, with his posh bit of fluff bringing up the rear. For a moment the kitchen was full of excited chatter as Fran poured wine and Becca tried to feed the cats and dogs. Kate tried to add some pasta to a saucepan of water without scalding herself, aware that all she could see in her mind's eye was a naked man.

Fran said, 'Kate, meet Al ...'

She turned from the hob, spoon in hand. 'We've already met, in the bathroom ...'

He laughed then, but she took his hand and was about to say something about not recognising him fully-clothed before mercifully he cut in, 'Er ... this is Jo,' he said, half turning to the woman hovering behind. 'Sorry, I didn't catch your name?'

'Kate.'

Jo kept her hands firmly locked inside the cuffs of her sweater, but the smile was genuine enough, though she looked almost blue with the cold and asked for a cup of tea instead of wine. Since she was the closest, Kate flicked the kettle on, and Jo mouthed a 'Thank you' to her, over Al's shoulder. She looked slightly out of place in Fran's kitchen, with her fashionable, pixie-styled hair and Chanel coat. Jo scanned the eighties' kitchen with, not disdain exactly, but Kate suspected she was not an animal lover. When her grey eyes followed the cats leaping from table to worktop and back down onto the dirty floor, they were positively flinty.

'Are you sure there's nothing I can do to help?' Fran asked, still in her fingerless gloves, struggling to carry a swaying bucket with a cloth over it, a stick poking out of the side.

'No, no, I've got it all covered, thanks.'

'You're an angel.'

'Is it OK to bring Butter and Marge in, Fran?' Al said.

'Um, yes … I don't think anything is on heat,' she said, rolling her eyes at Kate and then inclining her head in the direction of Al's girlfriend. Fran was never comfortable around false nails or fake fur, and continued to watch the femme fatale in her kitchen with obvious distrust.

Minutes later, George's arrival was heralded by the rushing of many dogs down the hall. Kate's brother-in-law made an entrance, swiping at the leaping animals with a rolled up copy of the *Financial Times*. He came across to Kate with a heartfelt kiss to her cheek.

'Lovely to see you, love.'

Before she could respond, George turned to Al. 'I presume that is your rust-bucket outside. When will you be leaving?' he said, smacking the newspaper against his hand like a truncheon.

'Can we talk about this later?'

'Nope.'

'Sit down!' Fran commanded, and George sat, obviously fuming.

Kate kept herself busy draining the pasta and adding chopped herbs, but the tension was so thick you could practically taste it. She placed the bowl of pasta and two cobs of crusty olive bread in the centre of the table and took her place. Everyone ate in virtual silence but the food was a good distraction and after a while, Fran nervously topped up everyone's glass, ignoring George when he scowled at his bottle of vintage Cabernet Sauvignon being offered towards Al.

'Oh, isn't it a lovely feeling when everything is bedded down for the night and fed and watered?' Fran said brightly.

'I wouldn't know,' George replied. 'In fact, I find it increasingly irksome that all the blasted animals round here are named after food, and yet more often than not, we have none in the house.' He held up his glass to Kate. 'Thank you, not only for this wonderful dinner, but also for providing a civilised interlude before I deal with our unwanted guest.'

George bent back over his plate and five sets of eyes settled on the top of his balding head. Becca poked out her tongue and Jo raised her brows at Al. 'What are we doing here with these mad people?' her eyes seemed to say.

'I didn't know you had a brother,' Kate said.

'I haven't,' George snarled. 'He's no brother of mine.'

Al threw down his cutlery and went outside and Jo bolted after him. They heard the slam of the back door and the screech of the bird followed. '*Shut the fuckin' door, why don't you?*'

Kate gulped down a slug of wine. 'Sorry …'

'Oh, don't be. It's George who should apologise,' Fran said.

'If there's going to be another argument I'm going to do my homework,' Becca said, and scraped her chair back.

'Please may I be excused from the washing up?'

Fran gave her a weak smile and time seemed to stand still as Becca's feet thumped up the stairs. They all stared at the tablecloth till she was out of earshot.

'I think we need to have a private talk,' George said to Fran, then turned to Kate. 'I do apologise, and I don't wish to appear rude but I thought this situation had been put to bed a long time ago.'

'Oh, don't mind me,' Kate said, minding quite a lot. What was she supposed to do now? She'd turned up in the middle of a family crisis and all she had to amuse herself with was a mountain of washing-up. She up-ended the remainder of the red wine into her glass and began to clear the pots from the table. George and Fran disappeared into the study. A guarded conversation ensued, and from what she could ascertain, it seemed Jo and Al were already arguing outside the back door.

She was drying the pots when Jo marched through the kitchen and ran upstairs, grey eyes like steel, her Liberty scarf flying. OK, so it was mildly amusing. On the point of calling it a night and going in search of a book, Kate almost escaped the kitchen when Al reappeared. He slid back into his chair, up-ended the same bottle she'd previously drained, then stared gloomily at the half teaspoon of wine that dribbled out.

'There's some warm white if you're desperate,' Kate said.

'I'll pretend to smoke instead,' he said, and placed a cigarette to his lips, then leant back and folded his arms. His eyes matched his Abercrombie denims and blue shirt. She wondered if the clothes were Jo's younger influence, but they didn't look in the least inappropriate, even considering the fact her daughter's boyfriend wore the same brand; albeit hanging off his backside. Al got up to push the kitchen door shut and Kate noted how well-fitted they were from the rear, too.

Even with the door now wedged shut, it was difficult to ignore the steadily rising voices from down the hall.

'I really thought all the animosity would be water under the bridge after fourteen years,' he said. 'I'm in a bloody desperate situation here. Nowhere to live, no job –'

'Fourteen years? So … what did you do?' Kate asked.

'You mean for a living, or what did I do to get everyone to hate me?'

'I think I'd find either of those answers interesting.'

He grinned at her, removed the unlit cigarette from his mouth, and turned it end over end on the packet. 'I stepped out of line.'

'Clearly. I didn't even know George had a younger brother.'

'I'm pleased you've noticed,' he said, 'that I'm younger.'

Goodness, was he flirting with her?

'You don't look related,' she said, and began to fill the kettle. 'George is dark, brown eyes, and so was your father from what I've seen of the odd photograph. Coffee?'

'Coffee, yeah. Best stay sober, eh? Could be a long night. Anyway, we're not blood brothers. I was adopted as a kid.'

'Oh … I see.'

'And the other answer … clown, freelance musician, full-time nanny, author –'

'You're an author? Would I know any of your titles?'

'*Was*. Doubt it. How about you?'

'I'm a senior sales associate for Bargain Home Stores.'

'That sounds good.'

'I hate it.'

This time there was the mildest frisson when she returned his smile. At least, that's what she thought it was. How long since she'd had even the *mildest* frisson? Too long.

24

Chapter Three

Al

Al was pleasantly distracted by Fran's sister-in-law. He would have stayed chatting, watching her cool, blue eyes lock onto his, had George not burst through the door.

'You. In the study. Now.'

'Charming,' Al said cockily. In reality, he was full of trepidation in case everything turned nasty in earshot of Jo and Becca and … Kate. Although there was some relief in knowing that the moment had finally come to move things on. Butter and Marge leapt up from under the table.

'Sit. *Stay*,' he said, but only Marge listened. Butter jumped up like a puppy, licking his face and snagging his shirt. Kate caught hold of the dog's collar and Al followed his brother, feeling like a schoolkid summoned to the headmaster's office. It never used to be like this. As kids, they were never apart. When their parents had been alive and worked Chathill as a farm in the early to mid-seventies, it had been paradise to grow up here – or at least it had seemed that way to Al. George, being eight years older, grew out of it sooner and went to university, and travelled. Then he came home one Christmas and fell in love with Fran from down the road. They married fairly soon after that and Fran moved in, drooling with the idea of turning the farm into a version of the Welsh Waltons.

Somewhere along the way, Chathill had degenerated into an animal refuge. Fran used to pretend she was interested in rare breeds and organic farming, but everyone knew the truth of it. Making money from traditional farming like their parents had was no longer making any real money, and Al suspected that Fran – denied of the big family she'd always craved – had solved the craving with a myriad of unwanted animals.

George waved him in to the study – a large room which used to be a second sitting room – and Al noted the kettle, the microwave, and the drinks cabinet.

'You live in here now, then?' he said, settling himself on the leather sofa. It was clean and comfortable, with an electric fire in the old hearth and an impressive mahogany desk dominating the room. Not a shred of animal hair to be seen, and the carpet looked new.

'Do you blame me?'

'You're asking for my opinion?'

'Yes, I am.'

'Well, the house seems to be a bit er, *bohemian*.'

'An understatement.'

'They're happy though, Fran and Becca?'

'But of course they are,' George said expansively, 'And we wouldn't want to upset the apple cart there, would we?'

Al watched his brother pour brandy into two cut-glass tumblers. He accepted the drink and waited until George was seated opposite on a refurbished Chesterfield chair, looking every inch the subject of an old oil painting.

'So,' George said, 'When are you leaving?'

'I'm not leaving. This is as much my home as it is yours, and I've nowhere to go. If you don't like it, pay me fifty per cent of its worth and I'll shove off.'

'You know I can't do that. We're just about keeping afloat here.'

'Sell up then!'

A brooding silence ensued. They both knew the futility of the argument. It was a repeat of fourteen years ago. The farm had been in the family for generations. To sell it was unthinkable, and it would destroy Fran and Becca. Al couldn't bear the thought of forcing them to live in a three-bedroom semi, and he suspected his brother was of the same opinion, although his current living arrangements were concerning. 'Why should we sell up?' George said. 'You're not even a blood relative, Al, and after what you did, I would simply contest it. Got plenty in the bank for legal expenses, have you?'

'My name is on that will.'

'Stuff the will. The will means fuck all. Try and force a sale and see how far you get. Be my guest.'

'It could take years, you know that!'

'I do. I also know you won't do it.'

'*Look* ... look, I just need a room. I'll stay out of your way.'

George rose, huffing and puffing, and went to the window. His big brother had aged a lot and although he seemed so much older, he was only fifty-eight, still smart in his suit and his squeaky leather shoes. He watched George pick up the black and white photograph of Mum and Dad, the one with shells around the frame, and felt inexplicably, deeply nostalgic. The kind of emotion that hit you right in the solar plexus.

Chathill, George, Mum and Dad, had been his life since he was five. It felt right to be *home* in so many ways.

'Come on, George, I'll get a job, help out.'

'Ha! What as?'

'Anything ...'

'What about that big swanky house of yours in Delamere?'

'Remortgaged with not much equity in it. Sold now, but half of nothing much equals piss all.'

George turned from the window and topped up his glass. 'Marriage down the pan as well, eh? What happened there then?'

'None of your business,' Al said, knowing full well George would likely wrangle a confession out of him in time, like he always did. Admittedly, even partially confiding in his brother made his problems contract

27

slightly, just like the old days when he'd got in a sticky situation and needed some mature advice. This time it was a serious grown-up mess; so sticky it needed a serious amount of solvent. On paper he owned two properties, but he couldn't live in either of them. On paper, he was married to the love of his life, but she wanted nothing to do with him.

He was about to confess to George that he'd 'accidentally' told Helen the family secret when George heard the falter in his voice and stopped him with an upheld palm.

'*All right*. All right … you can have a room. But believe this,' he said through gritted teeth. 'One step out of line and you're animal fodder. Get it?'

'Got it.'

Al was woken by Jo waving her iPad out of the window, presumably trying to get a signal. She sighed vehemently. 'It's hopeless.'

'What is?' he mumbled, rubbing his face.

'I need to forward an e-mail to Grayson.'

'Grayson …?'

'Yes! Grayson, my bloody boss.'

'All right, calm down.'

Marge trotted out from her secret nest of towels and Al let her jump into bed. He hadn't risked smuggling Butter upstairs; he was hopefully still shut in one of the stables.

'What's the problem anyway? I thought you were on holiday?'

'So did I. The American sector want more control of the charity site I've been working on. We're going to lose all funding if this isn't handled properly.'

'Oh. Right,' Al said and yawned, not understanding a word of it. He watched her clamber around the room in her La Senza bra and panties, searching for a signal on her mobile, holding it at different angles before resorting to standing on a chair. She began a heated conversation with Grayson and Al pulled the duvet over his head.

Jo had been up and down most of the night with stomach cramps, to the point where she'd woken Al on the verge of tears. It wasn't the first time Al had lain awake half the night with her, fetching cold flannels for her forehead and hot water bottles for her belly. Al blamed her job and all the deadlines she had to meet, although Jo would never admit to a weakness like that. She had a responsible career in the real world; a corporate fundraiser for several major charities. Al was never entirely sure what it all entailed but it seemed fraught with nasty meetings, a lot of stress, and important trips to the head office in London. Despite this, she loved, lived, and breathed the job.

Years ago, when he was writing a lot, he recalled getting the same buzz when his characters passed that point of being merely imaginary, and he got to play God and the Devil in the same day. The difference of course was that Jo got paid a substantial amount of money to do it for real.

Sometimes, he saw his books in bargain bins with 'three for a fiver' stickers across the covers, and he'd thumb through them, recalling that magical feeling of creation. They might not be worth much in the commercial world, but something of himself was laid down in those pages forever. Al could never put a price on that. Best of all, his daughter, Maisie, had all his titles in the original hardcovers. She kept them between special book-ends on her bedside table, with some of his old newspaper cuttings in a leather folder.

Priceless.

There was an argument of sorts. Jo wanted dropping at the nearest train station but Al persuaded her to come to the horse sale. 'You can't go now, I've promised Becca, and anyway, it'd be rude.'

'Since when has that ever bothered you?'

An hour later they were all crammed into the cab of Fran's old horsebox, with three ponies in the back. George thought they were going to the market and told Fran to make sure she got a good price for them; but ten minutes down the road they turned off, bouncing down a pot-holed track strewn with boulders. The ponies didn't appreciate the rolling about and sounded like they were kicking the insides to smithereens. Al was crushed between Kate and Jo, and Becca lay across their legs like a roll of carpet, her mud-encrusted boots in perfect alignment with Jo's designer denims.

Presently, they pulled up at some rundown outbuildings and an old guy with a wooden leg appeared. Fran and Becca jumped out of the cab and let down the ramp. Al watched with interest through the dirty windscreen as Kate followed them, her faded red hair blending into the late autumn landscape of dry moorland and broken stone walls. Fran slipped the head-collars from the ponies and they all trotted away, cautiously at first, then with more abandon, alert and cantering, leaping the foaming streams and calling to each other. It didn't take long for them to disappear from sight. Semi-feral retirement looked good to Al, although Becca's face told a different story. There was an echo of his own bittersweet childhood there, when the lesson of letting go and growing up seemed to be on constant repeat. When Al thought about his blood mother – he never called her his *real* mother – he wasn't entirely sure if that particular message had been hammered home hard enough.

Kate walked towards the cab, arms folded and head down against the freshening breeze. Becca caught up with her and Kate put an arm around her shoulders.

'Hey, they all looked happy, the horses,' Al said as they all clambered back in.

'*Ponies*, Uncle Al. Peg'll keep an eye on them, won't

he, Mum?'

'He's a diamond, is Peg.'

The lorry rumbled back down the track, even scarier with no weight in the back, and Al swayed, not uncomfortably, between Jo and Kate.

At Ruthin, the village was buzzing with livestock, burger vans, and street artists, providing an agreeable aroma of fried onions, fuel, and anxious animals. The arrival of the horse-box clearly signified a prospective sale and Al practically marched Fran past all the animal holding pens. She was easily distracted, not only by persuasive owners but by the sight of some of the less cared for occupants, and he couldn't risk George having a meltdown at this stage.

'Look at that pony, it's like a skeleton. It can hardly walk, its hooves are so bad. How can people leave them like that?'

'Fran, I *know*, but you can't help them all, love.'

They walked on, but she looked back twice.

In the old marketplace, the sales ring was noisy with whinnying horses and bellowing cattle, no doubt anxious to know their fate. Dominating all conversation, human and otherwise, the continuous babble of the auctioneer's patter took centre stage, punctuated by the sharp rap of a gavel before the next Lot was herded in. Al nudged Jo's shoulder. 'Don't put your hand up, you might buy five bullocks.'

She gave him a sardonic smile, then when her mobile suddenly sprang to life, rummaged in her bag. 'Oh … *brilliant*, there's a signal!'

Al watched her shove past everyone to get outside, one finger in her ear, already in a deep conversation. His gaze settled on the rear view of Kate, standing ringside with Fran and Becca. She turned to smile at him and those *eyes*. He didn't smile back and she quickly looked away. Hell, what was going on? She was a grieving widow and *he* was spoken for. He must be the luckiest fifty-year-old on the planet to have a sexy, thirty-two-year-old girlfriend like Jo.

He went to stand behind Becca, noticing that Fran had a well-thumbed catalogue, already clearly marked up as to which lots were possibly worth bidding on. Presently, a striking dappled grey horse was trotted up. White head, grey mane and tail, and a coat like dark cobwebs. The auctioneer ran through all the details in Welsh first, then translated. 'Lot 55 now, an attractive four-year-old, fifteen-hand Welsh cob gelding out of Arianwen of Angharad. Young competition horse, already placed. Needs bringing on.'

'Right, here he is,' Fran said, looking at her boots. 'Don't look interested.'

'Needs bringing on?' Al said, already baffled.

The horse was led around the small ring, its young leader fighting a losing battle to keep it at a sedate walk. It finally broke into a powerful trot and flew past, wide-eyed and spooking at the crowd. It looked dangerous to Al, strong and spirited, and he suddenly had a frightening vision of Becca riding it and disappearing over the moors like the ponies, but a lot faster.

'Fran, you're not thinking of –'

'*Four*? More like eight, if not older,' Fran scoffed, then when there was a lull in the bids, she nonchalantly waved her programme at the auctioneer.

Becca turned from the rail and buried her face in Al's chest. 'Oh, I can't watch. Just tell me when it's over.'

'Fran, are you sure about this?'

'I'm on the edge with my budget here, it's right on the nose,' she said furtively. 'I might need you all to turn your pockets out.'

Al studied Becca's stricken face, then dutifully went through all his pockets and handed over the hundred quid that Jo had given him earlier. Another bid went in, followed by a cool, confident return from Fran. The opposing bidder shook his head and moved away. The auctioneer counted down and seconds later the gavel sounded out and Fran was shouting out her name and bid number. A hundred pairs of eyes watched as Fran and Becca jumped up and down, clutching each other.

'Not like buying a second-hand car, is it?' Al said, and Kate laughed as she went through her handbag, spilling items on the floor as she searched for her purse. He hunkered down and helped her retrieve a battered lipstick, some loose change, and a set of keys. 'Not even had chance to kick the tyres or check the mileage.'

'He's a handsome beast though,' she said. She had creamy skin and full lips, slicked with a natural gloss. Beneath the wax jacket she wore a low-neck sweater and there was a flush of freckles across her chest and the considerable swell of her cleavage. Al drew his eyes away and got to his feet. 'So ... even if he's wild, he's still in with a chance? If he's got it all going on in the looks department, he's a winner?'

'Sure. Did you see the hocks on him? I reckon he can jump too.'

Was she flirting again?

'Bloody hell, we're short of about ... seventeen quid.' Fran said, tipping her rucksack upside down. 'You're right you know, Kate. He can jump anything. He's a bit green for his age but he came third in Flintshire Cross-Country Trials last season. Novice section ... but even so.'

Al spotted Jo's bright blonde head as it materialised through the jostling crowd. 'Hey, Jo! We bought a horse. Have you got any cash on you, love?'

'What for? I gave you a hundred this morning.'

'I've just given that to Becca. Wait till you see him,' he said, ignoring Jo's disinterested face. 'He's a right looker and he's got jumping hocks. Just needs, er ... bringing on. What is a green gelding anyway?' Al shot Kate a sideways glance, but she gave nothing away.

Instead, Fran pushed her face close to his. 'It's an immature male with *no nuts.*'

Al was about to laugh, then realised that Fran wasn't joking. She even shot him a mean stare before shoving her way back through the crowd. Kate and Becca followed, dropping bags and coats, still counting notes and coins. Suitably knocked back, Al suggested they find the local pub, which made Jo smile, even though he had to ask her for more money.

While he waited at the crowded bar, he brooded on Fran's words. It wasn't like her to snap, but maybe she had a point. Maybe Kate hadn't been flirting at all and he'd got it all wrong. From what Fran had said about her, she was likely still grieving. Leering down her top was despicable. And what was he flirting back for, anyway? He had Jo. Although when he looked to where she was sitting, Jo was glaring at him as well, tapping her watch. In the end, they only had time for one drink before he was hustled back to the lorry.

There was a small crowd of onlookers. It transpired that the handsome new horse wasn't interested in loading into Fran's old lorry, not one bit. He looked good though, despite having no nuts to speak of. At first, the advice was gentle and persuasive, but then sheer desperation manifested itself in the collaboration of four men, two either side. A rope was looped around the grey's hind legs and collectively they part pulled, part coerced the horse to take baby steps onto the ramp, shouting and whooping as they inched along. At the top, the horse stopped as if petrified in stone, like the horse on Trafalgar Square. Going nowhere. His nostrils flared, sweat poured down his flanks, his ears twitched back and forth. Al looked across to Becca, sensing her despondency and wishing he could help, but beyond the basics didn't know enough about horses to make a difference.

'Run another horse up first,' an old guy shouted. Fran looked like she'd had a lightbulb moment and trotted off through the milling crowd.

'Fuck's sake,' Jo muttered. 'How long's this going to take? There's only one train out of here on a Sunday.'

Fran quickly reappeared, leading the thin pony with the misshapen feet. It hobbled slowly into the lorry with barely a care and began to pick at the haynet secured to the back wall. The grey suddenly barged after it, the ramp practically buckling beneath its clattering hooves. A desultory cheer went up. Becca shot Al a relieved grin and he responded with a thumbs-up.

'Well, would you believe that?' he said.

'What, exactly?'

Al made no reply, noticing with irritation that Jo was busy texting.

'I'm sorry,' she said, seeking his hand. 'I'm tired, and cold. And I'm worried about this project.'

'Look, if you really need to go, I'll drive you all the way home later, but I think –'

'I *know* what you think, Al.'

They stopped twice to check and water the horses. Fran called in at the local food centre to pick up a joint of pork for dinner and pay an overdue bill.

Jo easily missed the train.

'Don't worry, I'll drive you back. Relax and have some dinner first,' Al said, knowing full well that she was fuming. The joint took a good while to roast too, but it went some way to easing the atmosphere, until Kate received a phone call on the landline. It was something to do with her sister, or her mother, Al couldn't be sure, but it seemed to darken the mood slightly, although Kate brushed it off as nothing.

'I'll go back tomorrow, it's probably nothing to worry about,' she said, resuming her place at the table.

'It didn't sound like nothing,' Fran said, cutting into an apple pie.

'Well, no, Annemarie is an expert on life and death situations. Mother has eaten some potpourri, apparently.'

Becca laughed. 'Oh my God, like, why?'

'Don't be so rude,' Fran said, 'Kate's mother is partially sighted.'

'Oh, it's OK,' Kate said, 'Even *I* laughed. She thought it was a bowl of fancy crisps. I suppose it might improve her halitosis.'

Al caught Becca's eye and she got a fit of the giggles. It always gave him a kick, making her laugh, but then he overheard Kate explaining to Fran and George that she was worried. Something about her sister being a liability, and that she should really go over and check what was happening. She looked down at her plate a lot. His earlier behaviour came back into sharp focus, but despite this, he found it difficult to draw his eyes away and stared at the darker roots of her centre parting, and then at her hands. She wore no wedding ring. Jo was standing in the doorway with her holdall, saying goodbye to everyone, and eventually all of this cut into his thoughts. He found his jacket and his newly acquired pork pie hat. An arm around Jo's shoulders, they dashed across the yard, avoiding the huge puddles.

The van wouldn't start.

To add to the general depression, it was dark and cold, wet and windy.

'Oh, for *fuck's* sake, Al!'

She unclipped her seatbelt and folded her arms.

They sat and stared at the rain sliding down the windscreen, until he became aware that she was crying, silently, which was far more disturbing than an all-out howl. This was so unlike Jo. Al had never seen her cry, couldn't imagine what would *make* her cry, if he was honest.

36

'Jo, what is it? What's the matter, love?' he said, and gathered her up in his arms, both surprised and pleased when she leant closer to him.

'I'm being pathetic.'

'I'll get you home, don't worry. I'll borrow Fran's car.'

She nodded into a tissue.

'It's this bloody job, isn't it? You need to tell Grayson to fucking back off and –'

'No, Al ... it's fine, really.' She pressed the palm of her hand into his chest. 'Go and sort out some transport, will you?'

Knowing he was being fobbed off, he kept his eyes on her as he slid out of the van, turned up the collar of his jacket, and flipped a well-worn cigarette between his lips. He'd get to the bottom of it – if that boss of hers had been taking advantage, then something needed to be done about it. Putting her under this kind of pressure was crazy.

Inside the house, Fran and Becca were washing up and Kate was sitting at the kitchen table, flicking through a newspaper. He felt a twit, begging for Fran's car.

'Oh ... but I've got to take Becca to rehearsals for school.'

Becca groaned and pulled a face, and so did Al. 'I'm a dead man walking.'

'Here,' Kate said, and flung her keys across the table. 'I need it back tomorrow.'

'Oh. Well, er ... thanks,' he said. She barely lifted her eyes from the paper, which Al took as a dismissal. Back outside, he walked past his brother's substantial, shiny 4x4 and dangled the keys at Jo. She quickly followed him to the Ford Fiesta, stowed her holdall in the boot, then climbed in the passenger seat.

'So, *Auntie Kate* must be the trusting sort.'

'How do you mean?'

'Attractive, isn't she?'

'Not noticed.'

'Yeah, right.'

The journey to Delamere was conducted in silence.

Jo lived in an apartment, four rooms in the middle of an incredibly fashionable, refurbished warehouse. Al was left in the sitting room while she went to run a bath. He studied his surroundings, an eclectic mix of old and new. Jo's taste in interior design was a mystery to Al; some of it was brand new, shiny, and angular, some of it retro, some of it Victorian. There was a leopard print chaise, for example, and then two bright blue modern armchairs, an antique writing desk, and an old gramophone. When he caught sight of his reflection in the massive mirror above the fireplace though, he was pleased to note that he didn't look out of place, and tweaked the pork pie hat to a jaunty angle.

Clearly retro in age, but kind of quirky.

He switched the floor lamp on. There was no need to draw any curtains or pull any blinds; the windows were so high it was pointless. That was a drawback to living in an old soap factory; the windows were listed and untouchable so some of the apartments got a window at knee level and so on.

Looking for somewhere to sit down – every surface in the room seemed to be covered with work-related files and computer stuff – he wondered what it said about Jo. A mixed-up, mismatched workaholic?

He knew he'd made the right decision in not cohabiting, although had his brother not relented, he may have been left with no choice. It wasn't that he didn't have feelings for Jo, far from it, but considering the mess he'd made of everything to date, Al concluded he was doing them both a favour, and, if he was being honest, he needed some breathing space. He was just about to shout through to the bathroom and suggest tackling her work-related stress when she emerged wearing just a towel. And when she pushed him flat on the sofa and straddled his lap, all thoughts of work-related stress were instantly erased.

'Feel better then?' he said, and she nodded slightly.

Her skin was soft and slippery with body oil and she smelt of expensive shampoo and a faint trace of Armani Code. Gorgeous. She touched her lips to his and the towel slipped to the floor.

'I'm sorry I've been a bitch,' she whispered, her face close to his. Al stroked her hair, but then couldn't resist pulling her across his body, manipulating the length of her spine until he reached her buttocks. *At last*, he thought, *a spark of love to lift the gloom of the weekend*. It wasn't the only thing that was lifting either. She was about to say something, but he cupped his hands around her face and kissed her. She reciprocated up to a point, but began to shiver, and hooked the towel back up off the floor. He continued to caress her, enjoying the feel of her breasts.

'Al, I need to *talk* to you.'

'Ah ... well, can it wait a bit?'

'No.'

'You can't throw yourself on me half naked, and then say you want to *talk*,' he said, grinning.

'Shut up, will you, I'm trying to be serious here.'

He sighed, and folded his arms.

She sighed, and looked up at the pink chandelier.

Her face crumpled. 'I've got something major to tell you.'

Chapter Four

Kate

Early on Monday morning, Kate deliberated switching her phone on again. She'd have to get out of bed and stand shivering by the window to get a signal, and anyway, did she really want to listen to another drunken tirade from her sister?

After years of being the favourite daughter – goodness knows how or why – it seemed Annemarie was shedding her sugar-coated disguise, perhaps through desperation, and certainly aided by alcohol. Her existence seemed to revolve around controlling their mother, (especially her finances) and finding a 'decent' man. Her concept of 'decent' was embarrassingly shallow. Top of the list was solvency (loaded), followed by looks (rugged), and then preferably younger, with no baggage. Of course, it invariably went wrong. It was almost the sort of criteria Kate's daughter, Tia, went looking for, but she was twenty-four and feckless, not a mature women in her forties with four children.

Her sister went hunting for men in all the bars and clubs they used to frequent when they were in their twenties. Kate had met Tia's father on one such Saturday night thirty or so years ago, enjoyed a long marriage which produced their daughter, but then ended painfully with a divorce. These days they were polite to each other, possibly slightly more so since Greg's death, but no amount of civility would ever erase the affair he'd conducted with her then-best friend.

Irritated by this train of thought – it was always

backwards and negative – Kate flung the quilt to one side and swung her legs out of bed. Grabbing her thick dressing gown, she crept across the landing and toward the bathroom. When she reached the double room which Al and Jo had been sharing, she stopped. The door was ajar, revealing a tidy bed, and curtains neatly framing the dawn sky. Quite clearly, he had either gone out before it was properly light or …

In the kitchen, Becca was both excited and nervous about riding the new horse.

'I'm not getting on him first, Mum. What if he bucks me off?'

'You get back on him,' Fran said automatically. 'Toast, Kate?'

'Just coffee, thanks.'

'Any further word from your sister?'

'No, and I don't know whether that's good or possibly worse than the wailing and sobbing of last night,' she said, reaching for the milk. 'I'll pop over and check though. Er … do you think I could have Al's mobile number? He doesn't appear to have brought my car back.' Fran spun around from the sink. 'Oh, well, that's Al all over,' she said, but rather than seem cross, Kate thought she detected a spark of amusement.

Kate *was* cross. Becca went through her mother's phone, then slid it across the table to her. Finding her reading glasses, Kate logged the proffered number.

'He probably won't answer though,' Becca said. 'He's useless with his mobile. Not even sure it's still working.'

'What about Jo, have you got a contact number?'

Fran made a harrumphing noise. 'Nope, never seen her before.'

She heaved a sack of carrots towards the back porch without a backwards glance. Clearly, the subject was closed. Clearly, it was too early to phone Al, although under the circumstances she had every right to wake him from his loved-up Monday slumber. Defeated, Kate followed Fran outside to help with animal duties and find a saddle to fit the new recruit, but rather than work off her annoyance it began to build.

A text arrived from Annemarie. '*I carnt cop wiv her shes doin my ead in. Wot if she starts eatin candles nex?*'

It was both childish, and chilling.

For a while she watched Becca astride the dappled horse, trotting in circles on the flat, worn-out section of tired grass they called a manége. It slowly crept to late morning and there was still no sign of Al or her car, and no message of apology. Kate scrolled down her phone. He was second on the index, in-between Annemarie and the AA. At least it rang out.

When he answered, Kate immediately began to talk over him, unable to suppress her impatience. She had to press the phone to her ear to drown out the wind and Fran's loud, shouted instructions in the background.

'Hello! You've reached Freddie Fun-Pants. I must be at a *party*! Leave me a message.' Quirky music kicked in and then a long tone. Was there anything more irritating than a recorded message when one was feeling mutinous? And it was delivered in a child-friendly, sing-song voice. She was about to leave a less than friendly response when she saw her car slowly reversing back into its place on the drive. *Finally!*

She strode purposefully across the field, arms folded, during which time Al remained sitting in her car, staring out through the windscreen. When she tapped on the driver's side window, his trance was only marginally broken. He turned to look at her and wound the window down, but his eyes were glazed, a trademark unlit cigarette stuck to his lip.

'Freddie Fun-Pants, I presume?' she said.

'Oh … yeah, keep meaning to ditch that.'

He climbed out of the car and dropped the keys into her hand. 'It must be eight, maybe ten years since my pants exploded for fun.'

'Fascinating,' she said.

'Sorry, I er ... I had some news last night and I've been a bit stunned ever since.'

She tried to look a little more solicitous at this. 'Oh. Well, nothing serious I hope?'

'It is pretty serious, actually. Best serious news I think I've had in eight, maybe ten, years.'

She watched him retreat towards the house, hat at a jaunty angle. It gave him a rakish, slightly theatrical air. No thanks for the lend of the car, no apology for his late return, and when she eventually set off for her mother's house it was to find a virtually empty fuel tank.

Al's arrival had been interesting at first, but overnight it had turned into a wet blanket. The previous day at the horse fair had been fun, although when she'd got back to her room and looked at her wild reflection, Kate wondered what on earth she'd been thinking, flirting with a man who not only had a girlfriend, but also an estranged wife tucked away somewhere too. So much for a cosy week with Fran, having a heart-to-heart about Greg. On the one occasion they'd managed to be alone, Fran had mostly filled her in about Al's impending divorce and how much she disliked his current girlfriend. George had remained closeted in his study for much of the time and the atmosphere was, not strained, but not exactly comfortable either. It was tempting to dream up some emergency and not return to Chathill; too easy given the phone calls from Annemarie, but then it would feel like her sister had control of her holidays as well. If you could call a week at Fran's place a holiday.

Half an hour later, she pulled into the communal car park at Rhos House. The flats were in a small block, a short stroll from the seafront. She pressed number 21 on the keypad by the door and waited a full minute before repeating. Her mother's voice came over the speaker.

'Who's that? Is that you, Annemarie?'

'It's Kate.'

'Late? I'll say you are. I've been waiting for over an hour.'

'Mum, it's me, it's Kate. *Kate*!'

'Oh. You should have said.'

The security lock released, and she pushed open the heavy communal door. Her nostrils were immediately assaulted by old cooking smells. No matter how careful the residents were, last week's lunch seemed permanently trapped in the lift. Two short flights of stairs and she was already tapping on the door before her mother had replaced the entry phone and shuffled down the hall.

'Well, this is a surprise,' her mother said, as if she'd not set eyes on her for weeks. Kate embraced her bird-like frame, shocked by how prominent her bones were. As well as the macular degeneration, she had problems swallowing food and often regurgitated her meal. Every time another problem came along Annemarie hovered like the spectre of death. The triple-heart-bypass five years ago had been the catalyst for all manner of hysteria from her sister.

'This'll kill her, this will!'

But she had survived it. It was Kate who did the three months of aftercare; Annemarie was too preoccupied with finding herself pregnant at forty and in the midst of a relationship crisis.

'I thought you were Anne,' her mother said, still refusing to add on the 'Marie' part of her name – her sister's addition. Her mother automatically filled the kettle, from the hot tap, Kate noticed. 'She was supposed to be taking me shopping but there's no sign of her. Will you ring her, see if she's all right?'

'No, I'm sure there's no need. So, you've recovered

45

have you?'

'What from?'

'Annemarie made it sound like you were choking to death.'

'Lot of fuss over nothing, I was all right after a drop of gin. Took the taste away,' she said, stirring hot water onto half a teaspoon of cheap instant coffee. The milk followed, far too much of it and from the look of the carton, possibly out of date. The mug was passed over and Kate repositioned it on the tiny work surface of the kitchen. Her mother went through all the cupboards to locate an ancient biscuit barrel.

'So who was there, at this *party*?'

'I don't know, I didn't know anybody, except that man from the bank, you know, the very tall one. Nice of Anne to ask me over though, sit here staring at the bloody walls some days. Even if I could see what was on the telly it's all rubbish, all that shouting and screaming.'

'Why was the bank manager there?' Kate asked. Thomas Clayton wasn't one of her sister's drinking partners.

'Oh, he just came to say hello and we had a chat about all the accounts, and before you get cross,' her mother said, wagging her finger, 'it was my idea.' Kate followed her through to the lounge and sat like stone on one of the chairs. Everything was a shade of beige, other than the animal-print cushion Annemarie had gifted her, which looked faintly ridiculous on the Dralon three-piece suite. The coasters were located, removed from their tatty box, and placed on the nest of tables.

'What was your idea?'

'Every time I go in that bank they want to upgrade me. Then they want to know about your dad's insurance and some car insurance, and then it's the Internet. What do I want with the Internet?' she said, horrified. 'And then there's all the numbers you have to remember.'

46

Half an hour later, Kate pulled onto her sister's driveway. It was a mere two-minute walk from the flats, a prestigious avenue of Victorian semi-detached properties, most of them with five or six bedrooms and at least two cars. Some of them – mostly those belonging to elderly residents – were in need of serious renovation, but the costs of keeping the many wooden window frames in good condition, or of keeping the roof in good repair, was often unfeasible. The same 'For Sale' boards had remained in place since the previous autumn.

Kate parked behind her sister's enormous 4x4, and went to open the porch door. The sweet scent of vanilla and rose hung heavy in the air as she collected up a huge bundle of mail from the mat. Robyn, her sixteen-year-old niece, let her in with barely a word, and Kate followed her into the kitchen, where she was making sandwiches with a noisy Jake, age six.

Her sister's house was beautiful, but it was also a dirty mess, and Kate resisted the urge to start wiping and clearing some of the work surfaces. Empty bottles were stacked up by the back door, clear evidence of a good night.

'Where's your mum?' she said to Robyn. The girl shrugged, eyes heavily made-up, pouting red lips, and a mass of tousled hair. She coated the bread with chocolate spread and gave it to Jake, who poked his tongue out at Kate, before ramming the whole piece of bread into his mouth. Robyn laughed as he posed for her, and she took picture after picture on her mobile.

'Robyn!'

'I dunno. Might be in bed, might be out. Look, can you watch Jakey for a bit?'

Kate ignored her and marched up the stairs, then listened outside the door to her sister's bedroom. It was open a tiny crack, dark inside with an overpowering smell of stale alcohol filtering through the gap. She was about to tap on the door when the sound of a man grunting, followed by a low female laugh, froze her hand.

What was she supposed to do now? Burst in, demand she take proper care of her children, and offer an explanation as to why Annemarie felt the need to be their mother's power of attorney with no discussion? She did neither. She just stared at her feet, then trod heavily back down the stairs. Jake was running around the sitting room with his fingers in the pot of chocolate spread, pausing only to drain all the dregs of drink from the mountain of beer and wine glasses littered across every surface. The potpourri was scattered beneath the table like confetti.

Kate closed the front door behind her and sat in her car. She looked up at the bedroom window, wondering who the suitor was. Not the bank manager, surely? Her mobile rang.

'Is everything all right? You've been a while …'

'Fran. Look, I'm not sure if I should come back –'

'Oh, don't say that! Al's cooking dinner for us. He's had some sort of news, I'm dying to know what it is, but he's acting all weird. So, er … what's the problem?'

'Annemarie.'

'Oh, her. Leave her! Kate, you are *not* to spoil your break. I'll expect you in an hour, OK? OK?'

She reversed the car and drove on autopilot, a billowing cloud of guilt following behind like a drogue parachute, a familiar feeling. When she parked the car at Chathill, she slammed the door with childish force. Almost instantaneously, Al opened the front door wearing a pink apron. He followed her wordlessly into the kitchen. Kate threw her keys and handbag down and accepted a large glass of wine from him. He watched her gulp down half of it, then went to stir something on the hob, glancing round warily as she pulled her jacket off.

'My sister is a … spoilt. Selfish. Bitch!'

Al nodded, slightly open-mouthed, refilled her glass,

then went back to the hob. 'I'm sorry about the car. Sorry I was late back with it. I'll fill it up tomorrow,' he said.

'Fine!'

She slumped into a chair at the table, surprised by her own venom, and watched his back view as he hunkered down and hunted through the kitchen units, a huge pink bow slung across his backside. The dividing shelf inside the pan cupboard collapsed, and the resulting crash made her smile.

'This kitchen needs a remake, like my life,' she said, then sighed. 'And like my manners. Sorry for snapping.'

He scrambled to his feet with a section of chipboard in his hands. 'Almost the same here, but I feel I may have just turned a corner. Come to a crossroads, anyway. Not sure if there's a choice in there, but it seems better than the usual, well-travelled route.'

Fran appeared at the back door, her arms full of halters and buckets. 'What crossroads might that be? I hate it when you talk in riddles,' she said, helping herself to wine. 'Don't throw that away, Al.'

'It won't fit back in, it's warped.'

'I know, but it will do for a pig board. It's perfect.'

'Well then, that's saved your bacon,' Kate said.

Al smiled, and held the eye contact just a second longer than was comfortable. He was attractive, in an off-beat way, and she couldn't help feeling pleased that the girlfriend had gone home. She needed banter more than anything. In fact, she'd almost forgotten how to laugh. The way Al had turned her mood on its head was … attractive.

Greg hadn't shown much of a sense of humour. Towards the end, he'd always taken her sarcasm the wrong way and her quips had occasionally resulted in a major sulk – although he preferred to call it depression. She'd tried very hard over the five years of their union to understand how much his beloved bike shop had defined him, both as a man, and as Greg. She couldn't deny that being made redundant at forty-three, just a few months into their marriage, too, had left a black hole in his life, but had she really counted for so little?

And then the cycling had started.

Al's roast beef was surprisingly good, and even George kept any scathing remarks to himself. Fran seemed preoccupied. In fact, she never lifted her eyes from the table other than to refill her glass, although once the food was consumed, and George went back into his study, she slowly came to life.

Becca moaned about homework. 'I hate Monday nights.'

'Me and your dad used to be a mean team,' Al said. 'He'd do our maths and science, and I'd do our English and art. So, what have you got?'

'Physics and trigonometry.'

'Ah.'

Everyone smiled.

The plates were sided, stacked up by the sink with a considerable selection of pans and oven dishes. Kate, Al, and Fran collapsed in the sitting room.

'So, come on, Al, tell us your secret!' Fran teased.

'It's still kind of private.'

'You've got a daft grin on your face, come on! Have you inherited a load of money from all those famous relatives?'

Kate tuned and half closed her eyes. She didn't want to think about money and relatives. The idea that her feckless sister had access to their mother's accounts was highly disturbing. Anyone who continued to draw benefits in the shape of family support, and whatever else she could get away with, rather than seek work was not going to be adverse to borrowing from Peter to pay Paul. The house was mortgage free, the legacy of her first marriage to a builder who'd bought it for a song and made it into a palace for her, Levi, and Jewel. So far as she was aware, said builder was still trying to get his share. It could have been resolved years ago, but Annemarie clearly thrived on all the conflict it created.

'Kate? You're miles away ...' Fran said.

'Thinking.'

'Is this about your bloody sister?'

Kate nodded, but before she could change the subject, Fran ran through a brief resumé of Annemarie's life, presumably for Al's benefit.

'Sounds like the synopsis for something by Jackie Collins,' he said carefully. Fran exploded into loud, hysterical laughter, clearly tipsy. 'You can talk, what about *your* life, mister?'

Al gave her a hooded look, 'How much have you had to drink? Shall I make some coffee?'

'*Coffee?*'

George appeared at the door, testy and anxious. 'That sounds like a good idea to me. Fran, I can hear you screeching through several stone walls and Beethoven's Fifth.'

'Oh, well, we can't have you disturbed, can we?' she said.

'Coffee?' George said to his brother, and Al dutifully sloped off to the kitchen, dirty pink apron still in situ.

'What plans do you have for the week, Kate?' George asked, throwing more logs in the burner.

'Some walking and reading definitely on the list. In fact, an hour alone in a bookshop would be bliss right now. Maybe some sightseeing too,' Kate said. 'You know, all the things you don't do because you live here.'

'If you find yourself wandering into Betws at lunchtime, I'd love to have you join me for lunch.'

'That would be nice.'

Al returned with a coffee pot and four cups. George, who made no move to help him find a space to put the tray, watched his face intently. 'And what are you going to do to waste time? There's a job centre in town, you may have seen it.'

'I need to sort out some transport, the van's had it.'

'Well, you can shift it from the drive, looks like a bloody hippie camp.'

'I'm going to make it into a duck house,' Fran said brightly.

'Over my dead body!'

'It might well be! Mr Fox is doing his rounds. Had my Muscovy drake today; just killed him and left him to bleed to death, but you don't care so I'm not discussing any of it with you,' she said dismissively. 'Al, tell us your good news, come on, let's change the subject. Is it something we can toast?'

Al looked distinctly uncomfortable. He almost rolled his eyes warningly at Fran. Kate wondered if she could make an escape to her room. Her stay wasn't turning out quite as she'd anticipated – in fact, she'd never known such an icy undercurrent, and it certainly wasn't helping to sort out the muddle in her head. She'd just needed a few days to get away from the house, from the sight of Greg's stuff all packed up in bin liners. The idea that she'd be able to talk to Fran in confidence about her marriage to Greg and her future seemed illogical now. The status quo of the family dynamic had changed considerably since the arrival of the black sheep.

She looked at Al over the rim of her cup. Who was he, this loved and hated adopted brother who used to be a clown? He lounged across the chair like a child would sit, with his legs dangling over the arm.

Fran had told her a little about his real mother, Ruby Martinez, a reclusive actress whom he understandably never talked about, since the woman had given him up for adoption when he was five and then rejected his olive branch in later years. Maybe this was why she sensed something in him that struck a chord in herself, although she couldn't quite work it out. Maybe a need for family roots? Greg had never been one for family either; he'd barely talked about Fran and George, let alone an errant brother-in-law. When she was a child, Kate used to love the idea of growing up and sharing secrets with a sister, and their relationship had been cosy until Anne started secondary school. Puberty had grabbed Anne like a whirling dervish, with Kate lagging timidly behind and eventually, picking up the inevitable pieces.

A wave of loneliness swept through her, taking memories and nostalgia with it and leaving an empty, hollow feeling in its cavernous place. Loneliness was a horrible state of mind, but easy enough to hide, a bit like the sad clown with the painted on smile.

George dragged the dogs off the sofa. 'News? What news is this then?'

'It can wait,' Al said.

'Oh, stop being a tease!' Fran said, knocking his foot with hers. 'You were singing in the kitchen earlier, so come on, spill the beans.'

'Fran …' he began, then trailed to a halt. He twisted round in the chair and made a pyramid shape with his hands. Something spat and hissed in the log burner, but all eyes were fixed on him.

'All right, I suppose you may as well know sooner, rather than later … Jo's pregnant. I'm going to ask her to marry me.'

Chapter Five

Al

There was a pregnant pause. Al could hear his own blood pumping. He hadn't wanted to spill the beans just yet, but Fran knew he was hiding something and she wouldn't stop nagging. And then there was his crazy state of mind, borderline euphoric. It seemed incredible, the best news he'd had since the lives of Tom and Maisie had begun, declared by the results on a little white stick.

Less than twenty-four hours and he'd already told four people, five if you counted the man in the kebab shop.

Jo would go mental.

He couldn't help it, the best times of his life had been when he was a full-time, stay-at-home, amazing dad and the most-wanted guest at every kid's party within twenty miles. It didn't get much better than that. Helen hadn't minded being the main breadwinner either, she'd been able to concentrate on her career at the bank. It was a pity his role had been seen as skiving by the majority. Some of the mothers used to think he was redundant, treading water while he looked for work; some had been just plain suspicious.

The idea that he'd been given a second bite of the cherry had transformed his crumbling world and given him a burning sense of pride and purpose. He'd even looked through some old manuscripts with a view to writing again. Book seven was just a mass of scribble, but maybe he could bring it back to life, give it some mouth to mouth, pen to paper. No, that was antiquated, he needed a laptop. And a car, he needed a car.

After the pause came the expected explosion. The mother of all explosions. George got to his feet, his face a mass of contorted anger. 'You fucking idiot! Pregnant? You're *fifty,* for chrissake!'

'Jo isn't.'

'Oh, so that's all right then!' he said, marching up and down the worn carpet. 'Why don't you go and live with *her* then? Huh?'

'We've got stuff to discuss first.'

'Like how you'll support another kid? Is that top of the list?'

'No, actually. I always put love first.'

'That was a good film,' Fran said quietly, '*Love Actually.*'

'No, Al, it's nothing to do with love, it's simply the result of *sex!*' George went on, his temples pulsing.

'Look, just pay me my share, and I'll get out.'

'Twenty per cent.'

'No chance. Fifty.'

'I can see you at the school gates now, a scruffy old granddad in a leather jacket, like some pervert in the middle of all the young mothers.'

'Off subject. Bit chauvinistic, old-fashioned views as well.'

'Better than being a sponger.'

Butter began to growl, a low sound to start with but then building in intensity until he bared his teeth as well, yellow eyes firmly on George. The angry hate and the mostly financial standpoint spouted by his brother was fully expected, although it was Fran's reaction that disturbed him the most. She looked tearful, haggard, and worn out. Normally she leapt to his defence, but not this time. Instead, she left the room without a backward glance, closing the door softly behind her.

Kate, her head thrown back against the sofa so that her hair fanned across the cushions, looked mildly shell-shocked, although she had a general air of despondency following her most of the time. Not that he was surprised under the circumstances, although he still didn't know all the details surrounding his brother-in-law's death. He'd been banned from the funeral, of course, and Fran had only managed to tell him the most basic of details over the phone, before she'd begun to cry. If they ever arranged a secret meet up, Becca was always there too and none of them wanted to spend precious time talking about Greg's death.

Thinking back, Greg was just a shadowy presence at family weddings and funerals. Something of a sports fanatic, and desperate to leave farming. When Fran and Greg's parents died, they inherited the converted chapel in the village and Greg had sold it for a song, buying a shop with his half. Fran had bought some knackered old horses and several hundred acres of wilderness.

George slammed the door on his exit and Marge leapt into his arms and licked his face.

'I bet Rod Stewart never got all this aggro,' he said to Kate. 'Or Des O'Connor.'

'Not publicly, no.'

'Is this a good time to ask if I can borrow the car again?'

A beat. 'I need it. I want to go into town.'

'Me too. Can I hitch a lift?' Another, longer beat, before she nodded her head in agreement. Not exactly over the moon with the idea, but he'd make it up to her.

Later, he charged up his phone and called Maisie. She'd just qualified as a vet and Al was proud of her. She listened to his news without interrupting and Al could see her in his mind's eye, phone to her ear under a mass of crinkly blonde hair, framing her heart-shaped face and delicate features. She always looked too pretty and fragile to be a vet, but Al had seen her in action once with a panicking horse stuck in a bog. The owner had been hysterical but

Maisie had calmly filled a syringe with tranquilliser, waded in up to her chest in heaving mud, and found the correct vein.

He'd watched her get a sling under the animal, quietly directing the fire brigade as if it were commonplace. There must be steel running through her petite core, but her dreamy nature, her blondeness, fooled everyone.

She laughed down the phone, sounding tinkly and far away. 'It's a bit soon, I mean, to be telling everyone, isn't it? How long have you been together?'

'Yeah, yeah, I know, only a few months. Perhaps you should keep it to yourself for now? I just needed to tell someone.'

'Have you told Mum?'

'Er … no, nor Tom. Face to face, when the time is right.'

'Good luck with that,' she said, a tad sarcastically because she'd always been on his side. 'Aw … Dad, you sound really happy. I'll be coming over for Christmas, maybe I could meet Jo?'

''*Course* you can.'

As always, his heart practically burst open with love for her. They said their goodbyes and disconnected, and Al pondered the repercussions of the baby and the family already in situ, and how it might all mesh together. There were only four years between Maisie and Jo. Was that good or potentially really bad? He'd not even met Jo's parents yet. A knot of tension gripped his insides, like being poised at the top of a roller coaster before the decent.

Late. His first lucid thought of the day always began with the same mantra. He was late because he'd sat up half the night sifting through badly-typed manuscripts. Becca woke him, hammering on the door, saying something about Kate waiting to take him into town and that she was leaving in twenty minutes.

In the car, the atmosphere was cool, much the same as the late autumn temperature settling over the valley. The last vestige of colour was slowly being sapped from the countryside, and the distant mountains were in soft focus, obscured by mist. Closer to hand, the fields looked sopping wet and worn out. They crossed the restless river. After a night of steady rain and then high tide, it looked especially violent, like a churning torrent of tea and coffee being sluiced down a drain.

'Is Fran OK?' he said to Kate.

'I haven't seen her this morning.'

'Oh, it's just that she seems ... Oh, I don't know, more manic than usual if that's possible. Distracted and kind of hyper.'

She shot him a quick glance, then looked back at the road. 'To be honest, I'm a little worried about her. She and George seem to be at loggerheads most of the time.'

'I think I'm to blame for most of it.'

She changed down a gear as they turned off the valley road and, as the low sun began to blink through the leafless trees, rooted about for her sunglasses. He passed them to her and she took them wordlessly, almost as if he wasn't even in the car. She seemed lost in thought, her profile a study of sad repose.

'I'm sorry for spoiling your weekend,' he said. 'I mean, all the arguments and everything. I don't know what you must think of me. If there's anything I can do ...' He trailed to a halt, knowing it was one of those throwaway remarks everyone makes when they feel indebted or embarrassed. With Al, it was more or less an even split.

After a long moment she said, 'You could help me clear the house of Greg's stuff.' Another sideways glance, gauging his reaction, no doubt. 'Would you? It's all packed up in bags and everything. I'd appreciate a hand getting it to the charity shop, though, it's sometimes awkward to park close enough.'

59

'Yeah, yeah, no problem.'

He was wondering how they were going to fix this up when she suddenly took a left at the roundabout and headed through Conwy, eventually crossing a stone bridge into a residential avenue of prestigious-looking properties. Just before the road began to climb to a steep incline, she pulled onto the wide drive of a modest-looking semi-detached house. She turned off the engine and met his eyes with a considered expression, almost an apology. 'I ... I know this is spur of the moment and a bit weird.' Her faltering words made him want to crush her up in a bear hug, but she seemed repelled by even the slightest touch of his hand on her arm.

'Kate, it's fine.'

Following her into the hall, he almost fell over a mountain of black bags, shoes, and books spilling out of them, and a bike propped up against the wall. The interior of the house seemed smaller than its decorative Edwardian facade would have you believe, with its fancy roofline and the long open porch. Although originally, he supposed, it would have been one residence combined with next door. He glimpsed a small sitting room on the left, a comfortable jumble of mismatched chairs and an open fire. The hall was a couple of strides, and then a snug with a pokey kitchen beyond.

She motioned to him to sit on the small sofa opposite the wood-burner and went about filling the kettle. On the wall opposite, there was a poster size black and white photograph of Greg astride a road bike, holding a cup aloft. He wore an expression of such intense exhilaration that Al found himself averting his eyes when Kate handed him a mug.

'It's a little overpowering in here, isn't it?' she said, 'I may give it to Fran, what do you think? I seem to have *thousands* of pictures of Greg with his bike.'

'Keen, was he?'

'You've no idea.'

She began to tell him a little about the guy's obsession; out on the bike for ten hours a day, every day, training for competitions. It didn't sound like a happy marriage and Al felt slightly uncomfortable hearing the details, but it was the most conversation they'd had and he had to admit, it was morbidly interesting. Then it was sons and daughters, and grandchildren.

'You're way ahead of me in the procreation stakes,' she said, 'I just have the one grown-up daughter who prefers not to communicate with me.'

'Busy, huh?' he said carefully.

'No, not especially. Just selfish.'

'What does she do?'

'She works in a nursery.'

'Children, or plants?'

'Children. I was shocked at your news last night,' she said abruptly. 'I suppose I should have congratulated you.'

He smiled at this. 'I wasn't actually planning on telling anyone, but you know how these things are.'

'I didn't love him.'

'Sorry?'

'Greg. I married him on the rebound after the collapse of my first marriage. I told him I wanted us to separate, divorce, whatever. He was deeply upset, but what did he do? He went out on the bike. He was killed outright on the road, undue care and attention, the report said.'

Al stared at her for longer than was absolutely necessary, with the mug of coffee practically burning his hands. It wasn't often he was lost for words but her eyes and her blunt manner imparted plenty.

'Are you blaming yourself, is that it?'

'Of *course* I blame myself!'

Almost immediately she apologised and raked a hand through her hair. He expected tears to follow but she was remarkably self-contained. 'I just wanted you to know. I don't want a shred of … of *sympathy*. And I want you to know that, that love on the rebound, that … *hopeless* seeking for something lost can be the most deceitful, selfish thing to do to another person!'

'You think I'm on the rebound, is that it?'

'That's for you to work out,' she said, then dropped eye contact and looked instead at the boxes full of bike bits and cycling gear stacked in the corner. 'I'm sorry, this was all a bad idea. And the stupid thing is, I'm not sure now that I want to see his gear dressing the local Oxfam window dummy on a daily basis, I mean, can you imagine?'

His mobile, now switched on all the time since the news of Jo's pregnancy, rang from the depths of his pocket and the *Muppets* theme tune quickly dispelled the mood, but saved him from thinking of a suitable answer. All he could see in his mind's eye was a Lycra-clad mannequin holding a puncture repair kit.

'Hi, love, are you OK?' he said, his eyes on Kate. He mouthed a 'sorry' and she took the mugs into the kitchen.

'Are you going to keep asking me how I feel all the time?' Jo said, then sighed. 'Look, I need to see you and I can't get over there. I have a job, remember?'

'I know. I'll come over later, if I can get transport. Hey, Maisie wants to meet you.'

A beat. 'Why? What have you said?'

'Nothing.'

'I need to see you, Al, it's important.'

'Jo, you don't have to worry about anything, all right? Jo?' She'd disconnected. Eventually, he looked up to see Kate watching him.

'How about this for an idea?' he said. 'I'll take all the stuff over to Delamere, there's bound to be a charity shop there.'

She folded her arms. 'You want to borrow the car.'

'When you put it like that, I feel a right heel.'

'No, actually, I think it's a good idea.'

Al was relieved; pleasing two women at the same time was impressive. Before he filled the car, with both fuel and the bags, she suggested they went about their respective appointments in town.

'I need to go to the bank and then I want some undisturbed time in the bookshop,' she said, her eyes hidden once again by dark glasses. Al suspected they were also hiding the gateway to a torrent of emotion, much like the swollen River Conwy, but held back by a fragile dam. She clearly had a serious guilt complex, too, but Al was no stranger to that and if he knew the cure he'd gladly have shared it with her.

'Funny that, I'm going to the bank and the bookshop as well, but I won't bug you,' he added quickly, 'I'll do it the opposite way about.'

A flicker of amusement crossed her face. She had very full, curvaceous lips, but the overwhelming feeling was one of relief that he'd made her smile. She parked in the main street. Llandudno was pleasantly deserted out of season and October half-term was well and truly over. Pulling his hat down firmly, hands stuffed in his denims, Al walked briskly in the opposite direction, trying to look as if he had a sense of purpose.

His business at the bank consisted of checking his balance, withdrawing some cash, and reassuring the manager that several thousand was due to hit his account very, very soon, and no, he had no intention of lighting the cigarette dangling from his lips. He didn't mention that most of the money would be withdrawn in order to purchase a car. Next door to the bank, the jewellers had some pearls in the window, but the shock of the price had him walking on – and anyway, what idiot buys stuff like that for an almost ex-wife?

The arcade was busy; bingo, slot machines, hot dogs, and tacky stalls. He loitered for a while and got rid of some small change, stopped briefly to listen to the busker outside Marks & Spencer, then having nothing else to do, spent the following half hour avoiding Kate in the bookshop. It was difficult because she gravitated to the same sections he wanted to go in.

Focusing on his practically non-existent technical skills, he loitered in the Teach Yourself section. Computing for the over fifties seemed liked a good bet, although there was nothing about publishing books in it. Maisie had been on at him for years to put his out of print titles onto the Internet and sell them as eBooks but Al didn't have a clue where to start. She'd even made a Facebook page for him but he had no idea what he was meant to do with it, and in any case, Helen had bagged all the computer equipment in working order.

Someone tapped him on the shoulder. 'I know you're here,' she said in a hushed voice. 'Stop hiding and sneaking about, you look shifty in that hat.'

'Help me with this then, I need to get a laptop or something so I'll need a guidebook. Which one should I get?'

'That's a massive, multi-dimensional question, Al.'

'Is it? Here's an easy one then, can I take you for some lunch instead? I'm starving, there was only cat food in the fridge this morning.'

It was tempting to go into The Sunnyside and have Helen waiting on them but the food was pretty dire, so they found a pub instead. Why would he want to hurt her again? He still had feelings for the woman; she was the mother of his children, after all. These random romantic thoughts about Helen were worrying, given his predicament.

Jo was all over the place with this development in their relationship. She just needed lots of reassurance that he wasn't going to disappear. As if! Maybe he shouldn't have told anyone about the baby, but it changed everything.

Only Maisie seemed to understand how and why, but maybe she had a better comprehension of life and death, and a deeper understanding of unconditional love. All of that combined with a scientific mind made her a good vet – a good person, in fact. He seemed to be always doing or saying the wrong thing these days, but at least he had amazing offspring. That was one job he was incredibly proud of.

He used to be proud of his novels. Helen used to like them when they were making money. She told everyone all about them; my husband the author, blah, blah. When he failed to deliver the next one, he got dropped by his publisher and Helen slowly became exasperated with it all, sick to death of discussing plot points and characters. Eventually, he stopped talking about them and Helen never asked. Jo had shown a passing interest when they were getting to know one another, but when she learnt they were set in 1982 couldn't help smirking. 'So they're *historical?*' Al had lost his sense of humour, and they'd had their first spat. Jo concluded that she never read anything anyway, she didn't have the time.

When Kate stood to go and order more drinks, the books she'd bought were nudged out of their brown paper bag and Al inclined his head sideways to have a look. He watched her head over to the bar. Nice legs, from what he could see. She was wearing pale denims with a long, tunic-style top, and flat boots. The ensemble would make a lot of women look frumpy but Kate had an air of confidence about her, something which broke through the thin veneer of fashion and said, 'this is me, like it or lump it.'

She placed two drinks down then gave him a rather critical look.

'Well, do you approve?'

'Yeah … very nice. I always liked blue.'

'What? *The books.* You've had them out of the bag,' she said, pointing.

'Oh.'

'Well?'

'I didn't really take them in, I was watching you,' he said, then began to tell her about Maisie's idea, about the piles of manuscripts gathering dust and animal hair at Chathill. He wouldn't put it past George to set fire to them, which made him feel incredibly anxious.

'I need to get them onto a computer.'

'You'll need a scanner for that,' she said, then studied him over the rim of her wine glass. 'Do you want me to do it? I can put them on a disc or a memory stick, and then you can load the books onto your new laptop.'

'Really? That would be amazing,' he said, wondering what she was talking about. She laughed though, and it altered her whole face, and made her seem vibrant with colour.

'So, what kind of books are they?'

'Mine? They're a spoof series about a private detective, but he gets easily distracted by women and, well, he never really solves anything.'

'Tell me about him.'

Encouraged, he began to tell her about Jim Silver. The conversation mostly lasted through lunch and a shared dessert, and he liked the way he was able to hold her attention, even when the sticky toffee pudding had gone.

'Should I rewrite the whole thing and make them current?'

'Absolutely not.'

'Niche?'

'Absolutely.'

Two hours later they left the pub to find it already getting dark, despite it only being mid-afternoon. It added an unwelcome misery to the house-clearing job, but Kate said it was good, the neighbours couldn't nosy in on what was going on. By the time they'd loaded the car with all the

66

bags and he'd dropped Kate back at Chathill, it was later than he'd planned. He climbed out of the passenger side, and she left the engine running, collected up her handbag and they collided on the changeover. He caught hold of her arms briefly and she offered a hurried cheek-to-cheek embrace. Her hair had a perfume like musky rain.

'Thanks, Al. I really appreciate you doing this.'

It was only seconds, two heartbeats, and then she was gone, running over the puddles into the house. Al adjusted the driver's seat and looked through the rear-view mirror at the considerable belongings of a dead cyclist squashed against the windows.

A steady drizzle smeared the car windscreen.

Chapter Six

Al

The drive to Delamere was miserable, that slow creep towards November darkness, the wind and rain stripping the last of the old leaves from the trees. He hit rush hour as well, and the traffic slowed to a crawl. One or two of the drivers in the middle lane were clearly on mobile phones, calling home.

Al used to do that, when he used to have a home and when someone was expecting him, making a meal or the children were playing up. He called Jo.

'Where the hell are you?' she snapped.

'Stuck in a jam, sorry.'

He could feel the animosity down the phone. She never used to be like this. It must be her raging hormones and she probably felt insecure, being pregnant and everything, but he was sure he could fix most of that.

'Look, let's go out for dinner, I'll tell you when I'm a couple of minutes away, run down and meet me.'

'We can't talk about this in a public place!'

The line of cars suddenly lurched forward and a bin liner full of inner tubes and pedals hit the back of his head. Al swore and dropped the phone into his lap, and for a while he could hear Jo shouting at his genitals, until the phone finally slid into the footwell. A whole heap of things balanced on the back seat keeled over into the passenger side, some of it still muddy.

Both charity shops in the village had been long since closed, of course, one of them with a clear sign, 'Do NOT leave items on the step outside'. Some brave fool had done just that, but he couldn't leave a whole car load, could he? It felt disrespectful, and Kate had been so grateful to him for shifting it all. Maybe he could store it in Jo's garage for a while. And then there was Kate's enthusiasm over the boxes of manuscripts in his room and the idea of sorting and scanning them seemed to present something of a pleasurable job to her.

'Do you mind if I make a start?'

'Help yourself.'

His mind on Jim Silver, he drove round to Jo's flat, and she must have been watching for him because she gave him no chance to locate his phone and call her first to warn her. She opened the passenger door and looked at the bulging contents with a blank expression. It didn't smell too good either. Lots of rubber. Before he could open his mouth, she slammed the door and walked purposefully back across the car park, leaving a subtle trail of a Jo Malone scent. Al switched the engine off and made after her.

Inside the flat, the atmosphere was strange, charged with some invisible fear. She'd left the door open but she had her back to him and her head was bowed in one of those classic 'don't touch me' poses. But Jo wasn't really like that. It was one of the reasons he'd been so attracted to her; her quiet independence, and she'd never displayed drama queen tendencies. Helen held the on-going award for that.

'Jo?' He touched the back of her arm and to his immense relief, she turned into him and he could hold her properly. 'I'm sorry about the car being full of tyres and pumps and … stuff,' he said into her hair. He started to explain about Greg, but she pushed him away and passed a hand across her eyes.

'Al, just … I need to tell you something, and I need to tell you before I bottle out.'

She steered him to the sofa and they sat next to each

other, holding hands. It felt like a Victorian drama and he didn't like the way she gave him the full eye contact. She looked especially pretty, dressed for a dinner he hadn't booked and she hadn't wanted to go to. Her grey eyes were dull and stormy.

'Right. Al.' She swallowed and looked down at their hands. 'Thing is, I don't want a baby right now.'

A beat.

'Marry me.'

There was a deadly silence, a yawning chasm of nothing, before she sighed. 'Oh, *Al*. Are you hearing me? I don't want marriage and children.'

It took several seconds to digest this, mostly because it was incomprehensible that a fit, healthy woman in her early thirties who was childless, and who had a man willing to marry her and take care of both her and the child, actually didn't want any of it. He must have looked gormless, he knew he felt it.

'Look, I've had some time to think,' she said. 'I'm really, really sorry and I *know* you would be right there for me, but it's just not going to work.'

'What's not going to work? Why?'

'*Why?*' She almost rolled her eyes, but then took several deep breaths and squeezed his hands instead. 'When I met you, I was so pleased that you had a family, a grown-up family that no longer needed you. We could just be a couple.'

'I see.'

She searched his eyes for a moment. 'You don't though, do you? Not really. Children were never on my agenda, you must have sensed that. I'm surprised they are still on yours!'

The tension shifted up a gear. In truth, he was slightly wrong-footed by her. Her perception of all matters emotional pierced his bubble like a heat-seeking missile, straight to target with a few well-chosen words. There was no hysteria and no sugar-coating. Snatches of Kate's conversation came back into his head, but Al had no need to remind himself. Jo was far too astute to be flattered by a marriage proposal. The female race had changed quite a lot since 1972.

'I thought we discussed it all last night?' he said.

She shook her head slightly. 'You did all the talking, remember? All about your family and how it was the best years of your life.'

'I was on a high.'

'I know, and I didn't want to –'

'*What?*'

'I was taken aback by your reaction,' she said slowly, carefully.

'Oh, which one was that? The caring one? Or the excited one?'

She got up from the sofa and went into the tiny kitchen. After a moment, Al realised she was crying. It was a silent affair and certainly not manufactured for his benefit. She turned to face him, and the cold realisation of what he saw there had his insides looping. This was it, the final countdown to destruction. His voice came out as if it belonged to someone else.

'Jo … *please.* Don't do anything rash. You'll regret it forever.'

'I'm sorry, Al. I'm sorry, but I'm booking a termination. I shouldn't have told you anything, should I? I should have just dealt with it myself. I could have saved you all this hurt, and myself all this anguish!' She crossed to the worktop where there was an open bottle of wine and sloshed some of it into a large glass. 'You just want to turn the clock back. You don't want *me*, you just want a baby.'

'I want both of you!'

She spun around, her eyes flashing. 'But I don't *want* to be a wife and I certainly don't want to be a *mother!* For chrissakes, Al, I can't say it in any other way!'

72

She yelled all of this, then downed most of the wine before he snatched the glass from her and slung what was left of the contents haphazardly down the sink. He upended the bottle as well for good measure. It felt better to be doing something physical, something which expressed how he felt because the blockage in his throat would not allow anything coherent to be voiced. He was astonished to see her lip trembling.

On the face of it, Jo came across as a tough cookie and played hard at work in a male-dominated arena, but emotionally she was a mass of contradictions to Al. Despite the fact that she took no shit at work and drew very hard lines on herself, she was always soft and loving towards him and he always took the lead in the bedroom. It was maybe the one area of her life where she was prepared to be submissive.

She told him she loved him frequently. He used to think she was a thoroughly modern woman who could have it all, but he hadn't factored in that perhaps she didn't actually *want* it all. She was maybe too intelligent to realise that having it all meant a compromise somewhere, but that was where Al came in, and until this evening he'd been sure of the goalposts.

'I'm so sorry, I know I'm hurting you,' she said.

He allowed himself to be steered back to the sofa again, adding to the sure knowledge that he had no control over the situation at all. His feelings, his grand gesture and the respect he felt for her as the bearer of life, held no weight whatsoever. She placed her hands around his face, channelling his full attention.

'I *know* you don't love me,' she said, almost in a whisper but the certainty of it, of her conviction, made him shudder inside.

'Of course I love you!'

'I know you don't love me, because you are still in love with your ex-wife.'

She kissed his silent lips, and then she kissed her way through the tears on his face until he stopped her, dragged her hands away, and held her wrists.

'Jo, I'm *begging* you. Please don't have an abortion.'

He didn't feel like staying over. Once she'd promised not to do anything rash, he wanted to be alone with his miserable thoughts. She was only a few days gone, so that meant he had time on his side. On the other hand, so did she; at least twelve weeks to book a no-questions-asked termination in a private clinic. That would take them beyond Christmas.

He sat in the cold car for a while, shivering and desperate to light a cigarette, but he found some sweets in the glove compartment and managed to resist. On the drive back to Chathill, his mobile rang somewhere under the seat. Thinking, or maybe hoping it was Jo, he pulled over and scrabbled around in the dark.

It was Helen, in a bad mood.

'At last! Where the *hell* are you? Do you not realise that your solicitor is trying to get hold of you? I've just been to the house and picked up two letters from Jones and Jones, one of them *weeks* old with a footprint on it. I've got them now, I'll send them on to you, shall I? I see all your stuff has gone at last, thanks for letting me know. Did you realise you'd left the back door unlocked? You *idiot*. Oh, and you need to hand the house keys over to the agent and you must have all the garage keys as well because I can't find a single set. Have you *still* not been in to the office in Delamere?'

'No, I forgot.'

'Oh for fuck's sake!' A long sigh, then a slow intake of breath. '*Right*, can you please, please respond to your solicitor, and get the house keys to the agent. It completes *tomorrow!*'

'Oh, sorry.'

'You sound like you've got a cold.'

'Yeah, don't feel too good.'

'Where are you anyway? I can hear traffic zipping past.'

'Dunno. In a lay-by somewhere.'

'What? Oh, don't bother answering that! Where are you staying?'

'Chathill'

'*What?*'

She disconnected angrily and he stared at the handset in mild disbelief, his guts churning uncomfortably with both hunger and probably stress. Where did she think he was staying? Like he had a choice?

He'd signed his house – and almost his marriage – away forever, and soon he'd be forced to accept the same fate onto his unborn child. So it was true, women really did rule the world. They certainly held all the cards. His mother held the trump card though, the one with the joker on it. He couldn't believe Jo had thrown that in his face.

'Why don't you have the baby and I'll look after it,' he'd said, or something like that.

'You mean give it away, like your mother did to you?'

'How's that the same? I don't even know who my real father was!'

It had been stupid, it was one of those throwaway statements people make when they've gone all round the houses with an argument, talked themselves into a dead-end, and then just hit out. All the same, he was surprised how much it got to him, even after forty-five years, the abandonment by his mother remained a touchy subject. Jo had apologised, of course, even hugged him, but it was too late by then. He wondered if his adoption and the disinterest of his birth mother had anything to do with his fierce feelings now.

Of course it fucking did.

He'd only ever met Ruby Martinez once, his mother.

How crazy was that? He'd tracked her down, when Bill and Doreen Black passed away in 1999. It had been easy, she'd been a well-known American actress at the point of his adoption, and a drunk, too. It was all well documented. The double bereavement had fuelled a despairing mix of sadness and deep curiosity about Ruby. It was strange to think that, although he'd lost a mum, he still had one, of sorts. He'd taken dozens of photographs with him of Helen, his wedding day, his children.

Al imagined Ruby would be so overcome by his appearance he'd be welcomed with open arms and enjoy a long, heartfelt reunion. At the very least he imagined he'd get some honest answers, about his father, and all the relatives he didn't know about. A second rejection had never been on the agenda, but in retrospect, that's what it had amounted to. The bitch didn't want to know.

That's when his life had imploded.

He turned the key in the ignition and pulled out into the traffic. An hour later, he could glimpse the midnight-blue sea in Llandudno Bay, a ferocious wind throwing the waves against a spotlighted section of The Orme.

You're still in love with your ex-wife.

The hotel looked quiet. He patted his inside pocket, the presence of the little packet a reassuring motivation to actually go and open the door. His heart leapt with gratitude to see her alone, on the reception desk, head bent over a diary and chewing a pen. She only glanced up at the last second, and at first there was a beautiful smile, but that was quickly replaced by something else when she recognised him.

'What the hell do you want?'

'I've brought the keys, thought you could take them where they're supposed to go.'

She held out her hand. Instead, he fumbled for the present and shook it out of its cheap paper bag. The excuse for a mussel shell rolled across the desk and she frowned at it, then frowned at him. 'What's this about?'

'Mussel shells have pearls in them sometimes, don't they?'

'This is from the arcade. It's *plastic*.'

'I know, but it's just symbolic, you know? Thirty years is pearl and we nearly made it, didn't we?'

'We *didn't* make it though, Al. Are you saying we were tat? A shell of a marriage is about right!'

'No! I'm saying a slightly belated happy anniversary, that's all. There's no hidden message. And we had a *fantastic* marriage until I fucked it up.'

'That's an understatement, but thank you for being so honest. Now get lost!'

Defeated and deflated, he placed his house keys and a bunch of garage keys onto the desk. Helen rummaged into her handbag and slapped down the aforementioned letters. Then she pulled her engagement and wedding ring off and slung them across the desk, and lobbed the mussel shell in his direction too, just missing his eye. By this point there were tears streaming down her face.

'Helen I –'

'Just piss off!'

With his eyes level with hers, he walked backwards down the hall, only coming to his senses when he collided with an umbrella stand and the evening bingo crowd trying to get through the front door. It was difficult to tear his eyes from hers, but in the end he had to.

Some twenty minutes later he drew up at the farm, not entirely sure he wanted to face anyone, but the second he got the car door open Fran came trotting out. She slowed down as she neared the car and spotted all the mess inside, himself included.

'Why are Greg's things in the car?' she said, tugging at a half-open bag. Her eyes roamed through the belongings crushed up at the windows and began to point out items she recognised. 'That's his yellow jersey from the Cymraeg Centenary Circuit.'

She began to stockpile things into her arms with a horrible desperation, looking more and more like the doctor out of *Back to the Future*, all wild, bulging eyes and mad hair. 'But *why, Al*?' Fran cried, rifling through a bag of shirts.

'What's going on?' Kate shouted from the doorway. The pool of light from the hall just about illuminated the scene and he could see his brother's bulk hovering behind Kate. Great. The day had started really well and then everything after lunch had been a downhill race to a smack in the face dead-end.

'Kate. I'm sorry but the charity shops were shut.'

'So … you brought everything back *here?*'

'I didn't know what else to do.'

'That's because his brains are in his pants,' George said. 'You look wrecked.'

'I've had some unwelcome news.'

'Oh,' Kate said, her face tight. 'Nothing serious I hope?'

'It is pretty serious, actually. Worst serious news I think I've had in a long time,' he said, and made to get past his brother.

'Blown you out, has she?' George said, then shoved his way outside. He caught hold of Fran, gently relieving her of the armful of clothing, and began to load everything into the rear of his 4x4. 'Don't worry, love,' he said to Kate, full of authority. 'I'll sort this out for you. My brother can never be relied upon to do the right thing.'

Doing the right thing. He thought he had done the right thing by Jo and the baby. He thought he'd done the right thing in being a great dad to Tom and Maisie but none of these things seemed to count for anything. The role reversal of men and women didn't work, either. The man's role was all about making money first and then being efficient in everything else. The woman's role was just about anything they fancied; from a cute, stay-at-home super mum to some ball-breaking bitch heading up the boardroom, ready for the company takeover.

He'd made a mistake a long time ago, quite a big one, he was the first to admit, but he'd done the right thing in the aftermath, hadn't he? He'd protected the one person he loved the most from the entire mess with his silence.

Until he'd told Helen.

Chapter Seven

Kate

Odd, that she thought about sex in such a sustained way since she'd found herself a singleton at the age of forty-nine. Sex was everywhere; films, books, even street advertising, but never a muffin top in sight unless you were in the supermarket, of course, and even then, there were subtle sexual signals at work. No limit to its power of seduction, or variety. The advert for yoghurt for example, was enhanced by a blonde thirty-something with her cleavage on display, a spoon halfway to her pouting mouth. She found it irksome, an insult to her intelligence, and deliberately avoided the brand.

In books, out of the public glare, it seemed the more extreme the better. Her daughter read books about multiple BDSM relationships – she'd had to Google the initials to understand what it meant – and had distasteful public chats about it through a book discussion group on the internet. The themes were along the lines of sex with two men at the same time, or two women and one man, or if you were bored by all of that how about sex with other people watching? Then there was a flashfiction section built around the plot lines from fairy tales but destroying them with various sexual acts along the way. *Alice in Wonderland and the Queen of Tarts explore the Hole*, or some such atrocity. No doubt the White Rabbit didn't get away unblemished either.

Their mother-daughter arguments around these subjects were prolific and frightening. Sad, that the only trigger for any deep emotion usually happened after one of her daughter's rants. It just made her weep, the memory of the little girl she used to be and the woman she had become. She seemed so hard, and selfish. Was it her fault? Maybe the divorce had made her like this? Did she expect to be used by men and so strove to get in first?

'Why are you even reading what I post on the Internet?' she'd snarl. 'My reading and sexual preferences have nothing to do with you!'

'Can you not see that I'm worried about the kind of men knocking on my door looking for you? Older, with a pair of bloody handcuffs!'

'Look, Mum,' she'd said, as if she were far more worldly-wise. 'I know what I'm doing. It's just a bit of fun. We even have a safe word.'

'Fun? And why would you feel unsafe?'

The key word, of course, was 'erotic' but it had a wide-ranging meaning. In all cases, it looked tacky and cheap to Kate. Some of the books were headed 'romance', and this seemed doubly insidious.

She's hot, he likes it when she's a dog and begs for it.

They argued about everything. Her musical taste had a pounding darkness to it with lyrics repeated over and over. *Wake me up inside.* Photographs on her Facebook page presented another battleground. Studded tongues pulled out, backsides showing, nipples poking through flimsy tops, her friend throwing up in a neighbour's hanging basket. Kate thought it was mindless and degrading, but perhaps that was her age, her generation, where women had fought for years for equality and respect, only to allow their daughters to throw it all away again.

Did sex really underpin one's existence and happiness? Did one need to be having lots and lots of sex? After all, it was only nature's way of procreating children, there was nothing more mysterious to it. Anything more was just self-gratification, wasn't it?

When she'd been with Greg, there was a protection

from the more blatant intrusion of sex. There was a presumption you had some sort of sex life. The truth of it had been very different, but behind the facade of marriage, it had all quietly taken a back seat.

She hadn't minded. At first, Greg's obsession with keeping fit and all the cycling had seemed a good thing, but then as time had worn on, watching his aero-dynamic body sliding into all that sweaty Lycra and padded underwear, had just revolted her. She no longer enjoyed the feel of him, either. He seemed to grow long and stringy, like a youth. It was likely tied up with his general need for cycling and she'd simply grown to hate his hobby, jealous of the time it consumed. Maybe.

And now there was a pile of his things in the sitting room at Chathill. Fran was clearly horrified that Kate had wanted to get rid of certain items of memorabilia, and clearly miffed that she hadn't been asked or consulted. She'd made an odd choice of items to cherish, and Butter had already made off with an inner tube. While all of this awkwardness was going on, George had taken control of the situation and emptied her car. Al slunk upstairs to his room like a teenager.

She was deeply annoyed with him for being unreliable and insensitive, but then she was curious about the bad news. He'd been such good company in the pub, easy to talk to, and unfazed by her outburst concerning Greg. She'd never confided in anyone about the morning of the accident but somehow Al had a way of drawing her out – or did he draw her in? He'd been so attentive, everything she'd said had been considered and absorbed.

When she padded back across the landing from using the bathroom some two hours later, she could see he was still sprawled across the unmade bed, fully clothed and staring at the ceiling with his trademark cigarette in place. She was almost past the door when he called her name, then when she stopped in her tracks, motioned that she perch next to him. He'd picked up her hand and rubbed it. The gesture was almost too intimate, but the warmth of it had her captivated.

'Kate, I'm so, so sorry –'

'It's OK, it doesn't matter. It's only *things*.'

She wished she could believe it; she did on the whole, but Fran didn't see it like that at all and had taken to wearing the cycling jersey over her jumper as she did evening chores outside, a huge number 9 just visible in the dusk.

The discomfort over the charity bags rumbled on. Kate found herself interrogated over a late breakfast on Wednesday.

'So, yesterday, you went into town with Al?' Fran said.

'Yes, then we had lunch. Can't believe how long we talked for. I guess partly my fault the charity shops were shut.'

'What did you talk about? Sorry, that's a bit rude.'

'Mostly books. I'm going to get his old titles out as eBooks.'

'Has he said anything about that girl? Jo?'

'No,' she said, truthfully.

Fran continued to be slightly off-hand with her, despite keeping to the loose arrangement that Kate had agreed to ride Stilton, Becca's new horse. Now she was faced with the reality instead of the wine-induced bravado from a couple of evenings previous, she wasn't so certain it was a good idea. Watching the hunter-fit horse career around the perimeter of his field sent her stomach churning with anxiety. She'd ridden as a teenager, a lot. But the seventies and eighties had been a long time ago. Her days filled with treasure hunts on the ponies of her youth were distant memories, and the sun was always shining in them.

She drove past one such trekking centre some days and it was sad to see it closed, given over to private liveries because it was easier, cheaper, less hassle. The horses looked sad and bored, pulled out at the weekends to trot round the same circuit, the pasture sick and unkempt because no one wanted the responsibility of it. Some days her heart was in her mouth when she saw young girls trying to get horses in or out of the paddock gate, cars whipping past with no thought of slowing down. It made her feel incredibly melancholy, a little like the sex issue with Tia had.

Greg had smirked and told her it was the start of the menopause. Maybe it was, but it was tiresome, this constant harking back to when things were better. It was exactly what her mother did, and she and Annemarie used to laugh with derision.

Stilton came to her with no fuss, nuzzling her hands for treats as she fumbled with the halter, first getting it upside down and then not being able to fasten the buckle. He walked with her across the muddy grass, his long, swinging stride keeping pace and it felt good just to be doing something different. The thought of riding again was something of a mixed bag, because although it felt good to push herself to feel something, it was a little odd to think that even fear was a welcome visitor.

Fran had her trotting on small circles and other shapes, requiring a surprising degree of concentration, and all of which confirmed how unfit and uncoordinated she'd become. Once upon a time her centre of balance aligned to the movement of the horse without thinking about it, it now required substantial effort. After ten minutes, she was running with sweat and had to stop.

Fran grinned. 'Just take your time, you have a natural seat. Obviously you've ridden a lot in the past.'

'Nothing feels natural, I assure you.'

'Let's do some more warming up and then you can finish with a canter.'

Her stomach sank, but she was determined to do it, to

feel the connection she used to have. She persevered until Fran declared them both good to canter. Stilton anticipated all of this long before she got to the right spot, and bunny-hopped with enthusiasm before bounding into too fast a pace for the size of the circuit, causing him to swerve round the bend instead of slowing down. Kate lost a stirrup and had to pull up, distinctly lopsided and holding on to the front of the saddle like a novice.

'Are you all right?' Fran said anxiously. 'He put in a funny one, didn't he?'

'I think I've bitten my tongue!'

They laughed together, and for a moment it was like it used to be. 'You recovered well though.'

'I don't feel recovered, not from anything.'

Fran smiled wistfully at this and patted her leg. When Kate followed her line of sight, she saw Al had been watching, hat jammed down, collar up.

'That was rubbish!' he yelled.

'Get over here and you do it then!' Fran yelled back, but he just grinned and tapped a cigarette over and over onto his mobile phone.

Kate jumped down from the horse, wincing at the jolt of pain it sent reverberating through her feet. So that meant she had no natural shock absorbers left either. Once Stilton was untacked, they both walked the horse back to his paddock. A cold wind snatched at her hair and Stilton's grey mane, blending both into a monochrome sky streaked with an odd hue. Early snow, or hail maybe, falling on higher ground.

'I think I enjoyed that,' she said to Fran with a smile. 'Although I need to do more exercise, clearly. My small excuse is that I was up half the night reading Al's book.'

Fran studied her face carefully. 'What did you think of it?'

'Well, I read it all in one sitting, very entertaining.'

'Yes he is, very entertaining.'

On the return walk to the house, looking at Chathill from a distance, she was struck by how shabby everything really was. Not that there was any welfare issue with the animals, but the whole place looked dismal, sagging fences patched up with planks of wood, and huge holes in the chicken wire, all pulled together with complicated bits of string. Once upon a time, George used to keep it all contained and tidy with everything in good repair, but it was as if he'd given up, and although she had to admit there were far too many animals for the space. She hated to think what it must cost to care for them all, let alone pay the feed merchant and the vet. Fran might be big-hearted and generous but it all came out of her husband's pocket.

The aforementioned invitation to lunch with George was scheduled for 1 p.m. at The Fairy Glen Hotel and Kate found herself pleased to be driving along the valley road to Betws. Hellishly busy in the summer, the town was virtually empty out of season, so there was no problem parking. The venue was typical of many establishments in the area; too big and too old to keep in good repair, but there was an appetising aroma when she pushed open the door. Gloomy, full of huge mirrors and portraits, Kate found her way into the bar area, which was a mix of eighties' carpets and curtains. In its favour, it boasted a very welcome, albeit fierce, log burner.

George waved and held out a chair for her at a small table by the window. She smiled at the chivalrous gesture and accepted a glass of wine and a menu. He told her he'd dealt with the charity bags, and that his brother was an abnormal waste of space. She thanked him, but chose to ignore the predictable slight on his brother. They ordered local lamb with roasted vegetables and Kate remarked on how well they seemed to know him, the barman and the waiter.

'Yes, well, I eat here virtually every day. Do you blame me?' he said, and topped up her wine glass. 'I bet you wish you'd gone away somewhere warm and exciting for your holiday, rather than the local animal sanctuary cum drop-out centre, hmm?'

'Have you brought me here to have a moan about Al and Fran?'

'Not entirely, no. But I wanted to have a frank chat. You know me, I say things as I see them. And I see you slaving away in the kitchen, cooking and cleaning, trying to scrub cat shit off the mat. What sort of a break is that?'

'Well, I've enjoyed it so far. I've been taken out to lunch twice, caught up on my reading, and this morning I rode Stilton, which I am very proud of.'

He almost smiled at her, then shot her something halfway between a laugh and a derisory grunt. 'And this is preferable to a week in the sun, being waited on, shopping and sightseeing?'

'In a way, yes. I'm with my family, or what's left of it. It's nice to be slightly unavailable for my sister. My daughter doesn't need me in any capacity and my mother ... look, to be honest I couldn't have coped with planning anything and getting to an airport, too much bother.'

George extended his big hand across the table and covered hers. 'You're still vulnerable from your loss, you need to be careful.'

They were interrupted by the arrival of the lamb. It was remarkably good and halted the conversation, which gave her time to think about his words and how she might change the subject, but she didn't get the chance.

'I saw you, with Al,' he said, dabbing his chin, eyes on hers. 'I saw you both walking through town.'

'We had a good day, as it happens.'

'Don't be drawn in by him, Kate.'

'Why are you at each other's throats, if you don't mind me asking?'

'Not at all, but you may not get a full answer.'

'Did you *ever* get on, in the past?'

His eyes locked on to hers and for a long moment, she thought he wasn't going to respond. When he did, it was with such gravity she was left with no doubt every word was from the heart. 'I loved my brother, Kate.' He took a moment to consider, draining his half pint thoughtfully. 'You know, Mum and Dad couldn't have any more kids so they went for adoption. I was dreading getting a sister, but from the day he arrived I loved Al more than if we were real blood, even when he told me I'd have to be locked in a glass case and be operated on by aliens when I needed a tonsillectomy. I wet the bed that night, thanks to him. And do you know, he stole every single one of my girlfriends? We fought like dogs over Bethany Brown.' He shot her a wry smile and screwed up his napkin. 'Oh, I'm no fool, he had all the looks and the charm. Still does.'

'What did he do that you can't bury the hatchet?'

'Oh, I'd bury one in his head if I thought it would solve anything.'

She sipped her wine, chilled by the look in his eyes. 'So why *do* you let him share a roof with you?'

'Much as I dislike the fact, he does actually own half the property. And much as I dislike the fact, my wife and my daughter think the world of him.'

'I get the feeling there's more to this than you are telling me.'

'There is, but you'll just have to accept it.' He pushed the pudding menu over. 'The pear compote is awfully good.' Once her eyes were drawn to the laminated sheet, he said, 'After Christmas I have a few difficult decisions to make, all of which will affect my family, my future. Al, much as I dislike the fact, is part of the general picture. I'll make my announcement in January.'

It sounded like a board meeting at the bank.

Afterwards, she wandered aimlessly around the town, disinterested in the tourist shops and unable to blank

George's words from her mind. There was nothing like someone else's troubles to water down one's own, and she realised that Greg and the funeral had taken a back seat. Was that a good sign or something else to feel guilty about?

Should she sell the house? She could give up her soul-destroying job. Greg had left her well enough provided for in that respect, but nothing would form in her mind. She stood on the stone bridge and watched the foaming river below bouncing over the rocks. She had a lot of time to stand and stare, and in a way she needed to, but then she sighed with boredom.

All this freedom, and she had no idea what to do with it.

The first day of November dragged itself slowly over the horizon. Peering through the curtains, Kate could see the dark shapes of the mountains groaning under a depressed sky. Closer to home, the farrier was busy in the yard, with four horses lined up along the stable block, including a restless Stilton. Becca was trying to soothe him, white hair all over her navy school uniform. The little mare they'd rescued from the auction sported medical-looking leg bandages and was watching with interest, both ears pricked. The acrid smell of burning hoof filtered through the small top window. It reminded her of the time a drunken Annemarie caught her long hair on the gas hob, singeing a good two inches off the length.

From the confines of her room, wrapped in an old dressing gown modelled along the style of an exploded duvet, she stuck her head out on to the landing, gauging the distance to the bathroom and wondering if she could get to it without being seen by Al. After everything she'd told herself about sex, here she was worrying about her sex appeal around a man she'd been warned off. A man with too many secrets, and a pregnant girlfriend.

As she crept past his room, she saw him standing on a chair by the window and having a hushed, heated conversation with someone on his mobile. The girlfriend, no doubt. Bathroom door firmly locked, she ran a deep, hot bath. There were parts of her body which had suffered quite severely from trying to stay in tune with Stilton, and the hot water was sublime.

Her shoulder blades and lower regions of her back felt like she'd been on a torture rack, and then there was always that curious, intimate place at the top of the inner thigh which always hurt like hell. Lying back under the suds she could hear another, muted argument in the kitchen below, between George and Fran, something about the cost of the farrier.

'I'm not a cruel man, Fran,' George was saying in a loud voice. 'I am a desperately exasperated man! And all of this … this hoof trimming and corrective shoes or whatever, all for a bloody nag destined to be shot. Oh, don't give me the doe eyes!'

'We'd never have got Stilton loaded if it wasn't for Olive. We need her to get Stilton to all the shows and competitions next summer, so he's settled in the lorry.'

'What shows? That's *more* cash! Entry fees, special gear, fuel!'

'Stop shouting! Don't you want Becca to do well and enjoy herself?'

'Yes, of course, but not at the risk of going bloody bankrupt!'

There was a heavy thud, like a door slamming, followed by the usual volley of profanities from the parrot. Presently, George's car purred down the drive and there was a welcome silence, broken just seconds later by a heart-stopping crash as something heavy, possibly made of metal, hit the tiled floor in the hall. Butter must have leapt the wobbly stair gate again.

As she reached for a towel, she heard the dog galloping

up the stairs, sniffing violently under all the doors, searching for Al.

Chapter Eight

Kate

Home. Her mobile sprang to life with two missed calls and a text. They were both from Annemarie. Disappointed it wasn't Al, Kate snapped her phone shut. She retrieved her bags and boxes from the car and set them down in the hall, then slowly sank onto the sofa to test her feelings. It was the same spot where she'd sat with Al just a few days prior, but this time she was faced with all the empty spaces, and the last traces of Greg were virtually gone. It was too cold to sit for long though and she was forced to flick the heating on and get the burner going in the snug.

The boxes of manuscripts went on the desk, next to her computer and the new scanner. She'd been making digital albums out of old family photographs and discovered she enjoyed the process, and although she had much to learn about compiling a book, having read some of Al's work the whole idea had caught her imagination. Al had been more than happy for her to take the novels, no doubt out of harm's way. Despite the challenge it represented, she couldn't help feeling gratified that he'd trusted her with them. The fact that it served as an on-going link between them was something she wasn't quite prepared to admit. She lifted the lid of the first one and smiled as she read the title page; *The Chronicles of Jim Silver*, by Alastair Black.

She was slightly peeved that he hadn't said goodbye to her. In fact, he'd laid low for the remainder of her week at Chathill, deep in thought with whatever problem the girlfriend had presented. On the occasions he did surface, it was with a rather tense solitude, which didn't suit him, and the argumentative battles over money from George with both his wife and his brother left Kate feeling frazzled. Fran had been her usual distracted self, as if nothing was wrong and mostly intent on getting Al's daughter to treat some of the animals.

'She's a vet,' Fran had explained, presumably for Kate's benefit. '*Such* a lovely girl.'

Al had half-smiled patiently, 'Yeah, but you can't expect her to do treatments for free. She has to account for the drugs, you know?'

'Oh, I know, but she could just come over and give me the heads-up about Olive and some of the goats, couldn't she? And she could help me with the worming, yes?'

'Christmas, maybe. She's got some time off.'

'Oh goody, tell her to come over for a few days, will you, please?'

'I can ask, but it's a bit like a busman's holiday for her, isn't it?'

Kate switched on the PC and checked her e-mail. Nothing from Tia. Her Facebook page though, was full of the usual party chaos and attention-seeking posts. 'I'm soooo pissed off right now.' A dozen or so *friends* wanted to know why, but she never enlightened them. Could mean anything, from a broken nail to a broken heart.

A message popped up from Annemarie.

'Back then? Next time you want to come into my house please have the bloody decency to knock or phone instead of creeping up the bloody stairs.'

'I did, but you were in bed with the bank manager.'

No response to that. She typed 'Maisie Black' into the search box and there were three to choose from. Easy to see which one was Al's daughter, even with the veterinary information – her profile picture screamed 'I'm Alastair Black's daughter.' Same dark blonde colouring, although hers was shimmery bright, and she had those long, denim-blue eyes. The main picture was a panoramic shot; an

African-looking landscape with gazelles in the background, a hunky boyfriend leaning on a Land Rover. In the 'About' section there was a long list of qualifications.

Her relationship list was clearly visible, all with profiles. Bursting with curiosity, she clicked onto brother Tom, Oxford graduate. Sister-in-law Bernice, something to do with higher education; two children in full-time nursery. Boyfriend Simon was practising partner at The Well Pet veterinary practice. Goodness, she'd be there all evening but it was too fascinating not to have a nose. Even though she was not privy to all the information, there was one over-riding, glaring fact; they didn't strike her as the profiles of people with a waste of space for a father.

Jo was something altogether different. Almost a thousand friends and everything on her page was public and incredibly busy, but sadly not very interesting or personal – other than a couple of arty, romantic photographs of her with Al in Delamere Forest. She slid one of them off onto her computer desktop, then felt embarrassed and deleted it.

Annemarie messaged back. 'How did you know who it was?'

'I didn't, it was a *joke!*'

'Just stay out of it!'

'I want to talk to you. I'll come by on Monday, shall I?'

While she was waiting for her sister to confirm, she browsed some more and looked at Alastair Black but his page appeared to be virtually un-used and carried only the briefest of detail; married to Helen, attended a school in Conwy, and then a list of his out of print paperbacks, and that was about it.. Even his profile picture was taken some twenty years ago.

Nothing further from Annemarie, clearly sulking. She plugged the scanner into the wall socket, googled various sites about formatting books, and tentatively created a file.

Christmas was beginning to filter into the retail world, with its usual blend of mercenary rubbish. Her job was one of those clock-watching affairs and the day passed painfully slow. Bargain Home Stores was a large, cheap department store, run on a shoestring but working false promise to its maximum leverage, on all levels. The elderly customers thought they were getting a bargain, of course, and most of the staff had been seduced by the promise of benefits which never quite materialised, because as soon as you were in sight of the prize, they always changed the rules.

The department managers were young, usually with business and computing degrees, enhanced with natural management skills in arrogance. The demoralising problem was that the younger staff really had the upper hand, which was mostly down to the speed of their computer skills on the increasingly complicated tills. It was one of the reasons Kate had elected to do an evening course in basic computing, and discovered that she actually enjoyed it, but it made little difference to the hierarchy of her job.

Once you became proficient on a section in the store, you would be moved to another one 'to broaden your opportunity to develop'. Knowledge was power, and the company didn't like that. They preferred the staff to be slightly dumbed down and compliant. Kate had long since given up trying to make a difference or to fight the inevitable. Some of the older women were quite kind and friendly but Kate found she had little in common with them. The bitching and bullying was rife, regardless.

As soon as it was five minutes to home time, she left the shop floor, climbed the stairs to the staff area, swiped her key card, and went into the locker room, then gratefully climbed out of the hideous uniform; loose black trousers and a gingham blouse with a name badge over the left breast. Her line manager, a huge, wobbly girl of nineteen – known in the stockroom as Wide Load, since no one could possibly get past her if she was standing in one of the aisles – made a show of looking at her watch and then gave her the eye. 'Thought you was on till three?'

'That's right.'

'By my watch you're stealing company time, I'll have to mark it up in the book.'

'Fine, you do that.'

Her rosebud mouth fell open as Kate closed her locker and hurried out of the confined space, down the stairs again, through the huge glass doors, and out into the gloriously weak sunlight of a mild winter's afternoon. It made her think about Stilton and the last couple of days at Chathill, when she'd finally mastered a controlled canter on a circle. The feeling of elation in the cold biting air, and then the shiver when she realised that Al had been watching her …

She turned her car towards her sister's house, but of course she wasn't in. A phone call revealed her whereabouts to be at their mother's flat. Kate cursed Annemarie's lackadaisical attitude. 'You could have told me!'

'She needed shopping doing.'

This was something new. Normally, Kate did the bulk of the doctor's appointments, the shopping, and the visits. On her arrival at Rhos House, Annemarie was in the kitchen with a cigarette, wafting the smoke out of the window. Mother looked pale, and she was nursing one of her Charles and Diana tumblers from the sideboard, the use of which was normally reserved for Christmas and funerals. A bad sign. Kate gave her a peck on the cheek.

'What's the brandy about, Mum?'

'Oh, you might well ask. I've had an excitement. I've been on a fire engine,' she said, then flapped her hand in the direction of the kitchen. 'You tell her, Anne.'

'A fire engine?' Kate frowned, looking from one to the

other. Annemarie threw herself down on the sofa and checked her mobile. 'It's nothing. She didn't want to come in the shop, said she felt faint and she'd sit outside and wait. So she sat on the kiddie's ride, you know, that Fireman Sam thing.'

'Oh, is that all? You had me worried,' Kate said, but her mother became deeply agitated and flushed at this. 'Yes, but it *set off*, and I couldn't get *out*. All the bloody bells were going off and it was jigging about, and oh … tell her, Anne!'

'Well, you've told her now.'

'Oh, I felt sick I did … and palpitations. I'll not get that song out of my mind for a long time, I can tell you. I thought my time had come.'

Her sister snorted with amusement. 'Attracted quite a crowd, be on YouTube tonight.'

'No lasting damage then?' Kate said.

'Only disappointment. No real firemen came to rescue her,' Annemarie cut in. 'The store manager pulled the plug in the end but he still wanted fifty pence, can you believe that?'

Kate said nothing as she genuinely couldn't think of anything to say. She knew there was a funny side to the story, but it just wouldn't surface.

'What's the matter? You've a face like a wet week,' her sister went on, 'You've just had a bloody holiday, it's me that's been holding the fort here.'

'For five days? My God, Annemarie, how did you cope?'

'Wish I could afford a holiday.'

'Get a job, then.'

'She's *got* a job now,' Mother said, and there was a certain pride and satisfaction in the statement. She drained the last of her brandy. 'It suits everyone, the arrangement.'

Kate waited until her mother had put the glass down on the mat, noticing out of the corner of her eye, that her sister was eye-rolling up to the ceiling.

'What *arrangement*, Mum?'

'I'm paying Anne to be my personal carer. I don't know why I didn't think of it before. It was my idea.'

'Personal carer? You mean simple daughter duties, the kind of things I've done for ten years without payment, and around a full-time job?'

'Well, yes, but don't you see? This way it's more fair. Anne has the time and she needs the money more than you, and you're always so *busy*.'

'At work, you mean? But I never *minded*, that's the point.'

Annemarie sighed and went to the bathroom. Her mother came across and clumsily embraced her. The brandy fumes almost made her eyes water. Kate had to hold her arms to stop her from wobbling over.

'I love you both the same,' her mother began in a low voice. 'But Anne is more needy than you, she's weak.'

And sleeping with the bank manager.

'You're not helping her by letting her take control of you, it's all for her own selfish means. And how much brandy have you had? You're not meant to be drinking on those tablets!'

'Shush, I know,' her mother said, and patted her hand as if they were conspiring, or she needed to be placated. 'Only a drop. And don't worry, I'll keep your sister busy, you wait and see. And take that ham home with you, it'll go off in this heat.'

Kate drove home feeling physically aged, but on the inside she was a mash of childish tears and building anger, although none of it surfaced properly and the containment of it all made her feel ten times worse. She thought about forcing some of it out once inside her own four walls, throw something at the wall maybe?

Her mobile began to trill and the screen began to flash. *Al calling.*

99

She took a deep breath and poured a huge glass of wine with her free hand and moderated her inner voice. 'Hi, how are you?'

'All right, I think,' he said. 'You?'

'Same, I think.'

'Guess what? I've got myself a secondhand car and a laptop. If all of this hadn't been the result of my divorce settlement, I'd be feeling like a teenager. I even got an argument about keeping my room tidy from big bro,' he went on, then sighed. 'Look, Kate, I'm sorry I didn't say goodbye and I haven't been in touch –'

'Oh, well, I suppose I was a bit hasty for the off,' she said, walking into the snug then and looking at the mess of paper. 'I've done the first book, by the way. I need you to check it before I upload it to any sites. Oh, and I need your email, and you'll need an e-reader app to check the formatting. And I'll need your bank details, and we need to discuss royalty percentages. Oh, and some possible marketing ideas, not to mention a cover and a decent blurb.'

There was a beat of total silence. 'Come again?'

'I suppose it would be easier if we did this face to face. I'll set up your laptop if you like.'

'I like.'

The phone died in her hand. Within half an hour, he was pulling onto the drive in what appeared to be a sporty-looking car, impossible to see exactly what it was in the dark, but clearly on the low side. He struggled to get out of it, and then struggled to get the boot open. Butter leapt into the vacated driving seat.

Kate hugged her arms around herself, shivering in the doorway, surprised but pleased by his sudden appearance, although slightly concerned that she hadn't had chance to glance in the mirror or run a brush through her hair.

'Are you leaving the dogs in the car? You can bring them in, I don't mind.'

'I've only got Butter, Marge isn't well.'

'Oh, nothing serious?'

'Not sure, I've left her in bed with a hot water bottle.'

She wondered briefly what any hovering neighbour might make of the bizarre conversation but it made her smile, and after feeling so tense, a very welcome diversion. Butter bounded in, and the dog seemed even bigger in the small space. Despite Al's commands to sit or lie down, the dog wouldn't settle until every corner of the house had been explored.

'He's looking for Marge,' Al said.

She poured him a glass of wine and topped up her own. After some deliberation about the lack of space, she suggested he bring a kitchen stool over to her small desk so they could sit side by side. It meant they were virtually thigh to thigh, laptop to laptop, shoulder to shoulder. His close proximity was distracting on all counts and his hand frequently brushed hers.

He watched and listened very carefully to everything she said, cigarette in place, eyes on the screen but occasionally flicking onto her profile. Two hours later and they'd covered all the basic stuff and she'd sent him an email with his book file in it, downloaded the e-reader app, and gone through the publishing instructions in the store.

His face lit up when he saw the title page. 'Hey, this is just … I can't believe you've done all this.'

'Now I know how, I can get the others done much faster. Shall we get this one on sale or do you want to wait and load them all together? What about cover images?'

'Hell, I don't know, let me think about it,' he said, then stretched and yawned. 'You're way ahead of me.'

Kate stared at his torso for a moment, then began to close down her computer. 'You know, I've read them all now. *Loved* them. So, who is Jim Silver exactly? Is much of it based on you? I couldn't help thinking about the adoption storyline.'

He looked at her with an expression she couldn't quite place, but he wouldn't break eye contact. Disconcerted, she scraped her chair back, almost landing in his lap, and put a hand out to balance herself. It landed on his leg, mercifully. 'Tea?' she said, and he nodded ever so slightly.

On her return with two mugs, he'd shoved another log in the burner and made himself comfortable on the sofa, arms behind his head.

'Not everyone *gets* them, the books.'

'Oh, I did,' she said, and smiled over her mug of tea.

'In answer to your question, there's a lot of me in there, yeah.'

He began to talk to her about his real, and his adoptive, mother, and she began to reciprocate, starting to feel better at getting some of it off her chest, when her mobile rang. They both looked at it, and then at the clock. And the irony wasn't lost when the shaky voice of her mother's next door neighbour came over the line.

'Kate? So sorry to call late.'

She scrambled to her feet, blood rushing through her ears. 'What is it?'

'I'm sorry, love, but I've had to call the ambulance for your mum. She … the paramedic thought she was having another heart attack.'

'Oh! *Mum*. Which hospital?'

Al's head shot up.

'Bangor. I've tried to call your Anne but there's no reply on any of the numbers.'

'I'll sort it.'

'You will let me know how she gets on, won't you?'

'Yes, of course.'

Al was already on his feet and grabbing his leather jacket. 'I'll drive you.'

She passed a hand over her forehead. 'I've had too much to drink, do you think I could get a taxi?'

'Kate. I'll drive you.'

Forty minutes later, they arrived at a dark, more or less deserted, car park. She struggled to get out of the car, and then Al struggled to lock it. Butter leapt up and pressed his nose to the glass.

'He'll be all right, he'll just go to sleep,' Al said, and then took hold of her hand. She'd never been so glad of the feel of someone's hand in hers. They pushed through the revolving doors and went up to the reception desk. Her mouth was so dry it took a couple of attempts to get the words out.

'Nora Allen? She was brought in by ambulance about an hour ago.'

The usual computer consultation revealed that she'd just been moved out of A&E to ward six, third floor. Al, caught hold of her hand again and negotiated all the lifts and the bewildering directions. Then she had to leave him in the waiting area because the ward was a closed one, single family members only sort of thing. She was led to a separate side room, seemingly full of hospital machinery and blinking monitors. Her mother lay beneath a single sheet and she looked lifeless, like parchment stretched over bone. After what seemed an age, her mother opened her eyes briefly and scanned her face.

'Who's there?'

'It's Kate.'

'I know why I'm in here, out of sight in a side room. I've got cancer but they won't say. They never tell you anything, they're all foreign.'

'No, Mum, you haven't got cancer. They think you've had an angina attack. Next door called the ambulance.'

'Renee? She can sling her hook. She never paid me for that twin tub, it was a good one as well.'

'Renee was more than thirty years ago! I'm talking about *Elsie,* next door to you at Rhos House.'

'Why didn't you say that, then?'

'I'm saying it now,' she snapped, then reeled herself in.

'Why don't you have a sleep, get some rest?'

'I'm watching *Family Fortunes* in a bit,' she said, then closed her eyes. There were a few more confused ramblings, the likely result of sedatives or painkillers. Kate sat on the chair at the side of the bed and watched the shallow breath escape from her mother's dry, parted lips. She touched the papery hand, lying claw-like on the bed, heavily bruised from drips being forced into shrivelled veins. She thought about the family photographs she'd been scanning, and how young her parents had looked in the black and white pictures, and how old she used to think they were.

The carefree holidays and the endless summers of the past somehow merged with Al and the way he made her feel. She felt cheated by it, that she should be attracted to a man who was engaged to a much younger woman, expecting his child, and ready to start again. Memories of her first, fairytale wedding floated into her mind and then the same round of parties and pony rides with her own daughter joined her landscape of regrets, lost dreams, and forgotten desires.

Several hours later, she woke with a cricked neck and a mild hangover.

A hovering nurse asked her about her mother's current medication. There was a long list which Kate always carried around with her, and the nurse seemed grateful for the information. She couldn't tell her very much, just that her mother was stable and that they were waiting for doctors and reports, the usual prognosis.

Kate left her contact numbers and then trailed back down the long corridor to the waiting room, surprised to find Al still there. His head was propped on his hand as he dozed, fingers splayed through his untidy hair and a light stubble shadowing his jaw. A cold plastic cup of tea sat on the low table in front of him.

He glanced up as she approached, and then he got slowly to his feet, looking tired and crumpled. 'Kate?'

And that's when the floodgates opened. It was like a dam bursting. She'd never known crying like it, real purging of the soul sobs erupting from some deep, untapped source, her eyes and nose streaming, none of it to do with the current situation. Al virtually held her upright and she allowed herself to sag against him, arms around his waist, head pressed against his chest.

After a few moments, she became aware of staff coming and going with trolleys and visitors starting to arrive. Her tears quickly subsided and she could have – should have – disentangled herself from his arms. But she couldn't; it felt so good, like the best rush of adrenaline she'd ever had.

Chapter Nine

Al

It was worrying to see her so distraught when normally everything about Kate seemed contained and controlled. At first he thought her mother must have passed away, but then he quickly realised that it was mostly relief, and maybe something else buried fighting to get out. He'd picked up on plenty of vibes as she was talking about her family earlier and coupled with what he knew about her marriage, reckoned some sort of mini meltdown had been imminent, if not necessary.

It had felt immoral though, to have her crushed against him in such a way, and he knew he was on dangerous ground given the responses it triggered to have her so deliciously close. He kept an arm around her shoulders as she blotted her face, and they went into the café. He ordered some breakfast, coffee, and bottles of water, glancing around at her every five minutes as he stood in the queue. When he got back to the table, he was relieved to see her face break into a smile when he wrapped up the extra sausages into a napkin for Butter.

'I went down to the car a couple of times, he was fine.'

'I didn't expect you to wait all night for me.'

'Why not? You've done plenty for me.'

He was thinking about his books; not just the work she'd put into the old manuscripts but the way she talked about them. Her insight had completely caught him out, fired him up, and focused his thoughts. She made him determined to carry on and write the final episode.

They talked about mothers. She felt guilty for getting

exasperated with Nora. She asked him about his blood mother, full of curiosity. He didn't want to dwell too much on Ruby and was scant on the detail. It was easy to be scant; he could sum it all up in two sentences and after all, she was the most un-motherly person he'd ever come across, and so moved the conversation around to his adoptive mother instead. Within minutes, Kate had picked up on his reticence and the comfort role was almost reversed.

When he thought about Kate and how short a time he'd known her, it didn't seem possible to have any sort of feelings for her. But then who was he kidding? He fell in like, love, or lust at the drop of a hat and he'd had a lifetime of trouble follow him as proof. From now on, e-mail would have to suffice. After breakfast, he dropped her back home and watched her run up to the front door without so much as a backward glance.

Relations with Jo continued to be borderline warm throughout November and into a wet December; a significant drop in temperature to when they'd met by chance in The Forest pub at Delamere the summer just passed. He'd bought her a drink and she'd listened to him moaning about Helen and his marriage breakdown with more than polite interest. Al went out of his way to impress that he was a bad catch and practically insolvent, and she'd pursued him relentlessly. She must have imagined he was after sex with no strings – which would have suited her – but the reality was that he loved the strings as well.

He was even fake at being a bad guy. Well, most of the time.

Jo had kept her promise about giving herself time to consider her pregnancy, and the closer Christmas advanced with all its family and child-related connotations, the more ground Al felt he'd gained. He *loved* Christmas, couldn't understand why anyone would feel turned off by it. Of course, children were the epicentre of the festivities and he used to look forward to it with manic devotion, whipping children and dogs into a frenzy of over-excitement.

Despite her reservations about everything, Jo announced she wanted to go into London for shopping.

'No way,' Al said. 'Can't stand the place, let's go local.'

'We can soak up the phoney atmosphere, go on the train, and stay over.'

'I haven't got that sort of cash, I'm trying to be sensible.'

'I'll pay. You can go in The Disney Shop.'

They travelled first class, and Jo had booked what she called a 'modest' hotel. Once there, she insisted on kitting him out with shirts and trousers, and then chose a new mobile phone for him. When they were in Liberty, she pointed out a silk scarf she fancied, dropping hints as big as incendiary bombs. So far as Al was concerned, it took all the pleasure and surprise out of Christmas Day, but when he told her this, she rounded on him.

'I've had enough surprises to last me a lifetime, thank you very much!'

'All right, no need to bite my head off!'

The evidence of morning sickness expelled any niggling doubt that she may have had a private termination behind his back. Her body was clearly adjusting to the pregnancy whether she liked it or not; although her mind wavered from being still set against the whole idea, to being maybe on the fence.

'I feel *shit*,' she said, on the morning they were due to catch the train home.

'It doesn't last long,' he said, catching hold of her hand. 'Twelve weeks, I think.'

'*Twelve weeks?* I have to go to New York in January, I *can't* be in this fucking state!'

She began to throw things into her case with

unnecessary force, and Al wondered how much longer they could exist in a relationship where he was keeping her sweet because he wanted the baby, and she was keeping him sweet *with* the baby because she was in love with him. That he'd admitted to this in his head was increasingly uncomfortable.

They struggled home on the train, Al carrying an enormous amount of toys and a single silk scarf. Jo spent most of the journey locked in the toilet. If he could have suffered all the discomfort for her, he would have done so, but there seemed little point in saying this since she batted away his offers of drinks and cuddles with a brooding silence.

The next hurdle was where and how to spend Christmas. Back at Jo's flat, they had an unsatisfactory conversation about it all. Jo wanted to go away. Al couldn't bear the thought. Christmas was about family. In the midst of locked horns, it seemed uncanny that his daughter-in-law called him about arrangements. Bernice had a hugely patronising tone, and the way she came up with a regimented plan over any social engagement added to his irritation. 'I thought Boxing Day, for lunch. Did you want to bring someone?'

Clearly he no longer qualified for Christmas Day. 'I've got a big pile of pressies for the kids, how about I pop round Christmas Eve?'

'Pop round? I'm not sure we'll be here, Alastair. It's a very busy day, what with the school fair and then the Christingle service.'

'Yeah? Count me in, I can help. Totally my thing.'

'Well, the thing is … gosh, this is awkward. We've got friends staying and Rupert and Barnaby will want to play with their children, you see. So, I thought … Boxing Day, lunch. Shall we see you at twelve, for drinks?'

'Is Tom there? Or maybe I can talk to the kids?'

'Tom's at work and the children are at their music

clubs, sorry. Look, can I ask what you've bought this time? It's just that, well, this year we've got a list. Those rats you acquired last year were *completely* unsuitable.'

'*Bernice*, Bernice … I'd like to see the kids either on or before Christmas Day, surely you get that? It's all done by Boxing Day!'

'The thing is, *Alastair* ... Oh, I do wish you wouldn't argue with me! I'm simply calling to invite you to lunch and –'

He lowered the phone, and weighed it in his hand for a moment before flinging it across the room. It fell to pieces instantly. The noise brought Jo out of the kitchen. She glanced at the bits of plastic against the cast iron grate and then at his apathetic position on the sofa.

'What did you say about not needing a new phone?'

He watched her legs walk towards him, and she cradled his head against her stomach, kissing the top of his head as she did so, and he was ashamed to find tears spring to his eyes.

A couple of days later, he called up Maisie on his complicated Internet phone. His daughter was the only person in the world who understood his frustration with Bernice and shared the opinion that basically, she was a bitch.

'She's such a control freak,' he said, and wandered over to the window for a stronger signal. Outside, the sky was like old pewter and a steady drizzle was turning everything underfoot to liquid mud. Fran was scurrying about in Wellingtons and a huge, ungainly overcoat, carrying buckets.

'Look,' Maisie said. 'Here's a thought. I've been scheduled in on the day before Christmas Eve. That's only next Monday, isn't it? I'm taking the boys to see Mum. When I'm done with that I could come over there with them?'

Yes! He explained about Fran's worming programme and she laughed. 'Oh well, I can kill two birds with one stone in that case.'

'The kids can help, they'd love that. *I'd* love it.'

'What, worming the goats? You need to get out more, Dad! If Bernice knew what we had planned she'd be on to social services.'

Al grunted in agreement, then Maisie took a deep breath. 'Anyway ... less of that, I have some news!'

'Will it make me smile?'

'Lots. But I'm not telling you till I come over.'

He tried his best to persuade her to spill the beans, but she wasn't having any of it. As they exchanged banter he grinned to himself, and moved the curtain back from the window. Fran was struggling with three horses in the yard as they pulled her over the slippery cobbles. The retired nags from the local riding school had arrived via a huge lorry, and not for the first time, Al wondered where the hell she was going to put them. In the blink of an eye, something spooked one of them and they all leapt in different directions. Fran, taken by surprise, was like flotsam on the end of a charging rhino. She quickly saw sense in letting go, but then tripped over and for a few seconds her slight frame seemed trampled by the hooves on the ground. Cutting his conversation short, Al lobbed the phone onto the bed and ran outside.

'Fran!' She was already up on her feet by the time he got there, leaning against a dilapidated fence, and panting and pointing at the horses. He caught two of them easily, both with their noses greedily buried in sacks of pony nuts. He couldn't blame them, they were like hat-racks. The other one had clattered over the dismantled jumping course: a selection of old oil drums and poles. He left it to pick its own way out and turned to look back at Fran.

'Are you hurt?'

'No, just lost my footing,' she said, then yelped and

112

clutched her ribcage. Her face suddenly drained to the colour of bleached straw and she slumped to the ground. She argued about going to get checked out, so in the end he just picked her up, carried her into his car, and laid her across the back seats with both seat belts pinning her down. Her lack of a struggle confirmed his suspicions.

Another afternoon hanging around A&E, this time in very damp clothes. An X-ray revealed that Fran had a fractured rib, but by far the most debilitating aspect would result from the bruising, which was quickly developing across her left side. There was another hoof-shaped imprint on her bony hip, which required cleaning and dressing. The nurse told her she was lucky the horses were not wearing iron shoes. They strapped her up, gave her a selection of painkillers and a tetanus shot, and wished her happy Christmas.

'What a mess!' she said, close to tears by the time they were back home, no doubt due to the shock. She could barely hobble around the kitchen, let alone resume normal duties outside. 'What a bloody miserable Christmas we're going to have with me like this!'

'I can help, and Becca will be off school in a couple of days.'

'What about all the cooking and shopping?'

'Seriously?' he said, trying to make her laugh. 'Fran, I don't recall you ever cooking Christmas dinner.'

'The farm alone is a full-time job, Al.'

She had a point. He rubbed his jaw. 'So, er … who'll be here over Christmas?'

'Just family. Why?'

'Does that include Kate? It's just that she's a whizz in the kitchen, and a natural with the horses.'

She thought about this for a moment. 'So are you.'

'But like you say, there's a lot of other stuff.'

'You fancy her, don't you?'

Where the hell had that come from? 'I *like* her.'

'In that case, *you* can ask her. Ask her if she'd like to spend Christmas shovelling shit and sweating over the stove and getting in the middle of all the arguments.'

'When you put it like that, I reckon she'll jump at it.'

Fran's bad mood was born out of frustration, he was sure. The fact that he'd created a good reason to ask Kate if she intended to come over to Chathill for Christmas was something he put down to him being sensible about the situation. It had taken hours to get round all the animals and start cooking dinner, while Fran lay on the sofa by the fire with the dogs, barking instructions and watching the Charity Animal channel on Sky.

He logged on to the Internet. No new e-mails, nothing from Kate. He read over their previous conversations and following the initial enquiry after Nora, it was all about the books, how to do this and how to do that. She'd found a graphic designer and they'd chosen a new image for Jim Silver. Other than his old agent, he'd never had anyone interested in his work to this degree, and he was slightly in awe of her expertise and enthusiasm. The first book had gone out onto the virtual bookshelf, but since he needed to get his head around promoting them, nothing else had happened. Occasionally, he looked at his book on eBook Emporium, and sent the link to Maisie and a couple of other people he used to know from his literary world, but other than his daughter, no one seemed to think his news was worth a reply, let alone a virtual pat on the back.

He'd fiddled about with Facebook too and Jo had helped him make an official author page, and it all looked very good but in truth he didn't have much patience with social networking and just wanted to get on with writing.

Jo had laughed when she'd looked at his personal profile.

'Seven friends? Who on earth has only seven friends?'

Al thought seven friends was quite a lot, but maybe he

needed to add a few more and look at all the book groups Jo had added him to, although from what he'd seen it was a horrible mix of posturing, boasting, and begging.

He typed 'Kate Roberts' into the search instead and a whole load of them came up, but she was unmistakable with that red hair. She responded to his friend request within seconds but before he could look properly or type anything, a private message from Jo popped up like an invisible eye.

'Hi, online at last? Found any more friends lol?'

'Lol?'

'Laugh out loud.'

He browsed Kate's page and looked at pictures of her and her late husband while he typed messages back and forth with Jo, but it seemed a bit indecent somehow, sort of secretive and shady. He saw it was Kate's birthday on the 21st of December, and she'd be fifty. That made her a Capricorn. Helen used to be an expert on all that stuff; she was always looking at a website called Star-Crossed, which plotted the planets and declared relationships to be either harmonious, difficult, or turbulent. He looked it up and carefully entered 'Scorpio man' and 'Capricorn woman' into the love section for analysis. Almost immediately, a row of five pink hearts flashed across the results box, followed by a red, flashing 'harmonious' sign held by a blushing, winking cherub.

He shut the page down, feeling slightly silly.

'Are you coming over tomorrow?' Jo had typed.

'Not sure, so much to do here with Fran laid off. You could come here though? I'll even let you use my homemade pig board lol!'

He deliberated sending a message to Kate, then decided to make an old-fashioned phone call instead, in case he posted something where he shouldn't. Kate took an age to answer. Again, all about the books until he steered the conversation elsewhere. He asked after her mother and

115

told her about Fran's accident. She sounded really down in the dumps and when they ran out of all the obvious things to say, he asked her what she was doing over Christmas.

'Working for most of it. I'm on the rota for sad people. The old singletons get all the unsociable hours, but at least a lot of it's overtime.'

'No chance of coming over, then?'

'I'll have to see how the land lies with Mum, and then there's Tia ... I'm fairly committed, if I'm honest.'

So basically it was a no. He told Fran and she laughed, but her shriek had a ring of hysteria to it rather than any real merriment. 'She'd rather work in that store than come to this madhouse!'

'Maybe she needs to earn a living?' George said, gently and sarcastically, then shook out his copy of the *Financial Times* and retired to his room with a large glass of single malt.

This was a new trait; condescension. Where a couple of months back Al felt he'd conquered a problem of sorts, now he began to feel uneasy. If he talked to Jo about it she'd want to dig out all the crap about their past and then it would be Helen all over again, which didn't bear thinking about.

Upstairs, Al dragged the Freddie box out and scored a pen nib down the parcel tape holding it all together. Inside, his Fun-Pants costume and all the props and paraphernalia belonging to his clown act gave off a musty smell. Marge got up for a look inside, then retreated and lay slumped on the mat, head on paws.

'Sad too, huh?'

Nothing, not even a tail thump. Another patient for Maisie. Gathering everything into his arms, he padded downstairs to the utility room and placed the billowing yellow trousers, the red T-shirt, and a sparkly green waistcoat into the washing machine and set it on a short, lukewarm wash. He didn't chance the black jacket and shoes. Twenty minutes later and the fibres from the felt buttons had made a mess of the door seal, but the suit came out looking passable. When he was throwing everything over the drying rack, his brother did a double-take.

'Christmas party work?'

'Nope. A free-of-charge cheering up job, that's all.'

This produced a sneer. 'God help us.'

Saturday the 21st of December wasn't a bad day weather-wise, which was good news if you had felt shoes. He decided to do the full make-up as well, then it was clear to any innocent bystanders exactly what he was doing.

When he rooted out his special bag it was to find the white foundation had separated a little as it was an oily base, but the face paints were still in surprisingly good condition, and there was just enough red left to draw a big, curving grin. He found some hair gel in the bathroom and made some passable spikes but his hair was too old and floppy and so he resorted to the smelly orange wig. He stuffed his pockets with some of Becca's sweets, grabbed the magic flowers, and managed to get out of the house unnoticed. His real fear was stopping at traffic lights. That stare-into-space moment, when the person in the lane alongside casually glances across, then looks quickly away to avoid any further eye contact.

Rounding the bend on Bodnant Road it soon became clear that Kate's car wasn't there. Of course it wasn't, it was the last weekend before Christmas. That meant she was probably at work. Hadn't she more or less told him this? Shit. He drove thoughtfully into town, slumped low in the seat and with his hat rammed well down, wondering if any of his plan was such a good idea.

Bargain Home Stores was a large unit on the new retail park. It was horrifically busy. The positive aspect was that he blended fairly well with all the general festivities of buskers and Father Christmas floats. He pushed through the huge glass doors to find the shop floor rammed with customers. He attracted a lot of stares, some smiles, and the usual screaming from children under the age of five. He waved at them all, handed out a few sweets, and had a good look around. The stock was cheap and old-fashioned, and he just couldn't imagine where Kate fitted into this artificial world. Maybe she was in one of the offices.

He spotted her hair.

She was dusting and replenishing a tower of children's games displayed somewhat unimaginatively on a large, flat plinth, with a plastic tree in the centre. When she turned around to delve into a box of new stock, he dodged behind a rail of underwear and caught his over-sized revolving dicky-bow on an empty hangar. Several flowery nightgowns fell to the floor but it was difficult bending down with a hoop in your pants, so he had to leave them there. A couple of small children giggled and pointed at him. He waved back and put a finger to his lips, then peered stealthily through a curtain of large, brightly coloured bras and knickers; colour-wise, it was a good concealment. Since the store was so noisy, it would be easy to creep up behind her and ashamedly, he couldn't really think of anything more original.

As if by telepathic agreement, she leant across the display, fully preoccupied with bunches of tinsel, presenting the perfect opportunity. Moving quickly on silent feet, he managed to get so close behind her that he could almost smell the rain-soft perfume of her hair. He touched his head close to hers. 'Happy Birthday.'

She spun around, almost falling over the empty boxes, but within seconds of looking him up and down, her attention was solely concentrated on his face. Fumbling in his pocket then for the hidden prompt, he cued the singing flowers, relieved as they dutifully opened into huge blooms with faces, their mouths a perfect O. To his dismay

118

a couple of the heads drooped, but they kept on singing 'Happy Birthday' well enough. After the first few bars he sensed complete and total apathy, and switched it off.

She still didn't smile, just stared with an ice-blue indifference.

'*Al?*'

'What gave it away?'

'You idiot!'

He should have agreed and left it at that. Instead, he snaked an arm around her waist and kissed her. It only lasted a few seconds and it was quite chaste but since she didn't recoil, he figured it made borderline harmonious. 'Come and have lunch with me?'

'Dressed like *that?*'

The harsh reality of this observation pulled him up short and he looked around wildly, aware then that a lot of customers were watching with interest. 'I'll buy something to wear. You don't look so hot either, anyway.'

'Well, thanks! Now, go away, I'm *working.*'

'You're too good for this place, let's just run. Live dangerously!'

She folded her arms. 'Why would I do that?'

'You need a reason?'

She softened visibly then, and there was a smile poised to light up her eyes, but then her gaze went beyond him, to somewhere behind his left shoulder. A burly security guard took hold of his arm.

'I've been watching you, Coco, on the CCTV. Now, if you'd like to come with me please, *sir*?'

Chapter Ten

Kate

As recent birthdays had gone, the day was certainly proving notable if not traditional. After some twenty minutes or so, Al was escorted off the premises and out into the fresh air with the rest of the world. She watched him walk through the foyer in his ridiculous outfit and the feeling of being trapped inside a glass bubble was painfully acute, as if she were the clown. Leaving the mess of boxes behind, she walked briskly across the store and shadowed his progress along the huge windows.

He walked unselfconsciously, with the flower heads hanging down and with an almost regal air. Within seconds, he was lost in the crowds and she was forced to go back to the job in hand. Wide Load was looking for her, arms folded under her enormous breasts, smug loathing emanating from every pore. The loathing was mutual.

'Tracy wants to see you in the camera room.'

'Now?'

'Straight away. Take the time out of your break, we're busy down here.'

Kate plodded up the stairs, swiped her security card at the staff door, and headed for the management offices. She knocked on the door of the camera room. The security guard and the store manager – a frightening twenty-three year old – asked her to sit and watch the monitor. They played the footage of Al entering the store, falling about in the lingerie section, and then creeping up behind her. She watched avidly, noting all the expressions on his face. When the flowers began to sing, she had the most uncontrollable fit of giggles, which quickly broke into proper belly laughs.

In the darkened room, the security man and the stone-faced manager had a problem with her attitude.

'Do you know this man?' Tracy said tartly.

'Yes, it's Freddie Fun-Pants.'

'I'm sorry, Kate, but I'm giving you another warning. Snogging on the shop floor is way out of line. And please, tell your friend to stay away. He is not to approach children and hand out sweets on these premises, and as for the stock damage, you can deal with that after your lunch.'

'Right, OK,' she said, wiping her eyes and blowing her nose. No sooner had she disposed of the wet tissue that the giggles started again. She walked back down the long corridor, one of shame. The locker room was empty, which was very good indeed. She pulled off the uniform and slung it, inside out and tangled up, to the back of her locker. When she looked in the mirror it was to find a greasy red smear of paint across her mouth and down one side of her chin. It was the devil to wash off. She took her time getting dressed, did her hair and lipstick, and then walked calmly out of the store, and kept on walking.

The quiet satisfaction of it thrilled her. Part of her wanted to go back in and be a fly on the wall for when they discovered she'd disappeared. They'd buzz about like demented bluebottles, checking the toilets, the stock room, and the fire escapes. In time, she'd write a full resignation, but for now it was gloriously simple. Watching herself back on that monitor she'd been horrified by the image of herself, working away in her snow-globe of existence. Until the arrival of Al, and then it was suddenly clearer.

She walked almost a mile along the wide promenade. The tide was roaring in, bringing with it a freshening sea breeze and throwing the loops of Christmas lights strung out between lampposts into a frenzied, flickering swaying, but despite the chill it wasn't unpleasant. Seagulls fought over the scant pickings in the bins, and the squawking reminded her of the half-price maroon and gold table settings at the store; the colour combo no one wanted this year, but were seemingly worth a fight if they were cheap enough. At the end of the seafront she came to a long wooden bench, and sat for a while until she was thoroughly cold, then walked briskly through the main shopping street and on impulse, straight into a very expensive hair salon.

As she sat in the chair, the implication of what she'd done sank in a little deeper. Yes, she'd hated her job, but it was the only aspect of her life that gave it any structure. Now, she had even more time to fill. Whether she had the strength to motivate herself without it remained to be seen, but then maybe she'd needed to kick the crutch away. And she had to admit, the relief of not having to deal with the store and all of its petty establishment rules was truly liberating.

At home, she soaked for an hour in the bath, read some of her book, and then cooked herself a fillet steak and opened a bottle of wine.

'Happy Birthday and Merry Christmas to you,' she said to the face in the mirror. It felt strange, having shorter hair, and she turned her head this way and that. It fell to jaw length now instead of resting untidily on her shoulders, and it was slightly graduated, longer at the front and sides, but revealing the nape of her neck. It was shiny and silky again too, like it used to be. The rich conker shade with bright highlights had been startling at first glance, but she was already getting used to that, and at least it no longer looked like Al's wig.

Taking her glass of wine, she went to her desk and made a list of phone calls and jobs. Speaking to Tia had become the priority, but as usual, there was no reply, and so enquiries regarding plans for Christmas were sent via a laborious text. Next was Fran, but it was George who picked up the call, and although he was surprised by her news, he seemed grateful for the promise of organisation and the offer of grocery shopping.

'How's Fran coping with her injuries?' she said.

'Badly. The animal in question is a pain in the posterior, it mounts everything in sight and no one seems to be able to get hold of it. Maisie's coming on Monday, so if she brings her gun with her, I intend to have her deploy it.'

Kate laughed but George seemed deadly serious and she wondered what kind of Christmas she was letting herself in for, although the thought of meeting Maisie filled her with curiosity. She deliberated then about calling Al. In fact, she was longing to speak to him, but what to say? She'd have to tell him she'd left her job and then he might feel guilty. The result of the whole episode was something she needed to talk about in person, then he wouldn't get the wrong impression.

Already disheartened with her list, she switched on her computer and connected to Facebook. The first thing she noticed was that Mr Black was online, although as usual there was no evidence of any public activity. Her own wall was full of standard happy birthday messages, including one from Al and one from Tia. And that was it. If the mundanities of her job could no longer get to her, then maybe sheer loneliness would kill her instead.

She was disturbed by someone pounding on the door and shouting through the letterbox. Annemarie. Admittedly, it was just after ten thirty so not excessively late, but not a very sociable time, or considerate either. She made her way groggily down the stairs. On the hall table, her phone was buzzing with an incoming message. It was a response to her text from Tia, 'no idea'. She peered through the curtains in the sitting room to double-check it was her sister, then went to unbolt the front door. Exclamations were made over her new hairstyle and the usual birthday greetings ensued, but Annemarie never settled on anyone for very long before she was back to her own agenda.

Her sister was in party mode. Full make-up, a tight dress, and towering heels. She was carrying a bottle of cheap fizz and a card. Kate followed her effervescent trail into the kitchen, where she proceeded to hunt out the champagne flutes and open the bottle.

'So, *sistah*, get yourself dressed and let's hit the town. A few of us are meeting at The Plough.'

'Not a chance.'

They retreated to the snug, and Kate flicked on the electric fire. Annemarie followed with the bottle and topped up both their glasses then settled herself on the sofa.

'You need a man. You're meant to be the sex siren of the zodiac, not sat here like fucking Cinderella with a posh hairdo.'

'Don't be ridiculous. I'm Capricorn, not Scorpio. That means cautious, slow, and steady, one foot at a time.'

'All the more reason to come out for some fun, then! Huh?'

'My idea of fun is not the same as yours.'

Annemarie sighed and crossed her legs, bouncing her foot with childish irritation. 'A very boring fiftieth to you then,' she said, and raised her glass.

'I want to talk to you about Christmas.'

Annemarie fluttered her long, manicured nails. 'Oh, I'm all sorted, listen to *this!* We've booked a luxury lodge in Scotland on one of those corporate holiday sites, you know, beauty salons, spa treatments … *everything* laid on. There's even a medical centre and a full-sized pool. *And* a kid's club. It sleeps six, which is kind of crazy, but Craig wanted the space.'

'My first question is, how can you afford it on child and housing benefits?'

Annemarie peeped engagingly over the rim of her glass.

'Craig's sorted it.'

'Craig? Is he the bank manager?'

'Yeah, well, funding manager or something.'

'What about *Mum's* Christmas? Now that you're her official keeper, I imagine you've got something planned?'

'Like what? You always secrete her here and it's not as if you ever go anywhere, is it?'

'No, but this year, I *am* going somewhere.' She put up a hand to stop her sister butting in. 'And I know it's only Chathill but I won't be around, for the first time in ... let's see, something like ten years? Since Dad died anyway. I fancy taking this year off.'

'Oh, well that's great! Thanks for telling me. So, what the hell are we supposed to do now?'

'That's simple,' Kate said, noting her sister's frown. For full effect, she drained her glass first and when she was sure Annemarie was fully attentive, delivered her killer line. 'Take her with you.'

'All the way to Edinburgh?' her mother said, as if Scotland was a war zone.

Kate nestled the phone under her chin as she cleared the fridge of its contents. 'Why not? Single-level living, pop-in medical centre ... think of the stories you can tell Elsie when you get back!'

'We're not speaking.'

Kate sighed and threw the last of the limp salad into the recycling bin. She hated this, the constant battle of gentle coercion, the subtle comments dropped into the conversation. It was exactly the kind of thing she used to do with Tia when any kind of change or challenge had presented itself in her toddler world.

The same tactics had been recently employed with a hearing aid in mind, but there was a long way to go. First

126

base with this enquiry had resulted in a prescription for olive oil, the prerequisite for syringing. Annemarie had managed to scupper weeks of steady progress by topping up the dwindling oil supply with some salad dressing laced with chilli.

Predictably, Annemarie had given up instantly with their mother's refusal to be taken from her comfort zone over the Christmas period, citing the *Family Fortunes* Christmas Special as the main stumbling block. Physically, her mother was capable of the trip. They'd patched her up at Bangor hospital with an extra stent in a partially collapsed artery, and within days she was back to being her stubborn self and making loud remarks about foreigners in public places.

'Look,' Kate began, none too kindly. 'I'm not going to *be* here.'

'Beer? I thought it was all whisky in Scotland?'

'For goodness sake!'

There was some sort of cry then and a thump followed by the loud tone of a disconnected line. She'd either dropped the receiver or knocked the huge telephone unit off the table. A couple of attempts to call back resulted in the engaged tone and a computerised voice. For a while, she continued to pack cool boxes, empty bins, and throw things into a case, but the grisly scenario of her mother lying prostrate, maybe with her head split open, eventually took over all rational thought. Monday was Elsie's shopping morning, and they usually went together but since communications had broken down, it was very likely that the body wouldn't be discovered until after Christmas.

Hugely frustrated, she loaded her car, then made the detour to Rhos House. Once there, she pressed her finger on the buzzer with continuous force. A frail voice came over the speaker and they went through the usual protracted exchange.

Entry granted, she marched up the stairs and waited

impatiently for her mother to unlock the flat door, slowly sliding all the bolts. When the door opened, Kate saw that she was already wearing the new dressing gown and slippers she'd gifted as a Christmas present. The phone lay upside down on the carpet along with a vase of flowers. Both the carpet and the phone was sopping wet. She set about clearing it up and plugged the phone back in, but it was totally waterlogged and showed no signs of life.

'You'll have to get Annemarie to buy another one,' she said.

'Where are you going anyway, all dolled-up?'

'I'm not dolled-up! I've had a haircut, that's all.'

'Must be a fella. Have you met a fella?'

'No!'

'No need to bite my head off. You're so bloody touchy!'

'And why do you think that is?' she snapped and wound the flex around the phone, then slung it in the bin. Now what?

The phone was her only lifeline.

Her mother retreated to the kitchen and began to run water and rattle crockery while Kate stood and fumed in the middle of the lounge. In one way, she was appalled by her own behaviour. It might be fuelled by frustration but there was a selfish undercurrent to it. The thought of what she intended; leaving her partially-sighted, eighty-six-year-old mother alone over Christmas because she wanted to flirt with a man was despicable. Al wasn't even available to her and the superficiality of this made it all the worse. She went into the kitchen and watched her mother fuss with bits of stale food and as she began to gulp back tears, realised with a shock that her mother was doing the same.

'Oh, Mum, I'm *sorry*,' she said, and went to enfold her bony frame.

After a long while her mother said, 'I don't want to go

with Anne. You don't *know* what it's like, being trapped in this body. I wanted to come to *you* because I wanted us to have mother-daughter time.'

Kate thought of Tia.

They were locked in this miserable embrace when Elsie shouted through from the hall, tapping on the open front door as she advanced.

'Hello? Nora?'

'Oh, here she comes, nosy old bat.'

Despite the supposed breakdown of communication, the episode of the phone was related in great detail, her mother relishing Elsie's attention. Elsie was shrewd. She knew exactly which questions to ask, when to feign surprise or shock, and most importantly, when to agree.

'I've come to ask if you're still coming to us for Christmas Day? We've got something to show you, a little cat. She's called Satin.'

'Statin? I'm on those now, did I tell you?'

There was no fuss in the end. Elsie even loaned a spare phone; not that her mother could use it, but she could receive incoming calls, and a trip was organised with Bert – Elsie's significant other – to buy a new, large-key version. Contact numbers and winks were exchanged, arms squeezed with understanding.

She was halfway to Chathill, enjoying the winter sunlight as it flickered through bare branches, when her mobile rang. She pulled over, pleased to see that it was Tia.

'Hello, love, at last! Happy Christmas.'

'I'm coming home, all right? Can you pick me up from the station?'

'Oh, Tia, I can't. I'm really sorry but I've made other arrangements.'

'What arrangements? Oh, you know what? Just forget it!'

'*Tia?*'

Her voice had sounded muffled, choked even, before she'd rudely disconnected. Her first thought was to call her back to see what was wrong, then she changed her mind and decided to text instead. If she intended going back to the house, she'd need to buy food and put the heating back on. Halfway through explaining all of this, in yet another longwinded text, she stopped herself and deleted it, then doggedly drove on.

When she walked through the front door at Chathill, carrying a huge box of groceries, Al was padding down the stairs and his initial reaction was one of surprise, then mild trepidation as she met his eyes. His gaze roamed over her face and she felt her skin heating under his scrutiny.

'Wow,' he said slowly, 'I like the hair.'

'Thanks.'

There was a new, taller stair gate, bolted to the wall with outdoor strength hinges. It looked awful and it wouldn't open properly so he resorted to climbing over it. 'I'm sorry about, you know … the other day.'

'Don't be! I think you may have changed my life,' she said, with dramatic effect, then went through to the kitchen. He followed.

'How do you mean?'

'OK, maybe a slight exaggeration, but Freddie gave me a kick start.'

'First time he's ever done that for anyone.'

'I did laugh, eventually.'

She filled him in on the events of the last couple of days as she went to and from the larder, in and out of the fridge. 'You wouldn't believe what it's taken for me to get here. Bring the turkey in, will you? Not the one scratching outside in the yard, the ready-stuffed one in the car.'

'Kate?'

'Uh-huh?'

'I'm glad you're here.'

'Me too,' she said into the depths of the freezer. She knocked the frost off her hands and looked up and smiled, surprised to see Jo leaning against the doorframe with her arms folded. There was something in her grey eyes which probed with painful precision. Kate looked away.

Around lunchtime, Maisie arrived with two very polite seven- and eight-year-old boys, Barnaby and Rupert Darlington-Black. Al, clearly in his element, introduced them – along with Maisie – to Kate and Jo, and for a while there was something approaching happy chaos in the kitchen as everyone exchanged news. Mention of Jo's pregnancy and the engagement was notable by its absence.

Kate doled out the mulled wine, enjoying the atmosphere despite avoiding eye contact with Jo. Maisie was every bit as engaging as she'd suspected and when the boys were being entertained by the sight of Fran's rainbow bruises, quietly scolded her father for calling them the Carling Black Label boys. 'If Bernice heard that, she'd have you strung up!'

'What's wrong with Black as a name? She always has to impress her fabby peeps, doesn't she? I don't see why she had to make it double-barrelled.'

'So she could get you over one?' Maisie quipped.

George roared laughing at this and raised his glass to her.

'I have no idea how my ex-brother has managed to produce someone as wonderful as my niece here. Maisie, if you see anything this afternoon on my property which needs putting out of its misery, you have my full permission to shoot.'

'I haven't brought the gun,' she said, her eyes flicking to Fran.

'Pity.'

Thereafter, Maisie was mostly commandeered by Fran, who'd made a long list of urgent animal inspections for

131

her, and it was to her credit that she took it all with good grace and went to get her veterinary bag from the car. Jo remained silent and watchful, like a spectator at one of those country house weekends where a Victorian mystery or some silly parlour game was acted out around them. For a newly-engaged woman with child, she was incredibly distant, and Kate couldn't help noticing, still ring-free. Kate felt sorry for her, mostly ignored by everyone except Al, who was clearly doing his best to humour her.

'Go and get some ponies tacked up, Becca,' Fran said, as they were clearing pots away. 'Let the boys have a ride on Kipper and Pickles.'

'The ponies are *filthy*,' Becca grumbled, clearly not in the mood for entertaining her cousins. 'I'm going out, anyway. I'm meant to be doing practice jumps with Megan Thomas, although there's not much point since you won't let me go to the hunt on Boxing Day.'

'You can't go by yourself,' Fran said, 'and that's final. '

'I hate hunting,' Jo said, and everyone turned to look at her. 'It's just mindless killing.'

'So is much of the food chain,' Fran snapped. 'And you city types want it all organic and free range as well, so tell me, how do you intend to keep Mr Mindless Fox at bay?'

'There must be other means.'

'Poison? All has a knock-on effect on the countryside, I'm afraid, not very organic. Then there's traps and guns. Have you ever seen an animal die in a trap? Huh? It can take *days*.'

'Fran, calm down,' Al said, but Jo piped up again.

'I don't know, just seems like something out of the past.'

'It's called our bloody heritage! It's called a time-honoured way of keeping our small farmers in business, but you wouldn't know anything about that. You still think it's a rich man's pastime.'

'What do you think?' Jo asked Al.

'I'm not a fan of mindless killing either,' he said quietly, his eyes never leaving hers. Fran looked broken by his admission, as if he'd betrayed her.

'You *hypocrite*,' she said. 'You have a short memory, farm boy.'

'I didn't say hunting was mindless. I know how Mum and Dad struggled to make a living here.'

'For what it's worth, and we could debate this all day,' Maisie said, 'but the worst cases of animal cruelty I've come across has been in the cities, mostly cats and dogs. There *is* a bigger picture, and fox-hunting gets an unfair amount of press. Take geese, for example, the hideous force-feeding that goes on, and the farming of ducks for their down, feathers ripped from their bodies while they are still alive.'

Fran nodded furiously.

'So, you're basically saying that the fox-hunting scandal is no more than a political scapegoat? That's rubbish!' Jo said, and Maisie bristled. Al looked caught between a rock and a hard place. Aware that she hadn't offered an opinion, Kate wondered if there was any point in saying something a little less inflammatory.

'I watched a hunt once, and I thought it was a bit like The Grand National, you know, the way it divides the nation? On the one hand I was moved by the courage and the partnerships, the risks man and horse took together. You can't deny that it brings out the best and the worst in human nature. I'm not sure you can have one without the other.'

Al's eyes flicked onto hers and there was an almost imperceptible nod of agreement, but the subtle exchange was picked up by Jo.

'I don't agree,' she said, eyes blazing. 'I hate gambling as well.'

'You would!' Fran said. 'What a bland and simplistic world you live in.'

George took hold of her arm. 'That's enough now.'

'I don't know what all the fuss is about, anyway,' Becca said, and turned to Jo to explain more fully. 'This one isn't even a real hunt. It's just like a treasure hunt but on horseback, following a trail. It's called a *drag*.'

'Er … let's discuss Boxing Day later, shall we?' Al said, and George's head snapped up.

'What's it got to do with you?' he quipped.

Al ignored this. 'Kate, come and help me with the ponies.'

'Sure. I'll get my Wellies.'

'Don't let the boys in the old feed store, the loft and the ladder are dangerous,' Fran said, and there was another small altercation with George about the cost of wood.

'Jo?' Al said, 'Come outside, you might feel better for some fresh air.'

'Umm … no, sorry but I'm going to head off, I'm not feeling so great.'

There was a murmur of commiseration at this but only Al went out to her car. He was gone some time and Kate was left with Maisie and the boys as they pulled on borrowed boots.

'There's spiders in these!' one of the boys yelped.

'Don't hurt them, Barney,' Maisie said, 'tip them into that bucket and we'll find them a new home.'

They ventured outside into a damp December afternoon, the fringes of Snowdonia's dark vanilla skyline already deepening with encroaching dusk. Of course, water and sky had no smell or taste, but somehow the aura of the landscape jumbled everything into a melting pot of heightened senses. The boys ran ahead with the dogs, scattering all the hens.

'This is a paradise playground for two small boys,' Kate said, breathing it all in, and Maisie agreed.

'It is, although it looks very run-down, not how I remember it.'

She wondered what Maisie knew of the brotherly rift, but it wasn't the right time, or her place to ask. Al and Fran caught up with them as they entered the barn and Fran explained about the latest recruits, the retired riding school horses.

'I had to bid against the meat man to get them,' she said bitterly, as Maisie looked in mouths and picked up feet. 'How could she send them to be slaughtered after they'd given their whole lives to her? Worked themselves into the ground in that riding school?'

'It happens, I'm afraid,' Maisie said, reaching for her stethoscope. Fran followed closely as she went through some of the other ponies. Eventually, Maisie asked Al to take the boys outside.

'Auntie Fran,' she said, 'I'm *really* sorry, but in my honest opinion one of these horses needs to be put down. I think it may have equine influenza as well, so you need to isolate it.'

The announcement launched her sister-in-law into an even deeper depression. Maisie continued her way around all the animals, with a distinctly subdued Fran limping behind. The untouchable horse who hovered on the periphery of the feed store and bothered the mares was, according to Maisie, a badly gelded stallion.

Al touched Kate's arm. 'I've a feeling this is going to end in tears. Maisie won't put up with any kind of misplaced sentiment.'

'Maybe George will see this as an opportunity to exert some control?'

'If my brother had his way he'd just shoot everything, including me.'

'When I had lunch with him last month, he said he would make some sort of announcement after Christmas.'

He stopped walking at this. 'What? How do you mean?'

She shrugged, 'I don't know, maybe he's retiring?'

'First I've heard.'

They continued to the paddock where Becca had obligingly tethered two Shetland ponies. Their winter coats were caked in dried mud but the boys enjoyed brushing them and Al showed them how to put the bridles on, making them giggle with far-fetched stories. Despite the obvious enjoyment of his grandchildren, it was clear he was ruminating over his brother's impending decision, and she began to wish she'd not said anything.

As the chilly bite of late afternoon turned to rain, they headed back indoors, rubbing hands and stamping feet, laughing at red noses and cheeks. On the kitchen table, there was a significant roll of cash. When Fran asked what it was for, George pushed it across the table towards Kate.

'Housekeeping,' he said succinctly, and turned to Fran. 'Our resident vet tells me we have an incorrectly gelded stallion in our midst, and some old horses which have been worked into the ground. I feel an odd kinship with all of them.'

She stuffed the money into her jeans pocket, aware that all eyes were upon her, but only George smiled.

Chapter Eleven

Al

Supper was early to accommodate the ravenous boys. His brother declined, announcing that it was his staff Christmas dinner dance and would Fran like to accompany him, *for once?*

Fran was in a thoroughly black mood, going over and over the list Maisie had put together. The animal treatments had been carefully costed out, minus any labour charges, so no one could argue it wasn't fair. Kate looked uncomfortable about the money lodged in her bag, although it wasn't as if she hadn't already spent it on everyone's Christmas dinner, and more. What rankled was the way his brother had enjoyed scoring a point in front of everyone. Unsurprisingly, Fran couldn't be persuaded to dress up and go out with him.

'I've nothing to wear,' she said, picking at the dirt under her fingernails. His brother looked at her with mild disgust.

'And whose fault is that?'

George climbed into a taxi around seven, and there was a visible sigh of relief radiating throughout the house at his departure, although his sister-in-law was never totally relaxed these days. Fran never seemed to eat, and sometimes her eyes looked wild and demonic, as if she were possessed.

'I'm worried about Kipper,' she said, waving the list.

'Kipper?'

'The horse Maisie says needs shooting. What if it passes on horse flu to Becca's horse, and all the others? I haven't got the money to get it sorted.'

Al sat down next to her and she shuffled up, then rested her head on his shoulder. 'George won't trust me with the housekeeping any more.'

He knew where the conversation was going, but if he was honest, he felt incredibly indebted to Fran. For years, she'd been a buffer between him and his brother whenever things turned ugly, and he knew how much she'd pleaded his case on his return to Chathill. 'I've got a bit of money left, if it would help.'

She lifted her head to look at him. 'Oh, Al! Would you do that? For me?'

'Yeah. Do what you have to do, right?'

'I'll never forget this.'

Becca had cheered up too. The Thomases had offered Stilton a space in their lorry, promising to keep an eye on her if she wanted to join them at the local meet. Fran, disappointed she wasn't fit enough to go herself, reluctantly agreed, and all the tack was brought into the sitting room to be soaped and polished.

The boys rolled about on the floor playing a rough, noisy tug-of-war game with Butter and an inner tube. Occasionally, if he was losing ground, the dog stole Becca's sponge instead and a chase ensued. Feeling weary at their energy but grateful to Butter for the first-class entertainment, Al stretched and yawned, clasping his hands behind his head. He saw Kate avert her eyes when the lower half of his shirt raised, and his heartbeat racked up a gear.

Kate. He kept thinking about the conversation they'd had in the kitchen, the one where she'd sincerely thanked him for playing the fool. And he couldn't stop taking sneaky glances at her ever since she'd arrived. It wasn't just the vibrant haircut and the way it lifted the colour of her eyes, it was the subtle details too; the way it nestled in the nape of her neck and skimmed the contours of her

138

cheekbones, the way her mouth curved with amusement. Part of him didn't want the complication of her, but *every* part of him wanted to kiss her again.

He had no idea where this left him with Jo. She was currently ignoring his calls. He'd tried to laugh off the flirty conversation she'd clearly witnessed between himself and Kate, but she was no fool. Jo was a sharp cookie and, from what he'd seen, handled all of her relationships with the same considered thought.

Kate was chatting to his daughter about the Jim Silver books, and that in itself gave him a feeling he wasn't sure what to do with, or how to categorise.

'Have you had a look at Marge?' he said to Maisie.

'Yes. I think she's pregnant.'

'No way! Honest?'

'Yep, pretty sure you're going to be a puppy daddy.'

Everyone laughed.

'This is as well as being a real daddy,' Maisie went on, 'and, er … it must be catching, because you're going to be a granddad again, too.'

The way she dropped this into the conversation threw him for a moment, and it was Kate who fully understood the picture before anyone else, and then Fran and Becca were both asking a million questions before he could get to his feet and get his arms around her. 'Come here! That's just the *best* news.'

'I thought you'd be pleased.'

'Pleased? That's the biggest understatement of the century.'

The baby had happened at the wrong time for her, career-wise, but Maisie approached it all with her usual practical determination. She was thirteen weeks, and planned to marry the following Christmas. Unlike himself and Jo, Maisie had been with Simon for many years, so there was no fear of a shotgun wedding there.

'This is just the *best* news,' he said, again. 'I've had all my Christmas presents in one go.'

'That's good, 'cos there's nothing wrapped for you,' Becca said.

'So, Dad? I plan to keep working. I think we'll be looking for a part-time nanny but I'll be needing every spare minute of your time for specialist babysitting,' she said, and the way she met his eyes was a delicious unspoken pact, it was a kick in the teeth for Bernice.

'You *know* the answer to that.'

She grinned and stretched. No sign of a bump yet. 'I probably need to get these boys back home, or my sister-in-law will think I've kidnapped them.'

Al carried all the bags and boxes, and loaded the boys' presents into her car. It was dark, wet, and miserable and he didn't want her to drive anywhere or lift anything, or manhandle big animals. Christ, he couldn't carry on like this, he'd be a nervous wreck.

She wound the window down on the driver's side and Al leant in to kiss her. 'Thanks for everything you've done today, bringing the boys, chasing that bloody horse ... I'd never have let you do any of that if I'd *known*.'

'I know, that's why I didn't say earlier. Other than creasing indigestion, I'm doing OK.'

'Indigestion? Bit soon for that, isn't it?'

'Dad, I'm *fine*. It's just a shame Jo went home, I wanted to talk babies with her. I'm sorry about that stupid spat, I should have kept my mouth shut.'

'Oh, I don't think she went home because of that,' he said quickly, but his daughter was no fool.

'Is everything all right?'

'No, not really. I wish I'd been sensible like you and not said anything till it was all set in stone.'

'Oh, *Dad*.'

Change the subject. 'How's your mum?'

'Bitter and lonely, if I'm honest. I'm spending Christmas over at Simon's parents', and I don't think she's too pleased.'

'Don't forget to bring my son-in-law over sometime, will you?'

'Boxing Day?'

'Yeah, why not?'

He kissed her goodnight, pulled a funny face at the fractious boys in the back, and stepped away from the car. She was about to wind the window back up, but stuck her head out again.

'Hey, well done on the books by the way. She's nice, isn't she? Kate.'

He nodded and smiled, waved at the boys. He watched the car bounce down the drive and indicate right.

'Yeah, she's nice.'

Full of a twisted sort of guilt, he tried calling Jo again, but her phone played the complicated message service relating to work. She wasn't even online, which was highly unusual. When she'd left Chathill earlier she'd been morose, deep in thought, clearly turning things over in her mind. They hadn't made any forward arrangements.

The tiny exchanges between Kate, Maisie, and Fran had been like shards of ice. Even Becca and the boys had irritated her with constant chatter, demanding his attention with questions, competitive taunts, and squabbles. Helen used to say he simply switched off from the adult world if there were any children within a ten-metre radius. Whenever they'd had dinner parties, Al was always more concerned with putting Tom and Maisie to bed while the guests, and the starters, sat stone cold at the table waiting for him. Helen always used to get drunk, and then they'd argue.

He was in Delamere village in just over an hour.

At least there was a light on in her flat. Crazily, he found himself shaking with nerves as he pressed the bell, as if his insides were pre-empting an imagined scenario, the one he'd gone over and over in his mind since the day she'd told him she wanted a termination.

She let him up the stairs and opened the flat door; surprised but not over-pleased to see him. He kissed her cheek and she frowned.

'What the hell are you doing here?'

'I was worried, I couldn't get hold of you.'

'There was no need,' she said, and indicated her busy desk, illuminated by an angle-poised lamp. 'I was just working, I had stuff to sort out before Christmas starts tomorrow and the whole world grinds to a halt.'

'Oh.'

'Look, sit down. Do you want a drink? Coffee, maybe a whisky?'

'No, no thanks.'

He sat vacantly while she made herself some tea. On her return, she cradled a mug in her hands and stood opposite him in front of the fireplace. It was almost as if they didn't know each other, as if the baby growing inside her had nothing to do with either of them.

'Guess what. Maisie's pregnant, and so is Marge. Wait till I find out which dirty dog is responsible,' he said, knowing full well it was a stupid diversion, but she shot him a lightning quick smile, then inclined her head to one side.

'Al, I have some stuff to say to you.'

'Right.'

'I've er … I've decided to spend Christmas with my parents, in London.'

His first feeling was one of massive relief, that it was something so inconsequential. For a wonderful, wild moment, he wondered if he'd get invited along, to meet Mum and Dad, but then as he studied her expression, he knew he was clutching at straws.

'Has this anything to do with what happened at the farm today?'

She half laughed and rolled her eyes. 'You mean was I

upset and intimidated by your string of female fans? Not at all. But it did make me realise how different we are.'

'What do you mean? Where's this heading, Jo?'

She took a deep breath and placed the mug on the mantelpiece.

'You know I have a secondment in New York, in January? Well, after that, I have the option of moving office. I've been offered a promotion.'

'And you're going to accept it?'

'Yes, yes I am.'

The hum of traffic was the only noise which broke through his jumbled thoughts. It was the sound of the world going about its business, unaware that a semi-rootless part of his was about to be pulled out of its fertile soil. He searched her face, willing her to say something about the baby, but not really wanting to hear it, because it would likely scar his insides forever. The second his eyes left hers though, she delivered the blow.

'Al, I ... I think we should finish.'

He'd been expecting a difficult conversation, but not those words, exactly. Ashamedly, the twist of fear and pain in his guts had nothing very much to do with Jo, but everything to do with his unborn child. She knew it, had known it all along, and now *he* knew it for certain.

His voice came out as a strangled whisper, 'Jo, listen –'

'No. Al, we have a seriously unbalanced relationship.'

She came to sit next to him, but he studied his clasped hands rather than look at her. Her voice, when she began to speak again, was gentle, so sincere. It turned his limbs to jelly, stripped him of bone.

'I watched you today, with your family, and your grandchildren. There was magic and truth there. You're a lovely, mixed up, funny man, Al, and I love you for that.'

A long moment passed as he digested this, but the second he moved to look at her face, she rose and went back to her superior position standing by the fireplace. 'I'd like you to leave now, before you start to tell me how much you care about me.'

'I do care about you!'

'Exactly. You don't *love* me. Look, I've tried to get my head around all of this, and I waited, like you wanted me to, but nothing's changed and I'm at the end of the line.'

'What about …?'

'I'll deal with it.'

'*Deal* with it? The mindless killing? Just where does all of this fit within your idealistic world, Jo?'

She swallowed hard and looked at the floor. 'I'd like you to leave, please.'

As much as he tried to absorb everything she'd said, he was also fully aware that he'd known these facts all along, so why did he feel so broken and unable to react? There was no fight in him, and even if there had been, he knew he was powerless against her decision.

He'd just have to deal with it.

He hardly remembered leaving the room, but swaggered down the stairs and let himself out into the night, leaning back against the outside door, his chest heaving with emotion. His mobile rang. It was Tom.

'Nice move, Dad.'

'Eh?'

'You and Maisie? Conspiring an afternoon at that tip of a farm. The boys are exhausted and their clothes are ruined.'

He let his son grumble on, knowing full well it was the result of an ear-bashing from Bernice. 'Are you coming over on Boxing Day or not? Bernice needs to know numbers for the prawn, wasabi, and samphire nests. She said you even put the phone down on her the other day. Honestly, you're like a child. Are you even still there?'

'Yeah, still here.'

A beat. 'So, Boxing Day? Yes or no?'

'Tom, can I call you back, son?'

A long, annoyed sigh, and the call ended.

In the kitchen at Chathill, Fran was rooting through a battered box of Christmas decorations and Becca was holding them up and laughing at them. Some of the decorations were the ones he and George had made, or had had gifted as children. The carrier bag he'd brought from the off licence cut into his hand and he wondered whether to just make a run for the stairs, but the kitchen door was open and they saw him the instant he stepped into the hall.

'Uncle Al, you promised we could get a tree,' Becca shouted.

'Yeah, in the morning.'

'Off to bed then, it's late,' he heard Fran mumble to Becca.

He trod heavily up the stairs, bottles clinking, and Becca followed, but thankfully dived into her own room. Kate was on the landing. She was wearing a modest, dark blue robe, but it did little to conceal her voluptuous figure. There was a triangle of fabric open at her milky, speckled cleavage, and he concentrated on not looking at it. Vanilla ice cream sprinkled with flakes of chocolate.

'It's all yours,' she said.

A beat. 'Sorry?'

'The bathroom …?'

'Oh, yeah, yeah.' He looked down at the floorboards for safety but found himself looking at her bare feet and before he realised, his eyes had travelled back up her body again.

'Well, congrats on gaining granddad status *again*. I've yet to get Tia to stay with the same man for longer than three months. It's going to be a busy time for you next year. Two babies, two weddings, a hundred and one puppies –'

'And a horse funeral.'

'Not funny,' she said, but then smiled.

He decided to come clean about his cul-de-sac future with Jo. 'Feel a bit of a twit now, telling everyone and getting all excited.'

She looked him directly in the eye. 'I'm sorry to hear that. We tend to think relationships get easier with maturity, but they just evolve somehow, still catch you out.'

He thought about this for a moment. 'Will you have a drink with me?'

She glanced at the bulging carrier bag. 'I'll go and find some glasses, maybe stoke the Aga.'

Clearly, she wasn't going to step into his room.

Back in the kitchen, she'd put three tumblers on the table, and Fran was telling her all about the decorations. She trailed to a halt when he placed a bottle of whisky, brandy, and one of gin amongst the angels, baubles, and fairies. It looked faintly blasphemous and drew an uncomfortable comparison to the background of carols on the radio.

'Name your poison,' he said.

'You don't drink, Al,' Fran said worriedly. 'Not really, not like this.'

'No?'

He unscrewed the top of the whisky and sloshed it in the direction of the first glass. Fran exchanged a look with Kate. 'What's happened?'

'Me and Jo are finished.'

'Oh, well, I think that's for the best,' Fran said.

'Really?' he said darkly.

'Yes, she wasn't right for you, Al. Not right at all.'

He downed the single malt and they both watched him top up the glass even though his eyes were practically watering. The last time he'd got really drunk was when that bitch Ruby Martinez had told him to go away. Helen had told him to go away eventually as well, and now Jo.

Kate found some ice and mixers and she was

dispensing these when George returned from his festive night out, pulling his tie awry and looking more bloated than usual. His eyes were drawn to the bottles.

'Is that my malt? It better hadn't be.'

'No. Want one?'

'Why would I want to drink with you, Al? Actually, I'm feeling a bit liverish. Fran, where's the salts?' He began hunting through the kitchen units, ripped open a packet of powder and ran the cold water tap, then began stirring vigorously into a mug. 'So, why are you all having a pow-wow in here?'

'Al's got some news,' Fran said, her eyes on his, seeking his permission to spill the beans. He saw no point in hiding the information and put a battered cigarette to his lips while his sister-in-law went over the non-event of the year on his behalf.

His brother laughed. 'Is that a fact? Our incorrectly gelded stallion runs true to form. You leave a fucking trail of disaster *everywhere* you go.'

'George,' Kate said quietly, 'Wanting to do the right thing by his unborn child is not the action of a weak man.'

'I'm sorry, Kate, but you don't know the half of it. What's she going to do about the kid?' George said to him, blunt as ever.

He thought about hitting him, but his brother was drunk, and he was quickly getting to the same stage. Neat whisky on an empty stomach wasn't a good idea, but then he was top of the masterclass for bad ideas. Out of the corner of his eye he became aware that Fran and Kate were both looking at George with varying degrees of shock and disgust, and that was good enough for him.

He kept his eyes focused on the Virgin Mary buried amongst the tinsel on the table, in the hope she'd maybe give him a short-term answer. Ironically, he remembered making the straw crib, so that was a no, then.

'Well?' George barked.

147

'I expect she's going to have a termination.'

'Intelligent woman, too good for you,' his brother said, and downed his liver-salts with a noisy flourish, then banged the mug down and wiped his mouth. 'Fran? I do hope you're not going to sit here and help him drown his sorrows, not with those painkillers you're still scoffing.'

She rose obediently from the table and followed her husband into the hall but in passing the back of Al's chair, kissed the top of his head. She continued to keep glancing back at him, blowing kisses until she began to ascend the stairs.

Al topped up their glasses, refusing Kate's offer of ginger ale.

'I don't know how you can drink it neat,' she said, 'but I guess if I'd just had your news, I might want to light that cigarette as well.'

They had a four-foot table between them like a barrier and her dressing gown was pulled tight across her chest.

'Despite what my brother says, I do actually have some will power.'

'Are you talking about smoking?'

'Partly. What you said earlier, about the best and the worst, that you can't have one without the other?'

'What of it?'

'Does that apply to everything in the universe, do you think?'

She leant back with a frown and the folds of her dressing gown fell open slightly. 'That's a big question. I guess in a broad sense, yes.'

'So, if you've had tremendous highs and then devastating lows in your life, is that better than feeling nothing?'

'Better than living in a single straight line you mean? I can relate to that.'

'Are you looking for some zigzags?'

She laughed. 'Better to have loved and lost, no matter

what the cost?'

'As a philosophy, as least you know you're alive if you experience both sides of the coin. When someone takes the knife out, you totally appreciate the meaning of joy.'

She held his eye contact and pushed her glass over to his side of the table for a refill. 'I didn't love Greg, not in the way I loved my first husband. I didn't think I could expect overwhelming passion twice, and I settled for something much less.'

'So, your first husband broke your heart?'

She nodded, 'Yes, he did.'

'I broke my wife's heart too.'

'Was it … love, money, or just sex?'

'None of those, not what you're thinking, although they all came into play. Rejection comes closer.'

'Love, then. Parental, maternal?'

'I think it may have been the more powerful driver, yes.'

He told her about Ruby Martinez, and she listened carefully, interested in his theory that his behaviours were down to female rejections.

'It doesn't work like that for everyone though, does it? If you're doing a Freud on yourself, you could easily blame your mother for everything and be a victim, so you can justify wielding the knife, but you're not guilty of that. I think you're just trying to be the very best, where she was the very worst.'

Oh, she was too astute. She was also beautiful, available, and grown-up, and there was no doubt he was drawn to the full package in the wake of his disastrous love life, although it seemed crude to think of her that way. The ink of his conversation with Jo hadn't even had the chance to dry, and the death of her second husband was barely old news, but he couldn't help thinking, wondering … if maybe Kate Roberts was the silver lining missing from his latest storm cloud.

'I'm going to buy a Christmas tree tomorrow, with Becca,' he said, swirling the remains of his drink. 'Will you come and help choose?'

'Case closed?'

'For the moment.'

She smiled. 'I'd love to.'

He got to his feet in a whisky fog, and she took the debris of their drunken past over to the sink. Her hair fell forward as she stacked pots and glasses, exposing the nape of her neck. Maybe sensing his gaze, she turned to face him, wiping her hands. If her intention to move closer had been nothing more than a chaste hug, then maybe he could have controlled it as such, but what actually happened was nothing like that. Instead of passing him by, she seemed to gravitate fully into his arms, and she was about to say goodnight – maybe she even actually said it? He didn't respond because he wasn't sure what drivel might come out of his mouth, so he went for the usual diversion and kissed her instead.

She tasted like a single malt after years of cheap blended scotch. How much of what he felt and tasted was down to the *actual* single malt he'd polished off was irrelevant. The caress of her hands as they roamed across the back of his shoulders, the way she turned her face to meet his, was a moment of blissful anticipation. Such soft lips, soft breasts pressed against him, and then all too soon, soft hands around his face and those ice-blue eyes, full of fire. OK, he was drunk.

'Night, Al,' she whispered.

Chapter Twelve

Kate

Rounding the stairs, she almost fell over Fran, who was perched on the third step, hunched like a pixie in the dark.

'Fran! What you doing there?'

'George is snoring like a pig. I was going to re-join you, but you looked ... intimate.'

'Oh,' she said, feeling about fifteen, tongue-tied, and caught out. 'Oh, you know how it is. Christmas ...' she finished lamely.

'Al has only been single for a matter of hours. You're my brother's widow,' she said to the floor, then squinted up at her. 'I'm a bit surprised at you.'

Kate felt her insides twist with a combination of embarrassment, the shock of Fran's reaction, and the idea that she'd been spying on her through the stair bannisters. Above all, it was deeply humiliating.

'I ... I'm sorry. Look, it was nothing,' she said, and squeezed Fran's shoulder briefly as she slid past. Once inside her room, she closed the door and leant on it, the blood surging, pounding through her head screaming liar, *liar!*

Who was she fooling? It hadn't been nothing at all, it had been an all-encompassing *everything*. She couldn't remember being held like that, ever.

Enjoying the warm contours of his body against hers had been painfully teasing in its brevity, intense and intoxicating. She hadn't quite opened her mouth to his. They'd danced on the periphery of each other and as a result, the ensuing tension was now considerable. She picked over and over it all as she lay wide-eyed on the bed, the room lit by a pearlised moon hanging in a heavily clouded night sky.

Feeling unrested, she rose early and almost leapt out of her skin when she found Al, slumped over in the kitchen chair with his head on the table. The whisky bottle was empty. She almost touched his hair, then thought better of it and set about putting the kettle to boil instead. The noise disturbed him and he lifted his head to look at her through bleary eyes.

'*Bloody hell.*' He rubbed the back of his neck, and then his eyes. When he got to his feet, the chair toppled over backwards with a clatter, causing him to stop in his tracks and grimace. 'Bloody, bloody hell.'

She passed him a pint of water, and two Alka-Seltzer. He thanked her, then slowly creaked up the stairs without so much as a backward glance.

Becca appeared an hour later to ask her for some painkillers.

'Menstrual cramps from hell,' she said, and grumbled that Uncle Al had passed out fully clothed on top of the bed, and who was meant to help her with all the chores?

'I've tried to wake him up but he just grunts,' she said, throwing her cereal bowl into the sink. 'I feel really horrible, and it's Christmas.'

'Don't worry, it'll pass,' Kate said, and reached up to get the first-aid box from the top kitchen cupboard. She rooted through it for the codeine she'd spotted in there, but there was none left and so had to resort to whatever she could find in her handbag. 'I'll help you feed the animals.'

Her spirits bottomed out when she saw the solid sheet of rain outside, but a couple of hours of physical activity was maybe the best cure for her mental and emotional melting pot of shame. Surely she was too old to feel like this?

A good hour later and George greeted them both at the back door as they flung off Wellingtons and shook out dripping coats with cold, numb fingers.

'Where's Al, I thought this was his job?'

'I don't think he's feeling very well,' Becca said, and then to Kate asked, 'Can we make some mince pies?'

They made mince pies. In the midst of rolling and cutting out the second lot of pastry, Al appeared, white and unshaven. There was a wonderful, steamy fug in the kitchen, an aroma of warm spices, wet dog, and wood-burner, and he smiled indulgently. It went a long way to lifting the gloom outside and the general mess littered across every surface. He scratched his belly and yawned, then slung an arm across Becca's shoulders, but she was mostly unrelenting.

'Sorry I was a grump,' he said, 'Can I have a pie?'

'Have you forgotten about the tree?'

'No! Have I ever let you down, *ever?*'

'I guess not.'

He pinched a hot mince pie off the cooling rack, tossing it from hand to hand. 'Go and ask your dad if Kate can borrow his vehicle, then we can get a decent-sized tree.'

When Becca disappeared, he helped to wash-up.

'I hope I didn't make an idiot of myself last night,' he began. 'Scrap that. I may as well just say sorry.'

'There's no need,' she said, passing him a bunch of utensils to dry, averting her eyes as their fingers touched. How much he actually remembered, she couldn't gauge. He looked pensive, but that could be down to any number of reasons since he had so many negative issues in his life, topped off with a considerable hangover. Her own face seemed frozen in time too, scared of saying or presuming the wrong thing.

He asked her what was wrong with Becca.

'Oh, just time of the month.'

'Ah ... I keep forgetting how old she is.'

They managed to escape the house before Fran surfaced, and the mood lifted a little as they bowled along the wet lanes towards the forestry plantation. After a full morning of rain, the smell of cut fir trees and logs for burning was delicious, and one long inhalation was almost enough to epitomise Christmas. They mooched down the muddied tracks between the long rows of trees, divided by size and type.

'Uncle Al,' Becca said. 'Do you think Mum is acting a bit weird?'

'How do you mean?'

'Oh, I dunno,' she said, twirling the fronds of a spruce between her fingers. 'Can we get one of these?'

'If it will make you smile.'

'She's not even bought any presents or sent any cards.'

Al exchanged a look, and Kate deliberated over telling him about the altercation on the stairs. She decided she couldn't very well do it with Becca in earshot, and anyway, she sensed it was only a small part of a bigger problem. 'Well, maybe we can kick start some atmosphere with one of these,' Kate said, reaching into the fronds. 'This one's a beauty.'

'Why are we getting a stupid tree anyway, we've no proper decorations for it,' Becca said, as Al heaved the huge eight footer out of the row and began to drag it towards the netting area.

'If you don't cheer up I'll put you feet first down that chute,' he said.

This was met with a scathing look, not usually part of Becca's personality. 'You wouldn't dare!'

'Are you challenging me?'

'Yeah, if you think it's so funny, why don't you do it yourself?'

She imagined that he would maybe grab hold of Becca and run with her to the chute, threatening to drop her in and then landing her safely to her feet at the last second.

But this was Al.

With one fluid movement, he climbed headlong into the short metal chute, inching along until the netting began to capture him, like a human chrysalis. Kate looked around wildly, registering that the place was mercifully quiet. Becca was open-mouthed with delighted shock, then shrieked.

'Uncle Al!'

He fell out at the other end, writhing on the ground as if he'd been born to some strange forest creature, a long knotted tail on top of his head. She laughed. How could she *not* laugh? Becca was soon hanging onto her arm, tears streaming down her face.

'I can't believe he's gone and done that!'

Kate tried to imagine Greg doing something as bizarre, but he would never have made such a fool of himself. Even Tia's father had employed strict limits on silly behaviour where it might be deemed marginally dangerous or getting out of hand, as he called most rough play. Although he'd been a good dad to their small daughter, he had far less interest in her now as a grown woman, having inherited two younger children with a second marriage. She wondered if Tia felt rejected, a little like Al.

In a very short time, he was cut out of the net and their selected tree was passed through the chute by two unimpressed forestry workers with very little festive spirit or sense of humour. Kate and Becca plucked all the needles off his sweater and out of his hair, grinning at the small audience of wary adults and amused children as they waited to pay for the trees.

At Chathill, their impressive purchase was manhandled into the sitting room and secured in a half barrel weighted with sand and rocks. Free from constraint, its wide girth soon filled a huge area, engulfing the telephone table, several dog beds, and an old piano, which had to be pushed and shoved along the wall, tearing a lot of ancient, yellowing wallpaper in the process. Of course, the tree was far too big for the room and the meagre collection of decorations was announced completely inadequate by Al. During the commiseration over the three kings, Fran materialised and admired the tree but avoided eye contact with any of them. Becca started to relate the chute story to her mother, much exaggerated, but Fran looked to be on autopilot.

'Right,' Al said, rubbing his hands. 'Who's for some Christmas shopping? Fran?'

'I haven't any money.'

'I can lend you a bit. We'll get really cheap stuff, use our imaginations.'

'Sounds fun.'

'Yeah. Kate?'

Immediately, all eyes were on her and Fran looked like a startled rabbit, so that the words which came out of Kate's mouth were not the ones in her head. 'Er, no, I'm all done. You go ahead and I'll get some dinner on the go for later.'

'Well … if you're sure?' Al said.

No, I'm not sure at all, she wanted to say, maybe even shout it as they all headed for the door and she was faced with the leftover debris in the kitchen, like a middle-aged Cinderella. And it was the age-old dilemma; she had no idea where she stood with Al. Maybe she was reading far too much into it and a breezy denial that the kiss had even happened was the best way forward. In the cold light of day it just seemed silly to feel so out of kilter over it, like the actions and thoughts of a teenager, but it was difficult to shake off.

She wandered over to the window, chewing her thumbnail, and saw the three of them squash into Al's car. George was hoovering his vehicle and watched with narrowed eyes before waving them off with a cheesy salute. Forty minutes later, a chicken casserole went into the oven and she cleared the work surfaces again. As dusk crept over Snowdonia, George came back inside and informed her that it already smelt wonderful, and opened an expensive bottle of wine.

'It's the season to be jolly,' he said, and poured her a generous measure.

Later, dinner was more jolly than she'd hoped and afterwards they dressed the tree with a huge selection of discounted baubles. Fran declared they were an absolute bargain from the pound shop. George said it looked hideous and was already listing starboard side.

'Why do you have to be so bloody miserable about it?' Al said, 'it's just a bit of fun, not a photo shoot for *Homes and Gardens*.'

Christmas Eve. The sitting room looked and felt very cosy thanks to Al and the effort he'd put in over the tree and making a good fire in the old hearth. Becca was happily wrapping secret gifts, casting sly glances.

Towards the end of the evening, when Becca went upstairs, Kate slid her own presents under the tree and Al shot her a smile. She tried to determine what kind of a smile it was and what it might mean, but then grew exasperated with the whole situation. In truth, she was irritated with both George and Fran. George was, as usual, ensconced in his study and Fran sat glued to Al's side, as if they were being chaperoned. Eventually, Al's drinking session, lack of sleep, and two hours helping Becca outside caught up with him, and his head lolled forward in sleep.

Kate made an apologetic exit to her room and Fran managed a tiny smile. Unable to settle, she tried calling Tia. No response, no messages either. Tia thought nothing of blanking her and of course, she'd done this before, but it was Christmas and if Kate were honest, there was a niggle of concern about where she was and with *whom.* The usual failsafe was Facebook, but since she'd completed publishing The Jim Silver Chronicles, the first page she looked at was a promotional eBook group which had shown an interest in Alastair Black. Some of the members recalled the books from their print days, and she'd read various conversations about him with interest. The discussion about Jim Silver was still going strong. Fascinated, she flipped over to the sales site and discovered that the first book was actually rating in the charts.

He'd sold thirty-eight copies without even trying. The thrill of it, the fact that she'd instigated it all was immensely satisfying. The anti-climax came when she discovered that Tia had removed her Facebook page. What on earth was that all about? It was difficult not to panic, not to let her imagination run wild. Calling Tia's father was a last resort really, but she scrolled down her phone and hit the number.

'Kate, hi.'

'Stuart, is Tia there?'

'Yeah.'

She took a moment to consider this, hurt and angry that neither of them had seen fit to let her know. Her daughter was a grown woman in her twenties and her sister a grown woman in her late forties, yet both of them had her constantly running on some sort of invisible elastic. Thank goodness Annemarie was away and someone else's responsibility. For a fleeting moment, she had the urge to tip the tables over in much the same way she'd done with her job.

Of course, one couldn't detach from family in an emotional sense, and *of course* she loved her daughter, despite the double glazing between them. It just seemed her carer's role, the big sister's role, and the mother's role had been around in her life forever. It was irksome that Fran was now somehow on the edge of this circle of control as well, denying her of any sort of relationship with Al, whatever that may evolve to be.

Fifty years; a lifetime of obligation. It had raced through her hands like fine sand and buried her before she'd actually died. Would she ever come up for air?

'Are you still there?' Stuart said, annoyed.

'Yes, sorry. Is she all right?'

'Er, not sure. Women's troubles, I think.'

'Women's troubles?' she snapped, then rolled her eyes. 'Have you spoken to her?'

'No, not really, she just turned up,' he said, then lowered his voice. 'Look, it's Christmas Eve and there's two other children here to consider. I've got to go.'

Christmas Day. She sent texts to her daughter and her sister, neither of whom replied, but steeling herself against their behaviour was easier after she'd gulped down a large Buck's Fizz. She hugged and kissed Fran, George, and Becca, ignoring the slightly wooden response from Fran. Al was late getting downstairs. He was scruffy and unshaven but still managed to look incredibly charismatic.

He clinked his glass against hers and his lips grazed her cheek. His eyes conveyed so much more though, spreading some warmth through her insides, a place where she'd felt so empty and alone, for too long.

'Me and you, Christmas lunch duty?' he said.

'Sounds good, yes.'

He disappeared outside with Becca, and Fran said she felt redundant.

'Come and help me prep the sprouts if you're desperate,' Kate said with a grin.

'No, I meant with the farm. I think I'll go outside anyway and see what I can do.'

'Right, yes, of course, whatever you think.'

George waited till she'd slammed the back door. 'I just despair, I really do.'

'Oh, it's OK, Al's helping with the cooking and from what I've seen, he's no slouch in that area.'

George up-ended the bottle of champagne into the last of the orange juice, his expression one of quiet deliberation. 'Yes, well. It's Christmas Day, and I've made a pact with myself. I hope I can make it last.'

Whatever his pact was based on, Kate could fully empathise. Feeling used and invisible was no recipe for a marriage. Al was just one of the mystery ingredients. She collected together the components for lunch, stuffed the turkey with her homemade recipe, and slid the main event into the Aga. How long it would take to roast was another mystery.

In her room, she sorted through various limited outfits she could change into. Everything was too tight and showed far too much excess baggage. In the end, she settled on a new loose sweater and her usual denims. Through the window she could see Al wheeling a barrow of used animal bedding, half a broken cigarette stuck to his lip, hat pulled down, and designer denims tucked into Wellies. He'd borrowed some huge old overcoat and with the collar turned up, his whole image was one of mild eccentricity. Or maybe he *was* Jim Silver, artful detective … and serial womaniser.

He was as good as his word with regard to the food. Showered and changed from outdoor duty, he set to work on the vegetables and made custard from scratch, which she stirred obediently with a wooden spoon. They talked about the books, their daughters, and respective sister and brother. His reaction to the book sales was difficult to gauge; he seemed more interested in wanting to know what readers were saying, rather than how much money he'd made.

Throughout all of this, his phone was busy with calls from his son and his daughter, his grandchildren. He spent an age talking to Rupert and Barnaby, the conversation peppered with funny characters and voices. Kate could hear their combined laughter across the kitchen, spilling out from the tiny speaker.

Despite the constant interruptions to the cooking, Kate had to admire Al's sheer, unadulterated passion for his children and grandchildren. It brought home to her how much pain Jo must surely be inflicting with her late, devastating decision to go ahead and abort his child.

'I can't decide whether to call Jo, wish her happy Christmas,' he said, as if reading her mind. 'Nothing feels right though, given what she plans to do. I mean, whatever I *think* I want to do somehow falls to pieces in my head and I'm left with a nasty taste.'

'No, I can imagine,' she said, keeping her eyes on the pan.

'I mean, we're clearly finished as a couple, and I'm dead set against what she wants to do, but the thought of her going through a termination by herself ... just makes me feel a bit of a cad, somehow.'

She watched him for a moment, intent on chopping carrots into batons and mixing almonds into the sprouts. She was further impressed by both his knife skills and his concern for Jo. On the other hand, thinking of Jo made her feel hopelessly frumpy and insecure.

Once the preparation was well in hand, Kate made a platter of sandwiches and it was agreed that gifts would be exchanged during their consumption. George gave Fran a beautiful cashmere cardigan and a pearl necklace. On opening the layers of tissue, Fran looked close to tears. 'I haven't got you anything like this!'

'If you wish to spend your allowance on pig swill, that's up to you.'

The sting of his remark was lost as Becca ripped the expensive paper off her riding clobber. 'I can't believe you've bought me all this,' she said to her parents, holding up leather chaps, a jacket, jodhpurs, and a hunting stock with a real silver pin.

'Can't have my girl riding to hounds in any old getup,' George said.

With a trembling bottom lip, she threw her arms around her father, knowing full well where the cash had come from. 'Thanks, Dad. I thought you didn't care about any of it, you know?'

'Just be safe, that's all.'

'I will, Stilton's just the best, isn't he, Mum?'

'Good horse you picked there, Fran,' Al said, and she nodded frantically.

Kate watched Fran and Becca unwrap the bulky parcels from herself; carefully unfolding full-length waterproof coats. Fran looked shell-shocked.

'It's too much,' she said, 'And you got one for Becca? They cost a fortune!'

'I've seen you both getting soaked to the skin. Hope you don't mind something practical. I used to hate practical.'

'Mind? It's bloody marvellous. I don't know how to thank you.'

'You just did.'

Fran seemed embarrassed, but the ice was broken after that and they got onto the rest of the gifts. Butter and Marge received smelly marrow bones, Butter immediately making a slobbery mess, but poor little Marge just wanted to be nursed, and climbed onto Al's lap.

Tom and Maisie had given their father an iPod loaded with every Morrissey track he'd ever produced, and Kate was reminded once again of her daughter's preoccupation with herself. She'd sent money to Tia, because it was all she ever asked for and anything Kate chose as a gift was never quite right. However, there had been nothing forthcoming in the way of reciprocation.

'Hey, I'm getting up to date with technology!' Al said loudly, earpieces in place, frowning at the tiny screen.

162

Becca exchanged a grin with her. 'Stop *shouting*, Uncle Al!'

'Am I?'

'Yes! Anyway, what did you win for me at bingo?'

He dragged the earpieces out. 'Aw, you spotted me in there, did you?'

'You kind of stood out.'

He threw a weird shaped parcel across to her and she ripped the paper off to find a pink hobby horse. 'I'm way too old for this,' she said, then located the package attached to the horse's pole and gave a whoop. It was a mobile phone. Her father looked thunderous, Fran detached.

'Oh ... *wow*,' Becca said, casting a sly glance at George. 'Dad said I couldn't have one until I was sixteen. Did you win this at bingo as well?'

'Funny girl. Come on, Kate, you've not opened anything,' Al said, shunting various parcels her way. A silk scarf from George, handmade chocolates from Becca, and earrings from Fran. While the others were busy examining Becca's spoils, she opened Al's present. It was a smooth, antique-looking wooden box, cute in itself. Inside, on a bed of washed silk, there was a tiny sheet of paper, rolled and held with a strip of ribbon, like an ancient scroll.

Full of curiosity, she unravelled the delicate paper and read the single sentence. The second she looked up, his eyes met hers, his expression perfectly serious. She managed to smile and nod but her hands felt clumsy and her heart was thumping uncomfortably. George saved her some thinking time by thanking her for the bottle of vintage single malt, and no one noticed her fumbling to put the paper and the ribbon back into the box.

'You're welcome. I just ... I just need to check the turkey,' she said, and escaped to the kitchen. Once there, she closed the door and read the words again.

I owe you something special.

163

Chapter Thirteen

Al

To Al, from Kate. He peeled the silver paper from the box. It was an e-reader with a silver finish, naturally. When he switched it on, it was to see that she'd already added his own books to the index.

Fran and Becca disappeared upstairs to try out the new riding clobber and George rose to stand over him, jingling loose change in his pockets.

'I don't know how you do it.'

'What?'

'Get women to buy you stuff. A brand new phone the other week, and now an e-reader. What are you listening to on that iPod, huh? "This Charming Man"?' he went on, making jazz hands. '"Heaven Knows I'm Miserable Now", "The Boy with the Thorn in his Side"? Written for you, all that Morrissey crap.'

'Back off.'

'For now.'

He waited until his brother moved, packed the e-reader back into the box, and deposited Marge into a nest of cushions, then went to find Kate in the kitchen. She was struggling to lift the turkey out of the Aga, her face flushed.

'Here, let me get that.'

'Oh, it looks almost ready, thought I'd take the foil off it for half an hour.'

'Yeah, good idea. Talking of silver stuff,' he said, sliding the roasting tin onto a spare patch of worktop, 'Thanks for the e-reader.'

'I just thought it seemed crazy, you not having one.'

'I mean what I say, about owing you.'

'You don't owe me anything.'

'I do. I just haven't worked out what it is yet. I'm sorry it didn't coincide with Christmas.'

She shot him a quick sideways smile and busied herself with basting the turkey and looking for a carving plate. There were things he wanted to say to her, but as usual they were never alone for any length of time and someone was bound to come bursting into the kitchen.

If he'd learnt anything from his relationship with Jo, it was that Kate had been right when she'd talked about marrying for the wrong reasons. Deep down, he'd known it was wrong with Jo, but he was only really ready to admit it now, because of the feelings he'd allowed to develop for Kate. With Jo out of the picture, the escalation of his desire to be with her was reinforced by that old green friend; subconscious permission.

Kate was a thinker, and he liked that. There was something deeply sustaining about being able to properly talk to someone. Despite this, Ms Roberts was incredibly difficult to read from a romantic point of view. It was that tough outer shell she presented to the world, but there again he liked the way she kept him guessing, and he'd never been one to shy away from making a fool of himself.

The truth of it was, he hated being single. He loved being in love. This hadn't changed since he was fifteen, a lifetime of seeking bonds like a begging dog, sometimes to the point of destruction. Was it wrong to make a play for Kate, so soon after Greg, and Jo?

'Um, amazing stuffing,' he said, helping himself to a big spoonful and dropping half of it down his front. He was scraping the mess off his shirt over the sink when she looked at him with a wide grin and the sudden realisation that he actually didn't need to say or explain anything to this woman washed over him with a mixture of relief and fear. One full-on smile and a lock with those eyes and his soul was exposed. It was like watching his life flash before him. Fifty years; a lifetime of drowning in an embryonic sac. Would he ever come up for air?

Later, their combined effort at Christmas dinner was amazingly good and he was pleased to see that Kate clearly enjoyed her food. Helen had always been on a permanent diet and Jo, well, Jo had been artistically perfect but he found Kate far more erotic. Her hair always smelt of the rain so it was a normal progression to imagine her body like a warm sea, deep and rolling, her skin the creamy foam of his desire ... OK, after a bottle of Chardonnay he was slightly drunk as well, but it happened a lot when he was in writing mode, these rambling thoughts. His inner eye constantly explored visual scenery, running like a film with dialogue whispering in his ear, sometimes mysterious, usually sensual.

His brother rubbed his big belly and belched, breaking the spell. He thanked Kate profusely for an excellent dinner.

'I didn't do all this by myself,' she protested. 'Al did lots of it, and this custard is to die for.'

'It's totally yummy,' Becca said, finishing her second portion with relish. 'Can I be excused to go and get ready for tomorrow? I need to find Stilton's numnah and pack some stuff to get changed into because we're going to the party thing afterwards.'

'Go on, off with you,' George said.

'Hold on,' Fran said, shooting a look at George, 'What are you doing about Stilton while you're at this "party thing"? He'll need rugging and feeding as well, you know.'

'I told you yesterday *twice,* but you weren't listening!'

'Tell us again,' George said gently.

Becca ran through a complicated itinerary, clearly

exasperated. George said he couldn't see anything wrong with it but Fran reeled off a list of things she'd need for unloading and settling Stilton next door for the night. Buckets, halter, bran mash, hay-net, stable bandages, night rug. Becca rolled her eyes and crossed her arms.

'Don't forget his teddy and his toothbrush,' Al said.

Becca giggled at this, then glared at her mother. 'I've got it all covered.'

'Right then, off you go,' George said again.

Fran pushed plum pudding around and around her bowl. She'd hardly eaten anything but she insisted on clearing up and making George help. In truth, he was increasingly worried about Fran. Since the accident she'd been on a steady decline. Her continued consumption of painkillers had not gone unnoticed, and clearly added to their already strained marriage. The fact that his presence in the house was likely adding to the general misery troubled him deeply but he had no idea what to do about it.

During the noisy clean-up operation in the kitchen, Kate opened her laptop, logged onto Facebook, and showed him the ongoing discussion about Jim Silver. It was strangely gratifying to find fans of the original printed books chatting about the series and expressing hopes for another one. New readers, the ones who couldn't recall the eighties, whined about it being old-fashioned. The more of these stupid remarks he read, the more he wanted to have his say. When Kate was engrossed in the paper, he added his comment at the end of the conversation, posting as Kate Roberts, of course. She soon cottoned on, looking up at the sound of his furious typing.

'What are you saying? I hope you're not being rude.'

'No. Just putting a couple of people straight.'

'Don't get me banned from the group, otherwise we can't snoop.'

He grinned, liking the way she said 'we' and loving the way she looked fiercely secretarial with horn-rimmed spectacles halfway down her nose.

'Have you managed to speak with your errant family yet?' he said.

'Mother is doing rather well. I suspect that's down to copious amounts of sherry, a special Christmas showing of *Family Fortunes*, and a cat called Statin. Tia is still blanking me, but at least Annemarie found time to send a two-worded text.'

'Merry Christmas?'

'A drunken, abbreviated version of that, but yes.'

He closed the laptop and went to sit next to her. The little box he'd gifted to her was on the coffee table and inside, she'd secreted the earrings from Fran and a decorative button which had come loose from her sweater.

'What have you done with the "I owe you" note?' he said, hoping she hadn't left it lying around.

'It's in my bra.'

Difficult then to keep his eyes on her face. 'I like your style.'

'Style? No one's ever said that word and my name in the same sentence.'

Totally unimpressed, she went back to reading the paper. He peered over the top and pulled it down slightly with one finger. 'So, er … have you any idea how I can fulfil my obligation?'

'No. That's down to you.'

'You like surprises, then?'

'No, not especially, but I'm thinking I need to change my outlook, be a little more spontaneous?'

'I think I might be able to help with that.'

She let the paper fall and crumple into her lap. Her breasts wobbled slightly with contained laughter, then when he picked up her freckled hand, she gave him that quizzical half smile over the top of her glasses.

'Look,' he began, 'I feel really bad about your job.'

'Why? It was my first spontaneous act.'

'Will there be more?'

She curled her fingers around his and it felt so incredibly good he moved forward to kiss her. She was about to either respond likewise, or say something, their faces just inches apart, when her eyes suddenly left his and focused beyond his shoulder. He twisted round to see his sister-in-law.

'Sorry, am I interrupting?' Fran said.

'No, just …'

She began to make a fuss about tidying the papers and all the old *Horse and Hound* magazines littering the table, which was way out of character. She was even putting them in date order. Kate raised her brows at him and he shot her a nod of understanding. It was like being thirteen and getting caught out by your parents. What the hell was Fran thinking, making a deal out of him and Kate? He hoped she didn't harbour any weird fantasies. No wonder his brother was giving him evil looks.

The first half of the evening passed in a mostly dignified silence with a good two feet of space between him and Kate. Not surprisingly, Kate excused herself and went to her room. If Becca hadn't been buzzing in and out he could maybe have had a chat with Fran, but then it seemed wrong to initiate something like that on Christmas night.

He let the dogs out for a last wee, then carried Marge upstairs. The good thing about not needing very much sleep was that it meant he could write until well past midnight without fear of interruption. When the children had been small, Helen had never missed a full night's rest, even when Tom and Maisie had been ill, because he'd always been on duty.

As he opened his laptop, he heard Kate creak across the landing to the bathroom. He was sorely tempted to intercept her on the way back, but there was something sordid and immature about that and he had the feeling she wouldn't like it, and anyway, he was trying to grow up. Instead, he set up his iPod and tried to concentrate on the complicated scene where Silver finds a lunatic in his garden and spots of blood on his best scarf. Morrissey began to warble and Al hummed along.

Boxing Day began with the neighbour's horsebox swinging into the yard. Reversing lights and loud bleeping woke him, and then the clatter of hooves and Becca shouting. When he padded downstairs and looked through the sitting room window, it was to see Stilton prancing across the yard in the gloomy half-light, wide-eyed and whinnying. The horse was dressed in his red travelling finery but spooked when he saw the ramp. Fran, in her dressing gown and Wellingtons, began to stroke the dappled grey's heaving flanks, her lips constantly moving, soothing. To his amazement, the horse loaded quietly – testament to Fran's hours of training – and the back doors were quickly bolted home.

The box revved up and released its air brakes. Becca kissed her mum and ran to get into the cab. She had a bridle hooked over her shoulder and her hat balanced on her hip, a long, dark plait of hair down her back. It seemed incomprehensible that she was fourteen now. He wondered if drag-hunting was more dangerous. When he thought about Becca's slight frame astride half a ton of galloping horse, leaping hedges and stone walls at thirty miles an hour, his insides somersaulted.

And yet, many years ago he'd done the very same thing alongside George and Fran, foolhardy with teenage bravado and too much stirrup-cup. He'd fallen from his borrowed horse many times, all through showing off. Although he'd enjoyed the farm and the country life it allowed, he'd never been a true horseman, it just wasn't in his blood. The inheritance of his mother's theatrical tendencies didn't mix too well with horses, and it was only

171

in an odd, random hindsight that he thought about it now. He sent Becca a text. 'Enjoy yourself. Don't take any risks will you? Love you.'

After a few minutes she responded with, 'I won't. Love you too.'

While he was filling the kettle, Fran came in through the back door and sighed heavily. The parrot reeled off a list of obscenities but even this failed to elicit a response.

'She'll be all right,' he said.

'She will, won't she?'

He nodded and spooned coffee into two mugs. 'Yeah, she's sensible too, not like we were. Do you remember us getting shot at for galloping though that crop of turnips?'

'I hope Stilton doesn't get too strong for her. She needs to set him up straight for each obstacle, he has a tendency to veer to the left. If he runs out and she gets left behind …'

Al let her carry on talking technicalities, knowing full well that it was her way of dealing with anxiety. He passed her a mug of coffee and out of the corner of his eye, noticed her swallow something.

'Are you still on those painkillers?'

'Yes! If I wasn't *suffering* I'd be with Becca now, wouldn't I?'

'Fran, I'm a bit worried about you, love.'

'Not now, Al, not today,' she said, and trailed back upstairs. She was still wearing her Wellingtons and the bottom of her dressing gown was covered in straw and horse manure.

Around mid-afternoon, Maisie and Simon arrived with Tom and the boys, and the house was filled with an agreeable distraction of disorganisation and much laughter.

His daughter sported an engagement ring and an air of happy contentment, and for a while, this radiated throughout the house. His pleasure was further intensified

172

by the sure knowledge that Maisie would never have to confront any demons of his own making. He'd given her a gold-plated, second-to-none start in life, and it showed. Likewise Tom. Gifting him and Bernice the money to set up their own accountancy business by re-mortgaging the house in Delamere had been a mere detail to Al. Helen hadn't been keen but then she'd got a big promotion and it had been easy to talk her round. In the aftermath of his impending divorce, he felt incredibly guilty about the financial debt and against his own solicitor's wishes, had split the house sale eighty-twenty in favour of Helen.

Simon helped carry the kitchen table into the sitting room and they located the extension for it in the barn. He cleaned the dung off and then once in position, covered the pitted and pecked surface with a huge, billowing white bed sheet. It had elasticated corners full of fluff and cat hair but since it hung almost to the floor, no one noticed. Kate had made an impressive cold spread with a whole salmon and the leftover turkey. Fran had started to help with the salads but became distracted with animal chores and wandered outside.

At the table, Al found himself squashed next to Kate on a garden bench, her thigh burning into his. Beneath the overhang of the tablecloth, he stroked her left hand and felt a jolt of electricity when she squeezed his fingers back. She was talking animatedly to Tom on her right side, who was a lot more chilled without Bernice in tow. Opposite, George was perched on Dad's old shooting stick, discussing small business finance with Simon. He could almost have fooled himself it was a happy family gathering if he didn't keep catching his brother's malevolent eye from time to time. At least he kept the drink flowing, although Maisie was only sipping orange juice, but everyone else was well catered for.

He heard the taxi first, rumbling and splashing through the water-filled potholes in the drive. Then he saw Helen

173

stagger out, slam the door, and pay the driver. As the car pulled away, she looked up at the house, swaying slightly and holding her bag upside down. When everything started to fall out, she began to scrabble on the ground, her dress riding up her thighs.

What the hell?

If he could have summoned any cohesive thought and got his legs to move, he might have darted to the front door and intercepted her before the taxi left, but he was well and truly trapped on the bench with no way of moving away from the table. He was in the line of fire with no escape. When the inevitable thumping on the door started, it was George who went to answer it.

Helen appeared at the entrance to the sitting room and the babble of chatter quietened as everyone turned to look at his almost ex-wife, her make-up smeared and her hair escaping some sort of elaborate up-do.

'Well, well. This is nice,' she said, pulling out a chair. 'I'll overlook the fact no one thought to invite me. White wine please, George.'

George poured her a moderate amount and she drank it down, then held out the glass for a re-fill. 'So, there I was, all alone in the hotel and I got to thinking ... how come that bastard ... Al, how come he has all the fun, eh?' She grabbed the neck of the wine bottle and poured it roughly in the direction of her glass. 'I mean, isn't it incredible that he's still so fucking popular after what he did, and yet here I am, all by myself while *he* ... ' She paused, as tears began to cloud her eyes and distort her voice. 'While *he* is welcomed back into the family home like some long-lost fucking hero!'

'I couldn't agree more,' George said. 'Help yourself to some food, soak up some of the alcohol, eh? Then you can tell us all about it. Played away with Blondie, did he?'

'I thought he was gay when I first met him, did you know that?'

174

'Mum, come on, don't do this,' Maisie said, and Al agreed.

'Helen, I think details about our relationship should remain private.' His mouth was bone dry, his insides the consistency of mush. The idea that she could blurt out anything and everything was beyond comprehension.

'You're an amazing actor to have kept such a secret from me all those years,' she went on, then began to stab a finger at George and Fran as well. 'And don't think you two are exempt.'

The colour slowly drained from his brother's smug face, then began to flush to a dark purple. Fran looked like she might pass out. An irrational part of him almost wanted Fran to pass out as a diversion, but it didn't happen.

'Hold on a minute. Hold it *right* there,' George said, his mind busily working overtime. He suddenly slapped both hands down on the table, his eyes boring into his. 'Just *what* have you told her?'

'He's told me everything,' Helen said sweetly, and pulled a huge bowl of trifle closer to her side of the table. 'And it all makes perfect sense now.' She hunted through the pile of cutlery for a spoon.

Lifting the tablecloth, Al wondered about getting underneath. He could see his brother, shifting his weight from one leg to the other, and he could see Helen's knickers as she sat with her legs slightly apart, totally sloshed. It was tempting to drop down there and curl up in a ball, but what would that solve? No, the only possible option he had at that precise moment was one of surprise. Without rocking the table too violently, he managed to crawl underneath and surfaced next to Helen's chair.

She seemed poised to begin some sort of rant, her finger ready to point and accuse. Thrown by his sudden, close proximity her nostrils flared and she inhaled deeply, steeling herself for battle. She was about to open her mouth and there was a brief connection when he looked apologetically into her eyes; the eyes of the woman he'd always love, as the mother of his children.

Then he pushed her face into the trifle.

Rupert broke the tension by tugging on his shirt. 'Granddad, can I have a go now, please?'

Simon was holding the bridge of his nose, his eyes sparkling with amusement. Maisie had a hand covering her mouth, her eyes mostly downcast. Tom was already collecting the boys' coats. 'I don't know what's going on here, but I don't think I want to know.'

Helen took a while to surface, coughing and blinking. Cream, custard, flaked almonds, and silver balls were liberally plastered all over her face and clung messily to her hair. She slewed most of it off with paper napkins, throwing them in his direction. He wanted to help her, ashamed of how miserable she was, ashamed of what he'd done to her in front of everyone, but she didn't give him a chance. She went through her handbag and fished out two crumpled letters, both of which she pushed dramatically at his chest.

'Decree. *Absolute.*'

Maisie took hold of her arm, flashing worried eyes at Al. 'Mum, come on, let's get you back to the hotel.'

'That's a good idea,' he managed to say.

The room slowly emptied. George even went to the door to wave them off. Al wiped the smears of trifle from his letters. They'd both been sent to Delamere Road, so presumably Helen had received them through mail re-direction at the hotel. Always the practical one. He unfolded his solicitor's cream embossed single sheet, and read the few lines without emotion. So that was that, then. His marriage of thirty years had been dissolved; invoice to follow. The other correspondence was overseas airmail, covered in foreign stamps. Curious, but not especially wanting any more drama or possible complications, he pushed it into his back pocket.

Kate was still wedged behind the table, and Fran remained staring at the floor, nursing a large glass of red wine. He couldn't read either of their expressions, but they both looked up expectantly as George closed the door behind him. He paused for a moment, scanning all of their faces.

'I was going to wait till Christmas was over before I said this, but in light of a certain *indiscretion,* I see no need to prolong my intentions.'

'What are you prattling on about?'

'This charade you've got us all playing, Al!'

'Helen won't say anything.'

He made a derisory noise at this, then picked up the turkey carving knife and waved the tip of it close to his face. 'I should have dealt with this fifteen years ago, but you couldn't keep it shut or even stay away, could you?'

'You know why. I've nowhere else to go!'

'Yeah, yeah, yeah,' he said, and thankfully moved the blade to a safer distance. 'So, here's what I've decided. My marriage is hanging by a thread. I'm reduced to a payer of bills, just like Helen.'

A brief muffle of protest from Fran, but George raised his hand. 'Let me speak, please. I'm taking voluntary redundancy. The bank's finished! I've already jumped, long before I was pushed.'

'They're closing the bank?' Fran whispered.

'I could have moved to another branch and carried on working, but I was tempted by the package they offered.'

'What will we do?'

'I'll tell you what *I'm* going to do. I've procured a two-bedroomed flat on the river estate, so I shall go and live in it. Ironically, it used to belong to the livery yard, just down the road. I suggest you get Chathill on the market before it's totally worthless; then, my *darling* wife, you and my *darling* brother may share the pathetic proceeds between you.'

'What about Becca?' Al said, barely taking anything in.

'My dear daughter is welcome to join me. There's even room for her horse at the aforementioned livery yard. But the rest of the menagerie out there,' he said, gesticulating wildly towards the window, 'Can go find another mug. And that includes *you*, Al!'

'Becca will want to stay here!' Fran protested.

'She can. And then she can go live with you in your council flat.'

'You can't do this to us!'

'What, exactly? Stop us going bankrupt? Stop paying the bills for this ramshackle excuse of a home? I think you'll find I can, and I will.' George took a long, careful look at her then plunged the knife into the Christmas cake. 'I've simply had enough. *Got it?*'

Fran looked broken, crushed by his words. Strangely though, George squeezed her shoulder in passing. And his voice was low, caring almost. 'I'm sorry, love, but I really don't know what else to do. Some might say I'm being cruel to be kind. I hope you'll see it like that too, eventually.'

His gaze swept across all their dumbfounded faces, and they stayed silent, locked in their own thoughts as his footsteps clumped up the threadbare stairs. Followed by the sound of a heavy suitcase dragged across the landing.

Chapter Fourteen

Kate

She had no idea what to say or do. It was awful, sitting there like a dummy while someone else's personal drama unfolded around her. On the other hand, maybe it was just as well George had exploded when he did. Although it had been uncomfortable, listening to him leave his wife, perhaps he'd done it to warn her, to expose the past complications with Al.

All three stared at the floor, deep in thought, Al chewing a nail.

George heaved his case over the stair-gate, cursing at the roaming dogs in the way. He loaded it into his vehicle and then began to remove items from his office. It didn't take very long and then he stuck his head round the door, as if he was just popping out for some milk.

'I'll call the agent, shall I? I'll speak to Becca, too.'

No one answered him, so he just nodded and left. Only when the engine noise of the BMW died to a distant hum, did Fran come to life.

'What shall I tell Becca?'

'We'll tell her together, don't worry,' Al said.

'*Together?* Will we, Al?'

'Yeah.'

'She'll want to go to Billy Williams' livery. He's got a big indoor manége and thirty acres of grazing,' she said, as if this was the most important conclusion she'd drawn. When she went from the room, Al looked at Kate properly for the first time, sweeping his over-grown hair back with a tired sigh. She wished he wasn't so handsome; it was far more difficult to be cool and detached in the presence of such rakish good looks.

'I didn't see that coming, did you?' he said.

'George? In a way, yes. Look, I don't know what's gone on between you and your brother,' she said, then when he made no reply asked, 'Is there history between you and Fran, is that it?'

Her mobile rang. A glance at the screen told her it was Tia, and there was no way she could ignore it. 'Hello, love! Are you all right?'

'No.' It was a muffled, tearful no.

Kate got to her feet and Al pulled the table back so she could get out and stand by the window, the signal hotspot. 'Where are you?'

'I'm at home; when are you coming back? I need to talk to you.'

'I'll get there as soon as I can.' The call ended abruptly, and she must have pulled a face.

'Problem?' Al said.

'I have to go, yes. My daughter needs me.'

'What, now? Right this minute? *Kate?*'

She ignored him and went to her room and sat on the bed, trying to decide if she was over the legal driving limit. She felt incredibly sober, although she knew through experience that two large glasses of Sauvignon Blanc were not to be trusted. The fact that maybe Al was not to be trusted either made her feel ashamed and embarrassed, which was faintly ridiculous. It was also ridiculous that she'd considered her daughter's crisis to be a well-timed life-saver.

Above all, she felt incredibly let down, as if she'd been teetering on the brink of something magical, and then someone had come along and told her it wasn't magic at all, it was a clever illusion done with mirrors. A cruel trick played by the sad clown in a circus of fools. Like being told that Father Christmas didn't exist, all those rug-pulling moments that build throughout childhood to culminate in the big one; the truth about love.

She began to throw her belongings into her case, zipping sponge bags with too much force. If she was stopped and faced with a breathalyser test, then so be it. Tia had clearly got herself into trouble over a man and the fact she was asking for help was some kind of miracle.

She dropped her bags at the bottom of the stairs, then saw Fran in George's study. She was sat at his desk, engrossed in sorting through a huge box of black and white photographs. Deep in thought, Kate entered the room and looked over Fran's shoulder. There were lots of family pictures; George and Al, standing side by side in school uniform, astride fat ponies, carrying fishing rods. There were country shows going back over the years, horse-drawn ploughs and the first motor cars, dates scribbled on the back.

And there were wedding photographs. George, slim and dark and linking arms with his bride. Al, in a crumpled linen jacket, standing to one side with both sets of parents. Fran trailed her finger over all of their faces.

'I married the wrong brother, didn't I?'

Kate, about to say her goodbyes, was further thrown by this. Fran looked up with enormous, intense eyes. 'My mother wouldn't allow it, you see. She wanted me to marry George. He was by far the better bet, she said. He's a bank manager. You can't go wrong there, that's what she said.'

Above the desk and reflecting her pinched face, there was a mahogany glass-fronted gun case holding a single shotgun. Beneath the gun there was a row of little boxes, presumably for holding shot. The cabinet was likely antique and despite the dust it looked like an attractive piece of furniture, although she couldn't help feeling relieved that it was locked.

She mumbled a reply to Fran, but her immediate

thought was to get out of the stuffy little room with its box of old memories. She slung her handbag over her shoulder and picked up the hurriedly packed holdall. A glance into the sitting room opposite revealed Al sitting exactly where she'd left him. He didn't look up as she opened the front door and walked briskly to her car.

Five miles down the valley road and the tears started. How pathetic was that? By the time she turned the lock in her own front door, her face was a blubbery mess. Her daughter emerged from the snug, holding a mug in one hand and a slice of toast in the other. She was wearing a dressing gown, wet hair bundled up in a turban, and sporting a pink face pack. When she spoke, she sounded like a bad ventriloquist, talking through gritted teeth.

'Why are you crying?'

'I've made a fool of myself over a man.'

Tia's mouth opened and some of the mask cracked and flaked off. '*You* have? No way!'

'Have we got any booze in?'

'I think there's some brandy?'

'Fine. Perfect.'

She scuttled off while Kate removed her coat and fiddled with the thermostat. She felt chilled to the bone. Tia returned, minus the face pack, rubbing at her hair, a damp, strawberry blonde tangle. Kate stacked up the logs in the burner, and they sat, side by side with drinks. Her daughter wanted to know everything about Al, refusing to speak until her mother had bared her soul. Kate was more than happy to talk it out and filled in an extensive overview for her, but Tia quickly lost interest with the more abstract detail.

'Did you sleep with him?'

'No! Why does everything come down to that?'

She seemed genuinely puzzled. 'So, how have you made a fool of yourself?'

'I started to develop feelings for him.'

'Big wow.'

Kate sighed at this, irritated by Tia's usual lack of sensitivity but mostly completely surprised by the conversation they were having. 'Anyway,' she said, desperate to change tack. 'I thought you had some sort of crisis?'

'It's nowhere near as interesting as yours. I've never seen you like this.'

'Like what?'

'Sobbing, opening up, *talking*.'

Kate nodded and looked at the ball of tissue in her lap. 'I know. I know I'm not very approachable, but maybe we can ... maybe *I* can change that.' She lifted her head to look at Tia, disappointed, but not entirely surprised, to see an expression of pity. 'Anyway, that's been my Christmas. What's this problem of yours?'

'I've lost my job.'

'Oh, me too.'

Tia's eyes widened. '... Over a stupid prat of a man.'

'Same here.'

'He posted a nude picture of himself with it all hanging out –'

'*Please,* spare me the details.'

'... On my Facebook page, underneath the playgroup Christmas party. How was that my fault?'

'You seriously want me to answer that?'

'A couple of the yummy mummies saw it and I got suspended. So I told them to shove it.'

'Was he worth it?' Kate asked, pausing before she lifted the glass to her lips, keeping her eyes facing forward onto the print of Greg adorning the chimney breast, as if the answer might be there. Through the glass of the brandy balloon, he looked distinctly distorted and wavy.

'No,' Tia said. 'Was he *fuck*.'

This admission was followed by a heaving sob.

Within a matter of days, Tia reverted to her prickly self. The atmosphere in the house changed from being a cocoon of cosy chats and wound-licking to bored sniping. They even exhausted bitching about Julie, Tia's step-mother, and although Kate had never lowered herself to do this in the past, the way it united them as mother and daughter was secretly satisfying.

In a way, bitching about Julie released some of the bitching she really wanted to do about the dysfunctional situation at Chathill. She couldn't decide whom she was the most cross with. All the months she'd wasted worrying about telling Fran about Greg, and now it seemed Fran's marriage was also based on some sort of lie. The hypocritical nerve she'd had too, warning her off Al! She felt sorry for George and Becca, maybe even Helen too, although she didn't have enough facts to have a real opinion there.

Tia was irritated by Kate's dithering, the way she picked the phone up then put it down again.

'If it bothers you, just drive over there!'

'I feel awful. About just dropping everything in everyone's hour of need; but then I think should remain impartial.'

'*Don't* go over there, then.'

'Oh, I don't know what to do! Stay away ... I think.'

'What's the big deal?' Tia said, already bored with her mother's pretend love life. 'Why don't you just *call* him?'

'It's complicated, that's why.'

Good grief, had she just said that?

It didn't help that she and Tia were both unemployed and suffering from not having enough to do. The dismal days after the New Year were like no-man's land, with Kate staring out of the window and Tia searching the Internet for a new life. The latest idea was a European au-pair job; preferably for an A- or B-list celebrity couple who travelled a lot, and included the use of a swimming

184

pool and a decent car as part of the package.

'Problem,' she said, after twenty minutes. 'I can't speak another language.'

They went to the local job centre.

There was the usual spate of cleaning and care-in-the-community opportunities, and then numerous dodgy tele-sales jobs. One temporary position for the council in the housing benefit office. Tia made exaggerated groaning noises and Kate sympathised, albeit silently. Basically, there was nothing with an exciting enough prospect to take her mind off Al, let alone something to tempt her daughter out of inertia.

Ironically, BHS were advertising for senior sales staff and Tia suddenly wanted to know how her boring, conventional mother had come to lose her boring, conventional job. When Kate told her about Freddie Fun-Pants she curled her lip.

'He sounds a right jerk.'

Later, as Kate began a pile of ironing, Tia made herself a new Facebook page. 'I need to know what's going on,' she said. 'Jobs and stuff.'

'You need to drop those silly friends of yours. Prospective employers check these days, you know.'

'I've got full privacy, no tagging or posting. No photographs.'

'Right, good,' she said, amazed that her daughter hadn't exploded in the face of her motherly advice, although it was doubtful she was actually listening. Her fingers flew over the keyboard, phone lodged under her chin.

'Is this *him?*' she said suddenly, tilting the screen towards her. Kate nodded in confirmation, the suspended iron hissing like an angry goose. She was surprised at the way it made her feel to see his headshot; tawny windblown hair, serious expression, silly hat. Tia raised one, perfectly plucked eyebrow. 'Actually, he's quite fit. For an older guy.'

A couple of weeks later, fully reunited with the World Wide Web, Tia announced she was going back to central London, this time to share a grotty-looking house. The other occupants consisted of two university students with rich parents, an exotic club dancer (sex indeterminate), and two smiling, ethnic characters, apparently making a fortune exporting baby milk formula to China. Kate was quickly exhausted and puzzled by all of it but didn't bother voicing any questions.

Tia showed her the house on an Internet house-share site.

'Oh, it has a little garden.'

'It'll be full of shit.'

'I see. And the prospect of this is better than staying here?'

'Hell yeah.'

She dropped Tia at the station and waved her off, tall and resolute again in just ten days. At least she'd signed to a reputable employment agency for nannies. Alone again, Kate turned the car towards Conwy, then on a whim took a left along the valley. It was bitterly cold and the smell of frozen rain filtered into the car. The sky was split open over a distant Moel Siabod, a dull illumination promising a few seconds of sunlight but generally the day was proving to be cold and wet.

There was a For Sale board on the main road, nailed to a tree at the top of the drive, and it gave her an unhappy jolt to actually see it. It was unlikely that anyone would buy Chathill and restore it to a working farm. It just wasn't cost-effective any more. The small parcel of land it had managed to cling to was probably its most valuable asset. At best, a property developer would buy it for a pittance and sell it as a 'substantial family home with paddocks'. Or demolish it and build three smaller starter homes. After a protest of sorts, the locals would say it was the end of an era.

The box of old photographs had her wondering at the nostalgia of it and the terrible heartbreak it would wrench, severing generations of a family to rubble. George's heritage. The only roots Al had ever known. The only life Fran had ever wanted.

Continuing on, Kate took a left at the next cross-roads and dropped down into a small hamlet which consisted of nothing more than a closed-up pub and a few detached properties. There was a smart sign for the livery yard at the start of a single-track road, crisscrossed by bridleways, and the roof of the indoor school was just visible through the leafless trees.

Close to the river front, there was a circle of newish looking houses, and a flat above the double-fronted newsagents cum post office. George's BMW looked too big for its surroundings, but at least it made an easy landmark. He must have been staring out of the window and came to the door the second she pulled in. He looked awful.

'Kate, love. I've been meaning to phone, apologise.'

'No need.'

She followed him up the narrow stairs and through the front door of his flat. It was surprisingly light and spacious, with stunning views of the swollen river and the dense, wooded hills beyond. He showed her the bedrooms, the second one clearly identified as Becca's, dominated by a new desk complete with computer, although there didn't seem to be many of Becca's personal belongings, and the still-wrapped horse-themed bedspread sat on top of a pile of bedding and pillows were clearly unused. The furniture throughout was shabby, but the kitchen and bathroom were both clean and modern, with gleaming white fittings, and she imagined how much this would please George. He bustled about, finding cups and filling the kettle. Neither of them knew what to say, how to start a conversation.

'How *is* Becca?'

'Fine. She's not sure about living here though. Too much too soon, I expect. Or it could be that she prefers life with Uncle Al. After all, I no longer fit down Christmas tree chutes or have a dressing-up box to rely on in times of adversity.'

She smiled at his sarcasm and they took drinks and biscuits through to the lounge. They talked about the view and the weather, and then eventually he said, 'I'm sorry for spoiling your Christmas like that, but I just couldn't carry on. I was at the end of my tether.'

'I totally understand.'

'The emotional scars are one thing but the financial mess is now as distasteful as the animal mess. Do you know, just before Christmas a one-legged man turned up wanting money to feed *seven* ponies! Seven ponies I thought she'd sold at market.'

'Oh.'

'We were all right until he came back,' he said. 'Like a fucking cuckoo.'

Kate wasn't sure it was possible to be a cuckoo in your own nest.

'It was bad enough having to live with him in the same bloody house!' he went on, starting to shout. 'And then, I find out he's told Helen! *Helen*, the biggest mouth in Cheshire and North Wales combined. I mean, how bloody stupid is he?'

'What did he tell Helen? Sorry, that's none of my business.'

He struggled to his feet then, jingling the change in his pocket and wandering across to look through the picture window. 'We made a *pact*. His side of the deal was to keep his mouth shut and *stay away*.'

'And Fran?'

At this, he seemed to crumple. He collapsed back down into his chair and rubbed his eyes. 'Fran is a mess. This has been building for years, you know? She needs help and I've tried. I've *tried*. Fran is in love with everything and everybody except me, have you not noticed? Even the bloody dogs come before me. All those broken animals she collects are her babies.'

Kate took their cups into the kitchen and stared at the shiny new sink. Despite her initial irritation she did feel concerned for Fran, locked in a world of make-believe and popping pills. She felt desperately sorry for her brother-in-law, usurped from his own home and estranged from his daughter through no real fault of his own. The only rather insidious action he'd taken was the one of conspiracy with the flat and the way he'd planned it behind everyone's back. Although, in desperation, could she really blame him? It was the same desperation which had driven Helen to speak, before she was silenced by the trifle.

'Will you divorce Fran?' she asked him.

'Divorce? All I want is for Fran to see sense.'

'And Al?'

'He'll get his thirty pieces of silver from Chathill. Final severance pay.'

They parted awkwardly, George clasping her hand and wishing her a happy new year. Neither of them knew quite how to proceed with each other, but she felt better having made some sort of gesture.

On the way home, she had to pull over to answer her mobile. It was her mother, in high spirits. Unlike everyone else Kate knew, she'd had a wonderful Christmas, but she could never recall everything in a single conversation and so relayed gossip as it occurred to her. Bert had sorted her out with a new, all-singing all-dancing phone, pre-programmed with everyone's numbers, including mobiles, which she could previously never manage. This was not a good thing.

She wanted to tell Kate about Betty Hislop's hysterectomy, although she couldn't bring herself to name actual body parts and so the conversation broke down into a tiresome guessing game.

'I had no idea, did you?'

'What?'

'That she'd had it all taken away,' her mother said, then dropped her voice to a whisper. 'Down below. You know.'

'You can't tell by just looking at her, you'd have to scan her.'

'I can't stand her either. What's it called when women have their downstairs taken out?'

'A refurbishment? A knock-through? You are allowed to say ovaries and womb, you know.'

'Yes, well. I'm coming back as a man.'

'You'd rather have a penis with a little brain in it, then?'

'I never brought you up to be so *vulgar*.'

'Cock and fanny would be *more* vulgar.'

There was a sharp intake of breath and a lot of tutting. 'You need to wash your mouth out with carbolic soap!'

Her mother disconnected on her. Kate opened the car window, enjoying the sharp air. She wished the clarity of it could stop her mind jumping from one issue to the next. Did they have an affair, was that it?

At home, she logged onto Facebook. A message popped up from Annemarie. 'Any chance you can have Jake? We've all got a bloody bug, been in the bog all Christmas.'

Al's page was devoid of activity as usual. He was very likely too busy, distracted with the farm, Fran, and Becca. Whenever she allowed her mind to drift, abstract pictures of him dominated her thoughts. Slumped in the hospital waiting room, fingers threaded through his hair. The bunch of singing flowers, the way he cuddled his pregnant dog. The silly voices he did for Barnaby and Rupert, over and over without losing patience. That fragile, scented scrap of paper tied with a ribbon.

I owe you something special.

Since he'd kissed her, held her, touched her, parts of her had shown signs of life. Is it OK to say that, Mother? Because she'd not thought of anything else since.

Around midnight the phone rang, disturbing her from a deep sleep. Since Tia had returned to London, she always kept her mobile switched on, as if it were some sort of lifeline. An invisible umbilical cord from the big bad city to the safe confines of a semi-detached house in North Wales. Well, she could easily turn that cliché on its head, and, given the current circumstances, it was more likely that she would be calling Tia. She grabbed her reading glasses and looked at the pulsing screen, saw it was Al, and her thumb wavered between "answer" and "reject". She switched the phone off.

Her mother accepted her apology with a lot of fussy embarrassment.

'It's not like you to say words like that.'

'No. Anyway, I'm sorry if you were offended.'

They'd been to the doctors, the chemist, and the supermarket. On passing her sister's house, they left a large box of Imodium and some bottles of Lucozade on the high shelf in the porch. Back at Rhos House, Kate unpacked the shopping. The lunchtime news on the television was so loud she had to virtually shout. 'I wish you'd get a hearing aid!'

There was no response because her mother was in the kitchen boiling handkerchiefs, pushing them into an old pan with a wooden spatula. Kate sighed and went to grab the remote control. As she fumbled with the unfamiliar buttons the tail-end of a news report had her look up sharply, and then she was waiting to hear it confirmed, urging the local news and weather to finish so they'd go to the recap. It was more or less a single sentence, accompanied by a black and white picture of a beautiful blonde woman in her thirties, with upswept hair and long blue eyes. She'd died alone, age eighty-six. Star of *Nine Good Men* and *Running on Empty*.

Ruby Martinez was dead.

Another bombshell. One which raised a different list of emotive questions. She didn't really want to think about another earth-shattering issue. She was already overloaded in that department, but she couldn't help wondering how it might make Al feel, the death of the woman who'd rejected him as a five year old and then again at a thirty-six. Should she call him, send a card? Did he even know she was dead? Was it normal to call her daughter and discuss matters like this?

Tia was always running somewhere, heavy traffic noise and the wail of sirens in the background. 'For Chrissakes, Mum. *If* anything happened with freaky Fran, it was years ago! Answer me this; is he married?'

'Divorced.'

'Are *you* married?'

'Widowed.'

'There's the frigging answer then.'

Kate rolled her eyes. Tia's world was black and white, it was so simple, but everything in Kate's head made her feel distinctly grey, and undistinguished.

He had some kind of history with Fran.

His mother's dead.

Chapter Fifteen

Al

Kate had ignored his call. He was prepared to beg in order to plead his case but when several days passed by and she also ignored his e-mail, Al forced himself to accept that she'd blown him out. She was no longer interested in him as a friend and a token book agent, let alone a possible love interest. Shortly after this though, Jo also unfriended him on Facebook, and this seemed the final insult, but then the landline phone account was terminated, and so they lost the Internet anyway. Becca was unimpressed and sighed a lot.

'I thought you didn't bother with it,' Al said.

'I kind of need it, for school? It's OK, I'll go round to Dad's, he's got a high-speed connection.'

He didn't blame her in the least, but the effect it had on Fran manifested itself in her deteriorating health, and trying to get her to see sense or agree to talk to a doctor continued to fall on deaf ears and she'd virtually stopped eating. He craved Kate's grounded advice about this, about all kinds of things, especially over the letter.

The letter. His first thought had been to tear it up, burn it. It was creased and crumpled because he'd screwed it into a ball and thrown it at the wall, only to smooth it out and read it, again and again. Sometimes he felt sick when he read through it, then at other times he wanted to bang his head on the wall and scream in silence. It seemed wrong to have to suffer twice for the death of a mother.

So far, he hadn't acted on its brief instruction. There was a long, foreign-looking phone number he was supposed to call. He really wanted to erase the whole thing from his mind and not have to deal with it in any shape or form; physically, mentally, or emotionally. In some ways, it drew an uncomfortable parallel with his brother, but they'd been through exhausting weeks of remorse years ago, and although he wasn't keen to resurrect this aspect, he went to see George anyway.

Considering it was four weeks or so after the Boxing Day debacle, his brother remained mostly hostile and unreasonable. He was making himself a meal for one, something Chinese. Al wanted to tell him he should have cooked the rice first and he was chopping the peppers too small, but the knife looked sharp.

'Kate's been round,' George said, triumphantly.

'What did you tell her?'

'Nothing! But she's not stupid, she can join the dots. What the fuck did you tell Helen for? She's got a mouth as big as the bloody Channel Tunnel!'

'I was desperate, and we had a cash-flow problem.'

'Snap!'

'Listen, this situation with the farm. It's killing Fran. I *know* you. You'll be just as gutted to lose Chathill, all that work Mum and Dad put into it. Someone offered thirty per cent below the asking price this morning, it's just crazy.'

'Not my fault, I'm afraid. I've been the only one earning for, let's see, forty years?' He paused to scoop bean sprouts into a bowl. 'If it doesn't sell we can auction it, get rid. You see, if you love something the idea is to nurture it, feed it, and keep it safe. Blind, selfish love is a very dangerous place to be.'

'Stop patronising me. I know what love is.'

'No, you don't. If you knew what it was you'd never have taken something that belonged to me.'

'I didn't. They're both at home, waiting for you. The rest of it's in your head.'

'Now who's a patronising little git?'

'Just come back and let's talk it through. I think Fran needs to see a doctor, that's the main issue here, not your misplaced pride.'

George hit him, a backhander with a wok. He'd hit him before, of course, but never with a hot pan. Searing heat and sharp pain shot across the left side of his face. Most of the damage was concentrated on his left eye and brow bone as the impact came just as he moved his head, purely a reflex action. As the metallic taste of blood seeped into his mouth, the realisation that George was close to crying fully compounded the shock. It was like going back fifteen years when it had all still been raw.

He went from the flat, his head reeling and his shaking hand covering his split lip. In his car, he angled the rear view mirror so that he could see his smashed face, and rooted about for a tissue. Bloody hell, the situation was becoming intolerable. After a short while, he started the engine and drove the short distance home. Once parked, he switched the engine off and leant his forehead on the steering wheel, feeling sick and dizzy.

Home. The prospective purchasers who'd turned up earlier that day had consisted of two men in sharp suits with a builder in tow. They'd viewed everything with indifference; taking photographs, measuring, knocking on walls, and tutting. He'd felt violated by them; thank Christ Becca had been at school. She'd been on such a high after Boxing Day, and it had fallen to Al to talk her through what was going on without alarming her.

This was no mean feat, since her mother's detached behaviour had only added to the worry of it all. On top of this she was overtired from the exertion of riding fences all day and was up and down all night claiming she felt unwell.

Outside, the buyers had baulked at the mud underfoot and turned up expensive coat collars against the high wind, giving the paddocks nothing more than a sweeping glance.

Looking at it through their eyes, he couldn't blame them. His rusting camper van, home to twenty-two half-dead battery hens and three ducks, and the brown, one hundred per cent dead Christmas tree rolling around the paddock didn't exactly help to sell the place.

He had mixed feelings about selling Chathill. It was difficult to get past the emotional ties, and he'd had the best idyllic childhood here. The long summer days, when wild honeysuckle thickened the hedges and dusk infused with the liquorice perfume of sweet meadow hay, was like drinking the elixir of summer itself. Good times, although they hadn't realised it then, and now it was all about looking back.

They'd lived more life than what could possibly lie ahead.

He may have been born on the other side of the world, but there was something magical buried in the hills. Even subdued by bleak January and obscured more often than not by shifting mist, the distant mountains were startling. It was astonishing how many different shades of greys, greens, and browns there actually were, how many variations of sepia and granite. A hesitant flicker of pale sunlight would sometimes break through and highlight the stone wall roaming across Tal y Fan. Al saw it through an artist's eye and as a teenager he'd spent hours daydreaming and trying to paint it all. Eventually, he gave that up and turned to writing. George had framed his abstract daubs and sold them at the local show, maintaining it was all for charity.

They'd spent the substantial profits on local ale and cider.

In the end, it was all about money.

The ensuing low offer for Chathill had been predictable and the agent had treated it with disdain. Al could simply dig his heels in and refuse to co-operate with anyone, even deny them access to the property, but then what? The future was grim, with virtually no money coming in and everything in a steady decline. There was a possible trump card, of course, one which only *he* could bring into play.

Sole beneficiary.

His first thought was that it would be some kind of cruel trick, and *why?* Why had she done this, after a lifetime of no contact? Half of that lifetime had been spent searching for her, another massive drain on the finances *and* his emotions. It was the first nail in the coffin of his marriage, and subsequently due to his deplorable behaviour, the final nail in the coffin of his relationship with George.

After the visit to his brother's flat, he tried to soothe his battered face with ice cubes packed into a plastic freezer bag. There was nothing in the bathroom cupboard to put on the cuts and burns, nothing of any use. No doubt in the morning he would be multicoloured with a closed eye. He told Fran and Becca he'd been mugged.

'But where, Al?'

'Just outside here, soon as it got dark.'

'You're a lousy liar. You've been out somewhere. Have you been fighting?'

'Don't be silly.'

Becca was more concerned that the hay had run out.

'What am I supposed to feed Stilton?'

Al put an arm across her shoulders. 'Let's have a talk.'

Becca caved in, in the end. The following morning, he drove slowly behind her as she rode Stilton to the livery yard, his car full of rugs and buckets and his eye throbbing painfully. The yard was a swish place, full of teenage girls and a full set of show jumps in the indoor school. There was a loose box already prepared for Stilton, everything paid for. Even on that first day, she was soon lost in a crowd of new friends, billing and cooing over the new arrival and comparing tack.

A couple of days after the horse was settled in, Becca

tentatively suggested to her mother that she might *try* living at the flat. After all, Stilton was within walking distance, her father had promised to drive her to school instead of having to catch the bus, and there was a brand new computer in her room. Fran seemed curiously unaffected.

'Are you sure it's going to be OK?' Becca whispered to Al.

'I think you'll be doing your dad a massive favour.'

'Seriously?'

'Yeah, and I think we have to face some truths about the farm.'

She nodded sagely at this. 'Mum's going to be all right though, isn't she?'

He scrunched her shoulders and kissed the top of her head. 'Yeah, don't worry, I'll talk to her.'

Actually, he had no idea what to do about Fran and the farm, or indeed about any of his relationships or his finances, let alone *the letter*. The only adults he had access to talk to about all of this were his grown children, although he couldn't bring himself to tell them about the wicked witch they'd had for a real grandmother, now deceased.

Following Boxing Day, Tom had been his usual aloof self, not wanting to get involved in the crossfire, clearly ashamed of Helen's drunken visit and pissed off with Al for being so childish. Maisie was rather more astute and kept to problem solving, which was her forte. She listened patiently to the recent developments.

'Look, the veterinary practice has just won a huge contract with an animal rescue centre. If you're desperate, I can get some of the animals collected and re-homed there.'

'Desperate all right, yeah! I'll have to talk to Fran first, that's the tricky part.'

In truth, all the parts were tricky. He took Becca to her

198

father's flat, and she traipsed up the stairs with her stuff. She was quiet and pale throughout the whole ordeal. Al remained on the pavement and leant against his car with his arms folded. On sight of his closed-up eye, George had the decency to look sheepish.

'Well ... thanks for bringing her.'

'At the moment, it's better for her to be here.'

'We agree on something, then.'

Al nodded. They always used to agree, deep down they probably still saw much of life from the same perspective. After all, they'd been brought up with much the same values and viewpoints. Al always felt it only accounted for half of who he was though, the other fifty per cent was still out there somewhere, rootless and drifting.

The following morning, he told Fran he was going to the doctor's about his eye and he'd make her an appointment for a check-up. This was met with the usual indifference. She peered at his face.

'Did George do that? Tell me the truth.'

'He's angry, that's all. I just didn't want to say in front of Becca.'

'He's a *pig!* Why can't he leave the past behind?'

'Fran, it's not just about that,' he said gently. 'He can't cope with me being here all the time, but it's about other stuff as well. We need to have a serious talk.'

'You're never serious, Al.'

'I am today.'

He told her about Maisie's offer of finding new homes for the ponies, the pigs, and the ducks, and maybe some of the dogs. To his utmost relief, she nodded ever so slightly, in the affirmative. 'But what about us? Where will we go? Stay together, that's the main thing.'

'Let's just take one step at a time,' he said carefully.

But even one step needed an effort of some sort. It was disconcerting to feel so totally worn out and his eye was streaming and painful. The doctor asked him to look up at the ceiling and manipulated his lower lid, squinting at his left eye with a tiny torch. 'How did this happen?'

'My brother hit me with a wok.'

'Have you reported him for assault?'

'He didn't mean it.'

'Bit old to be fighting with pans, aren't you?' He began scribbling on a prescription pad. 'Flucloxacillin ... and then something for the burns. Could have been much worse. Come and see me again if the eye doesn't improve. Do you need any painkillers?'

'No, no thanks.'

'Is that all?' he said, tapping away at his keyboard.

'Not quite. Can you come round and see my sister-in-law? I think she might be having a breakdown.'

'What makes you think that?'

The answer to this was complex and, of course, hopelessly lost in the red tape of the health service the second he opened his mouth. Apparently, Fran had to make the first move. How stupid was that? He drove to the chemist to collect his prescription in a black shroud of despair, then on impulse walked into the grotty pub on Mostyn Street. He'd never been one to drink by himself, but the circumstances were extenuating. Sometimes, staring into a crystal ball of beer could produce the most amazing obvious solution.

When his mobile trilled in his pocket, several other solitary drinkers looked up as if it was the call they'd all been waiting for. It was Kate. Al stood up and knocked the table, spilling beer from his untouched pint.

'Kate, hi.'

'Where are you?' she said sharply, no hello or preamble.

'In the pub.'

'There's been an accident. Fran –'

'What accident?' he said, grabbing his jacket off the

back of the chair.

'Just come back, all right?'

It wasn't the kind of sign he'd wanted. When he arrived back at Chathill, the sight of Kate's car gave him a warm buzz that soon vanished when he saw the scene around the ambulance. Fran was strapped onto a stretcher, out cold from the looks of it. Kate, white and shaken, had a blanket across her shoulders. She did a double-take at the sight of his face, but he ignored this.

'What the hell happened?'

'I found her on the floor.'

'Where?'

'Outside. It's OK, she was coming round, talking.'

George arrived, skidding dramatically to a halt, and began barking questions at everyone but only Kate knew the answers. Well, some of them. It seemed she'd turned up at the farm and discovered Fran's dog pacing and whining in the hall. She'd followed the collie to the old feed store where she discovered Fran spreadeagled on the ground, surrounded by a jumble of floorboards and straw.

'I told her not to go up there!' George yelled.

'What are you shouting at Kate for?' Al said, 'Fran's been telling you for weeks about the state of that shed!'

'And what have *you* done about it? It's you who bloody lives here!'

'I wedged it shut, closed it off!'

'Oh, shut up the both of you,' Kate said.

One of the paramedics closed the back doors of the ambulance and informed George that their destination was Bangor Hospital, A&E. There was a slow, awkward departure as the vehicle bounced its way down the drive, and George climbed back into his car. He immediately slid the window down and said something about collecting Becca from school. Kate said she'd go for her, and he nodded a curt thanks, then they stood in the rain until the ambulance reached the main road, poised for the wail of a siren. To his relief, there was none forthcoming, which had to be a good sign.

'We should go up there too,' Kate said.

'In a while, let's give George some space.'

She agreed and followed him inside. He made for the leftover Christmas brandy, grabbing two glasses and waving them. 'I need a drink. I don't know what other disasters are waiting to happen, but I've had enough of this year already and we're only just out of January.'

To his astonishment, she came and put her arms around him. It felt so amazingly good that he planted the bottle and glasses elsewhere, hugged her back, and inhaled the scent of her. 'Scrap what I've just said. I don't know what I'm saying.'

'I'm sorry I ignored you.'

'I don't blame you.'

She pulled back from him slightly. 'What the hell happened to your face?'

'My brother.'

They sat at opposite sides of the kitchen table with the brandy, and face to face, it felt awkward. 'Right,' she said, scrutinising his wounds. 'Tell me what's going on here, I need to know.'

The silence was almost too acute, loudly punctuated by rain water dripping into a bucket somewhere. It was the sort of loaded silence that made his flesh crawl for no good reason. 'Fran and I ... we shared a kiss once, and she's always had a bit of a thing for me. I think she still does.'

Kate took a deep breath and pursed her lips slightly. For a moment he just stared at her beautiful, disappointed face as the cogs worked away in her mind, trying to slot it all together and no doubt finding a big hole in the middle.

'Well, thank you, for being honest,' she said, 'Is that all?'

'There's backstory.'

'I'm sure there is.'

Since she didn't object, he began to tell her about the dark time he'd lost his adoptive mother to a heart attack, just six weeks after the death of his father. The double bereavement materialised as an obsession to find Ruby. 'When I eventually disappeared to go and meet this woman, Helen was furious with me for squandering all the family resources, mostly down to hiring private detectives. She kicked me out for a while and at the time I thought we were finished. And then when I finally faced Ruby she told me to clear off, that she wasn't interested in me or my family and how dare I track her down. George and Fran came to my rescue. Well, mostly Fran.'

'I think I can fill in the rest.'

'I got drunk a lot – *we* got drunk a lot, on homemade elder wine. Not very original, or clever.'

She dropped her eyes from his and studied her nails and he reached across and touched the tips of his fingers to hers. 'There's nothing going on with us, there never was.'

She leant back in her chair and folded her arms. 'She told me she married the wrong brother. That intimates rather more than a stolen kiss.'

'That's a load of bullshit. I've never had those kind of feelings for her.'

'In a way that makes it worse! And I don't know, for sure but I suspect she may still have feelings for you.'

'I don't *know* what's going on in Fran's head. I'm not sure I want to know. I think I need to get away, wrap up this sale, and *get out*.'

He suddenly scraped his chair back and set about making coffee. There was just enough of the ground variety to make a cafetière for two. By the time he'd gone through the motions of boiling water and measuring the Columbian dark roast, his angry anxiety had tempered.

Kate said, 'Once, my mother ordered a catheter in a posh hotel.'

He flashed her a quick smile but she didn't smile back,

just watched him with enigmatic eyes, no doubt still digesting everything he'd said. He hoped that telling her the truth – at least a small part of it – would be the wild card in his favour.

'Is it the *only* way?' she said. 'I'm talking about selling Chathill. It seems such a waste, for all of you. I'm not convinced George is as blasé as he makes out about the farm. Or Fran, come to that. It all seems blown out of proportion to me.'

The letter, secreted in his inside pocket, began to burn against his chest. He pulled it out and threw it across the table to her and she scanned the few sentences with a deepening frown. 'Oh, I'm *so* sorry Al. I saw a news clip about her death, it was one of the reasons I came over to see you. I wasn't sure if you even knew.'

'Why are you sorry?' he said, then raised a hand in apology. He still didn't know how he felt; angry, sad, full of regret? Mostly he just wanted to kill something.

'So, have you called the number?' She handed the letter back.

'No. I'm not sure I want to.'

'Why on earth not? It could be the answer to all your problems!'

'I know, it's just –'

'What? *Pride?*'

Was it? He couldn't accuse his brother of misplaced pride and then succumb to the luxury of it himself. 'Maybe …'

'For what it's worth, I think you need to do it anyway, then you can draw a line under it.'

'Closure, is that what they call it?'

She half smiled and nodded and he knew then, he knew that he *had* to call the number and make the trip, and steel himself to whatever he discovered; maybe even banish some of the demons from the last trip. 'Do you fancy an adventure? I still owe you something special.'

'Does the reading of your mother's will cover all that?'

'I've no idea. It wouldn't be *just* about the will. It could be about us, spending some time together, somewhere it doesn't rain so much. You know how you said it was only one of the reasons you came over?'

'Uh-huh.'

'Then why not come with me?'

She pushed the plunger down slowly through the coffee and it seemed like there was a long suspension of time and a deep intake of breath before she actually spoke.

'I don't think so.'

'Think about it, please?'

Shortly after the coffee, she went to collect Becca from school, with a view to continuing on to the hospital, and he felt surprisingly positive to the point where he braced himself to shave the burnt part of his face.

Of course he had to wait till the evening to call Ruby's lawyer because of the time difference, but he asked Maisie to send someone to collect whatever animals they could take. It was a horrible decision carrying out this act behind Fran's back but now that he had decided to make the overseas trip, with or without Kate, it was more a question of practicalities. The place was done for anyway. Even if by some miracle he managed to acquire enough money to put it all right, it wouldn't fix his brother's marriage, would it?

Telling Kate about the biggest mistake of his life had been a snap second decision, a little like the time he'd blurted it out to Helen, as a last resort. The fact that he'd told Kate the truth but not the whole truth, was a risk he was prepared to take. At least she hadn't screamed and run away. In fact, she'd carefully applied the eye cream for him, and he could still feel her hands on his jaw, angling his face to the light.

It was dark outside, cold and wet, but he managed to beg some hay from next door in exchange for gifting the ex-battery hens. He went to take a look at the shed where Fran had fallen through the first floor, presumably trying to get to the remaining couple of bales up there. A call from Kate revealed that Fran had a broken arm and a sprained ankle, mild concussion, and dehydration. It was lucky Kate had turned up when she did, otherwise they may have been adding hypothermia to the list.

He shivered and kicked at the pile of wood and the rotten ladder, then fondled the warm ears of Fran's Border Collie, Fig. The dog followed him like a shadow, catching his eye whenever he glanced in its direction, as if fearful for the future. The sheepdogs had followed him and George everywhere when they were children, like surrogate parents, barking and whining if they went near deep water or climbed the forbidden crumbling ruins of farmhouses.

'Don't worry, your time's not quite up,' he said to the dog. 'Unlike mine.'

Maisie had agreed to temporarily home the three dogs, until matters were sorted out, whatever that meant. At least miserable Marge would be in good hands. She must be due to give birth any day if the amount of dirty looks and snarling was anything to go by.

When he couldn't put it off any longer, when he couldn't think of any more excuses, he picked up the letter, and dialled the number.

Chapter Sixteen

Kate

Tia seemed fascinated by it all.

'OK, so … now he wants to take you away, somewhere hot? And you're running this by *me?*'

Kate stood looking out at her dismal garden, sodden with February rain, cupping the phone under her chin as she stacked pots in the sink. It seemed such a long time since the sun had shone.

'Actually, it's more to do with the reading of his mother's will.'

'Yeah, well that part *is* a bit weird, but then so is dressing up as a clown. Where is it, anyway?'

'New Zealand.'

'But you hate flying!'

'Who said I was going to go? Who said I was going to get *involved?*'

'Why does agreeing to go away with him mean you're *involved?* Can't you just look at it as a holiday? You know that simple concept? Get drunk, have sex on the beach, and get a nice tan?'

'You do that with *all* your male friends? Anyway, I don't tan.'

Tia just laughed. Kate tried not to be too starchy about it, since the lines of communication were thrumming very well between them. It helped that Tia seemed to have found herself a reasonable job, a sort of Girl Friday with childcare.

Whenever she allowed herself head space, to try and make a rational decision about going with Al to New

Zealand, all she could think about was them both rolling about on a beach, waves crashing on the shore. Utterly ridiculous. She blamed Tia for this image but maybe that was unfair, because when she'd been standing in the kitchen at Chathill, trying to drop eye cream in the right place without blinding him, she was filled with the same intense feelings, with no help from the idyll of sea and sand. Oh yes, the sexual attraction was there, tied up with the dangerous quantity that was Alastair Black but so often, one went hand in hand with the other.

She thought about this aspect quite a lot. He was steady in some respects; funny, caring ... OK, *occasionally* unreliable. But look how good a father he'd been, and his marriage had lasted some thirty years, hadn't it? So now he was divorced, useless with money, and likely had unresolved issues with his blood mother. Then there was the pregnant ex-girlfriend who'd had an abortion, leaving goodness know what scars. Frequently beaten up by his brother, both physically and emotionally, because he'd kissed his sister-in-law and her feelings for him had been resurrected on his return to the family fold.

Stop.

Did a marriage break up and a brother's love turn to hate over one forbidden kiss? Deep down, she doubted it. So he was possibly a liar too, by way of omission. She sometimes wondered if she was too old and sensible to have a bad boy love interest, but then Tia's face would appear like an apparition on her shoulder with that lip curl. And he wasn't really bad, just misunderstood. Good grief, had she really thought that? The soul-searching went on, but she kept coming back to the bottom line; he was Jim Silver and she fancied him to the point of combustion.

They were talking again, mostly over the phone and Internet. When she saw his name flash on her phone screen, there was a delicious moment of anticipation before she accepted the call and heard his voice. She tried to remember if she'd felt like this with Greg, but nothing came to mind. He always had specific times when he'd phone. Al had no such order in his life and would call her randomly, whenever something popped into his head. Marge had given birth to one huge puppy. He called to discuss this when she was shopping, suggesting she went to the butter counter to find a good name. To be caught out in the supermarket, feeling like a giddy teenager at the age of fifty was deliciously disconcerting, but it felt OK. It felt very good indeed.

The trip was planned for the beginning of March and apparently, the money for two return tickets had automatically been forwarded to him via the solicitor in Auckland. This information had put Kate in a lather of uncertainty but Al told her it had been part of the will.

'It was one of her last wishes,' he said. 'For the funds to be made available to me and "one other" to get over there.'

'That was thoughtful.'

'Or just weird.'

'Stop being so suspicious! You need to have an open mind and be prepared to forgive. It's over now, whatever legacy she's left.'

A long sigh. 'This is why I need you to come with me.'

'To be the voice of reason?'

'And many, many other reasons. I need you to control the eye cream.'

She laughed silently. 'I'll think about it.'

A week later and she still hadn't decided for definite, although she had borrowed a home waxing kit from her sister.

'Are you seeing someone?' Annemarie said.

'What makes you think that?'

'I can't remember the last time you waxed your legs in *February*.'

'Yes, well.'

'I'm off men. Bastards, all of them.'

'What's happened to the bank manager?'

'He gave me something special for Christmas. It's itchy and very unpleasant.'

'Oh dear.'

She bought a new suitcase, went shopping for clothes, had her hair cut and re-coloured again, and made an appointment for a manicure. At home, in the privacy of her bedroom, she went through her new outfits, and that was where her initial enthusiasm rapidly began to diminish.

'Am I too old to wear this wraparound sarong thing?' she said to Tia via Skype. 'Be honest.'

'Ugh. My God, Mother that's *horrific*.'

'Too honest.'

'And you really need to wax your top lip.'

'How's the job?'

'Great; and I actually really like her as a boss.'

The job was the best thing since sliced bread.

Working for a singleton with a high-flying job was right up her daughter's street. The female in question was working from home because of health complications with her pregnancy, but Tia seemed to enjoy running all over London, popping into smart offices and driving her employer's swanky car to the deli. If they continued to get along well, there was an option for Tia to move into the company apartment with her – a posh address popped into her mail inbox – and later in the year, to travel to New York, which was of course, the icing on the cake. Kate was pleased for her, it was the first time she'd ever heard such enthusiasm for paid work. She listened to Tia chatter on as she discarded the sarong and added it to the returns pile, then finally sat on the bed and looked at the screen positioned on the dressing table.

'Well, I'm really pleased for you.'

'I'm not allowed to blab about her too much, because of the baby,' she went on. 'She already knows she's having a girl, how cool is that? Anyway she doesn't want the father to know about it. Maybe he's violent or something?'

'Oh dear. What's her name anyway?'

'Jo.'

Kate felt all the air being sucked from her lungs. 'Does she work for a charity fundraising company?' she said, her voice an octave too high.

'Yes, why? What is it? *What?*'

When she'd double checked the facts and Tia had stopped screeching at her they had a protracted conversation about Jo and Al. At mention of the supposed abortion, Tia became increasingly open-mouthed and kept interrupting. 'But you *cannot* say anything! I'll lose the best job I've ever had!'

'All right, calm down.'

'I can't believe this, I just *can't.* And if he's been with *her,* how come he fancies you? She's incredibly pretty and way younger.'

'I just want to forget we had this conversation.'

'Suits me!'

Tia disconnected from Skype and Kate switched off the laptop. She could scream with frustration; or maybe it would be more sensible to open a bottle of wine and just forget all about Mr Black and his increasingly complicated love life. It was true, she was a million times older than his previous partner and looked ridiculous in beachwear. She'd been hovering on the point of telling Al she'd be glad to accompany him to the other side of the world, but seriously, could she hold on to her daughter's whopping great secret?

Oh, and she had an old lady moustache too.

She opened a bottle of wine.

Fran remained in hospital, presumably due to the concussion and her general lack of eating and drinking. Although Al had mentioned that he'd talked to someone about her general state of mind *before* the accident, he didn't really hold out much hope of anyone acting on the information.

Kate took some magazines and chocolates, relieved to see Fran sitting up with a tiny blush of colour on her face. Her initial visit with Becca had not gone well. There was nothing especially gruesome to see other than a plastered-up arm and a strapped-up ankle, but Fran had been weepy and frail. She claimed she couldn't recall anything about the accident or whatever else had occurred on that day.

George had been brusque, laying the full blame on Fran for not eating, until Kate said his overbearing attitude wasn't helping. The bluster was all a front, of course. She suspected it was the mental health issue, and despite its mostly innocuous presence, he was somehow desperate to place the onus on something physical and easily fixed.

She wondered about making an offer for Fran to stay with her for a while. It would be a neat way of opting out of the trip with Al, it would solve everyone's problems and considerably ease Tia's anxiety. But then she thought about the steep, narrow staircase to her bedrooms and bathroom, whereas the flat was perfect in that respect, and if she was serious did she really, honestly want to play the martyr? *Again?*

'I've got to have counselling, and I'm on antidepressants,' Fran said, as Kate placed the reading matter on the bedside cabinet. There was a card from George and Becca, and a small framed photograph of Fig, from Al. He'd drawn a thought bubble on top of the dog's head.

Woof! I'm on holiday with Auntie Maisie. Missing You.

'Oh, well, if they help, that's the main thing,' Kate said, unable to draw her eyes from the picture. His handwriting seemed curiously intimate. Maybe because it reminded her of the Christmas note. Upright, bold letters with elaborate scrolls on the tails, almost like an autograph.

I owe you something special.

'I had a talk to one of the doctors,' Fran said, biting into a truffle. 'His wife breeds alpacas, so I said I'd love to have some and then I remembered Al told me all the animals have gone to a rescue centre and the farm was up for sale! I'm so cross with him.'

'He's only got your best interests at heart.'

'Everyone keeps saying that, but I don't understand how.'

'What else did the doctor say?'

'That I could probably go home at the end of the week.'

'That's great. Will you go to the flat ... with George and Becca?'

'What flat?'

Fran remembered, eventually, but it took a lot of patient prompting and then she suddenly burst into tears and said she missed Becca so much but George didn't want her, not really. And what would happen to her without Chathill? Kate felt her own chest heave with the sad futility of it, and decided she'd collect Fran herself at the end of the week and nurse her better. Al would just have to deal with his own business. Fran's need was greater.

She found her way back to the car park with a renewed sense of commitment, planning a detour across country to Chathill, feeling it only fair to tell Al about this decision face to face, and while the carefully worded conversation was fresh in her mind.

Late February, and it was a sparkling day. Flashes of brief sunlight lit up the wet roads and pools of water in the fields. There could, of course, still be snow to come, but not this day, this glimpse into spring, when the air was softer somehow, intoxicating. Subtle changes in the colours of the countryside underpinned this feeling of vibrancy. Horses and cattle moved with a different gait, birdsong was commented on again, and the low pastures were flooded with bleating lambs calling to the ewes.

This part reminded her of Fran, those desperate maternal longings, buried for years but still capable of eating away at sense and sensibility. This was likely the part George couldn't cope with.

The hedges bordering the drive to Chathill were straggly with long brambles and the pot holes worse than ever, but she was surprised by the rest of it. Walking around the back, the lack of animals was the first overwhelming difference, and then Al had clearly been on a mission to clear up on a major scale. She spotted him, cigarette between his lips, shovelling something off the ground and into a skip. He looked out of place concerned with manual labour, too aristocratic by far.

When he saw her, he speared the garden fork into the manure heap and ambled over. He grinned, and her initial plan, which had seemed so secure in her mind less than an hour ago, already began to crumble at the edges.

'Don't come too close, I stink,' he said, wiping his hands on a rag.

'Thanks for the warning. Wow, you've been busy. The eye looks better.'

'Yeah.'

'I've been to see Fran.'

'Right.'

They walked across the paddock, and already it was looking refreshed with the bright shoots of new grass. She told him about Fran's condition and her thoughts about George. He agreed with everything she said. They stopped walking when they came to the fence and she dropped her bombshell about collecting Fran and looking after her.

'*What?*'

'We can't just leave her. Where will she go?'

'How about back to her husband?'

'How's that going to work?'

His answer was to grab hold of her hand and march with her back towards the house. 'I'm tired of this, this constant side-stepping. We're going to sort this, once and for all.'

'How do you mean?'

'We're going over to the flat, sort it out. You're coming with me so we can't start a fight. Then you're going to pack a suitcase.'

'Am I?'

She looked up at the mercurial blue of the sky and hoped the clarity of it was a positive sign. Al went to have a shower and get changed while Kate paced slowly up and down the hall, chewing her thumbnail. There were boxes stacked up and off-white spaces on the walls where pictures used to be. Presently, he reappeared in clean denims, a slight waft of musky aftershave in his wake as he looked for shoes, then searched her face, caught hold of her hand again, and pulled her gently through the front porch and back outside.

'I'll drive,' he said, and wrenched open the car door for her. They set off and the engine noise put paid to any conversation.

'This is a horrible car,' she said, trying to yank the seatbelt across, and he agreed. When they arrived, she climbed out and had the same mechanical problems trying to close the car door but he told her to leave it open.

'Who's going to pinch it? It's one of the perks of having an old banger.'

Al leaned on the doorbell for the flat and George answered quickly, looking at their faces with deep concern furrowing his brow.

'What's happened? Is it Fran?'

'No, she's fine, getting discharged very soon,' Kate said.

Al butted in, 'We've come to talk to you. Did you know she was coming out?'

'Yes! I do make calls and visits, you know,' George said, looking from one to the other. 'Does this take two of you?'

'Kate's here as referee, and to help knock some sense into you,' Al said.

They trooped up the stairs in single file. In the lounge, they stood in an awkward triangle, George fidgeting with the coins in his pocket and Al with his arms crossed.

'Kate and I are going on a trip,' he said. 'So you're going to have to get yourself together and bring Fran back here and look after her.'

'Don't tell me what to do!'

'He doesn't mean it like that,' Kate said. 'Look, I had a talk to Fran this morning. She misses you dreadfully.'

'Oh?'

'In her mind, you've taken Becca and the farm away. She feels utterly alone and abandoned.'

'Ditto,' he said, flashing a glance at Al.

'Oh, stop scoring points off each other,' she said, and shot a warning glance at Al. George turned his back and went to stare though the window. There was a long sigh, but when he turned around his expression was softer, as if he'd seen a different light rising from the river. 'You're right, of course. All of this ... this animosity has to stop. It's not helping anyone.'

'So, you'll collect her and look after her?' Al said.

'Of course I'll look after her!'

Kate pushed a placatory hand at Al's chest. 'George, all she really needs is to be with you and Becca.'

'Are you sure she'll want to come here?'

'I think she will. Just talk things through.'

'Talk to her, yes,' he said, as if it were an alien concept. Kate remembered her father being of the same persuasion when it came to feelings. George had plenty of emotion on his face though, as if he was struggling to keep it all contained. And then exactly as her father used to do, he changed the subject.

'I should tell you, we've had a massively upped offer

on Chathill this morning. Agent says we should consider.'

Al nodded. 'Oh, right.'

'Al's done an amazing job, clearing everything and packing up,' Kate added.

At this, George looked at the floor as if considering his words before lifting his eyes to carefully study his brother's expectant face. 'I should come and help; there's all Fran's things to pack and there are things I'd like, those pictures of Granddad's, and Mum's rings.'

Al shrugged. 'Fine, come and get what you want. It's all yours.'

Kate thought Al was heroically compliant over this, as if George had more right to them than he did. After all, it was his family too.

'Well, I think we should accept this offer,' George went on. 'And then can we put *all* of this mess behind us? Can we do that, finally?'

'Yeah,' Al said, nodding with equal conviction.

'And I'm sorry about your eye. I shouldn't have hit you, it solves nothing.'

'Forget it, I probably deserved it,' Al said, and offered his hand. After a few seconds' hesitation, George was about to reciprocate but then Al moved to clasp him in a hug, patting him fiercely on the back.

It was a good moment, emotionally tense but perfectly timed. They left the flat in comfortable silence, satisfied that a void had somehow being crossed which had wiped out weeks of tension. She looked at Al in a new light. He could be decisive when he needed to be, and the idea that wanting to be with her had triggered this motivation was something to savour.

They'd travelled a couple of miles and reached the bridge before he spoke, ramming the car into a lower gear. 'Well, that went better than I thought. It was because you were there. George thought he had us all backed into a corner but Fran's accident had it backfire on him in a way.'

'I'd like to think it was because both of you were ready to see sense. Let's just think about future plans, no point in constantly looking back.'

'I'll drink to that,' he said, and swung into the pub car park. He killed the engine and it coughed to a stop.

'What will you do after the sale of the farm?'

'Buy something else I guess, but don't ask me what or where. First things first, can I confirm these flights?'

'I want the window seat. I'm not very good on planes,' she confessed, then turned her head to look at him. 'Oh ... *passport.*'

'Don't tell me ...'

'I can go to the offices in Liverpool today and get it renewed.'

'I'm driving you there, right now.'

She laughed, 'No chance, I'm not going all that way in this car. I can drive myself, thank you.'

'So you're coming with me? We're going to get this will business out of the way first, and then share some down time, erase some bad memories, make some new ones. I'd like you to be part of that, if you want to?'

'Yes, I'd like to, very much.'

Now that she'd actually said it, she realised how true the words were. Her fears about his integrity and honesty were completely overshadowed, simply by his close proximity. He picked up her cold hands, rubbed them, and kissed them, and she loved the way he did this. Then he leaned across to kiss her cheek but she turned her face and met his lips instead.

The connection was startling.

It blew everything else out of her mind. She knew then, knew she was going to sleep with Alastair Black, whatever the consequences, to hell with all of them. It was just a holiday, with sex. If Tia could do it, so could she.

Chapter Seventeen

Al

'I mean, if you had a kid somewhere in the world wouldn't you want to know about it, how it was doing? It would kill me to think I was estranged from any of mine,' he said to Kate, but she made no immediate reply.

They were hanging about in Singapore airport, waiting for another long haul, their overnight connection to Auckland. Kate looked tired. She clearly wasn't a great traveller, suffering from lack of sleep after a twelve-hour flight from London Heathrow, followed by eight hours in a noisy transit hotel. After a two hour wait back at the airport, they were finally inching along in another queue.

'I think you're working yourself up too much along this theme,' she said, hitching her handbag over her shoulder.

'Sorry, I promise not to bang on about it. I'm feeling a bit spooked. Not knowing what's in the will, that sort of thing.'

'You mean it might be something *awful*, like money?'

'Very funny. I hope so, actually. I've booked us in to a five-star hotel in Auckland, I think we'll deserve it by the time we get there. *If* we ever there. I'd forgotten how punishing this trip is.'

'Have you booked *two* rooms at this swanky hotel?'

'Yeah.'

'That's a waste of money,' she said, and calmly proffered her passport to the smiley Malaysian guy at the security desk. For a moment, he was thrown by her words, by the casual way she'd dropped them into the conversation and how much they shifted the axis of his

219

feelings. They sky-rocketed into a place he'd imagined would be off-limits. In the transit hotel, she'd given no indication that the two-room arrangement was unnecessary. In fact, she'd apologised for not taking up the suggested whistle-stop tour of Singapore, preferring instead to grab a shower and get some rest. As it turned out, this was pretty sensible – but then that was Kate all over, which only went to accentuate her out-of-character remark. He had to remember though, that since he'd booked the accommodation, they'd shared that high-voltage kiss in the pub car park, not that he could forget it, ever.

Once on the aircraft, he removed the deluxe head support from its extensive Chinese packaging and recoiled slightly at the bright pink colour, which was not indicated on the box. Even before it was fully inflated it seemed to take up a lot of room. Kate shot him a mischievous look when he began to blow into it.

'You could have just bought me an eye mask.'

'This will be much better for you,' he said, feeling positively heroic. He inhaled deeply, as if he were about to dive into deep water, and blew into the tiny valve. After a good five minutes he began to feel dizzy, and it had ballooned into something which was clearly not a neck support.

'*Shit,* what is it?' he said, trying to open it out in the small space provided between his lap and the row of seats in front. One of the cabin-crew gave him the evil eye as she sailed up and down the aisle, checking for loose bags and the like.

'Kiddies' paddling pool?' Kate said, pointing to the decorative line of fish.

The hostess homed in on him as he was trying to deflate it but the valve must have been faulty and it remained billowing and semi-inflated, like a giant amoeba.

'Have you got anything sharp?' he whispered to Kate.

'I'll have to pop it.'

'Nope, security even removed my tiny tweezers.'

Apologising for the second time to the passenger seated on his right, he stuffed it in the overhead locker and avoided contact with some six hundred pairs of eyes.

'Made in China, huh?' Kate said, a big smile on her face.

They arrived to glorious full sun, slightly punch drunk and having no idea what day it was, let alone something as precise as the time, and made their way through the concourse of Auckland airport. It was considerably smaller and a hundred times more rustic than the oriental glamour of Singapore, but they didn't take much notice of their surroundings. Following the general crowd, they headed silently for bag reclaim, Al struggling with the semi-inflated paddling pool. He'd purposefully left it behind on the aircraft but some kind American tourist had caught up with him and he was re-united with it.

Kate still had the energy to find this funny.

It wasn't quite as amusing having to stand with it at the reception in the hotel but Kate took control at the desk, cancelling the two small doubles and booking instead one larger room with a king-sized bed. He followed her obediently to the lift with the bags and the paddling pool, while she organised the key cards and took them to the twenty-seventh floor, room eighteen.

Room eighteen had a view of the small, white city which comprised city centre Auckland, the harbour just discernible, glinting in the distance behind the tinted glass of the floor to ceiling window. It could be any city in the world so far as Al was concerned, it was a bland combination of columns and boxes. Traffic and pedestrians passed silently, many feet below.

'It's not called the SkyCity Hotel for nothing, is it?'

Kate was spreadeagled across the bed, luxuriating in its

horizontal space. When he slid alongside her she turned to nestle into him. 'Hey, don't go to sleep, it's fatal,' he said, smoothing hair off her face. 'We need to stay awake till we're in sync with the sun and the moon. It's only around midday.'

'What will we do to stay awake?'

He whispered close to her ear. 'Go find a chemist?'

'That's so romantic.'

'I could have got something at the airport but heaven knows what they might have turned out to be. Bloody Chinese firecrackers or something.'

'Al, unless you have some horrible disease, what on earth do we need contraception for?'

'Now who's being an old romantic?' he said, kicking off his shoes.

'I'm trying to see it as one of the advantages of getting older. And in case you haven't noticed, I'm post-menopausal so there's no way you can get me pregnant.'

A shadow must have crossed his face or his eyes may have betrayed him, because she caught hold of his hand and twisted her lip. 'Ugh, sorry, not very tactful.'

'Let's not go backwards, huh? I've got a trail of stupid mistakes with relationships I'd rather forget.'

'I know.'

'Here's something you don't know; how I feel about you.'

'Forwards then?' she said, and pressed her lips to his, silencing his declaration of love. In truth, he'd started to have serious feelings for her the day he'd watched her badly riding Becca's horse. Fire and ice, that's how he saw her. Such cool eyes and reasoning, but fire hot hair and sensuality. His own fire was already fully stoked and she said something about sex being easier for men and how nervous she was. 'Unlike you, I'm extremely out of practise. Can we pretend to be virgins?'

He couldn't help laughing. 'Virgins, at our age?'

She shot him a coy expression, but this admission coupled with her bold sensuality was sweet, and oddly arousing.

'Does sharing the shower come under general foreplay?' she said.

'Yeah, go and switch it on.'

He watched her shuffle off the bed and go into the wet room, a delicious sense of anticipation swirling new life into his body. There was a bottle of champagne in the mini-bar. He didn't look at the price and managed to swig a good third of it while she was running the water, then poured a large glass and tapped on the shower screen. She peered round the door and wiped her face, droplets of water still trickling from her hair.

'How gorgeous,' she said, and took the cold elixir from him, downing it in one. He reclaimed the glass, refilled it, and placed it on the vanity unit, then he stripped off his travel-worn clothes and stepped into the cubicle with her. The double shower was so powerful, for a moment all he could do was stand immobile and let it blast his body while he devoured her naked proximity. She was every bit as beautiful as he could have imagined, such delicate freckled skin.

'We met in a shower, do you remember?' she said.

How could he forget? He began to soap her body with the complimentary geothermal soap from Rotorua Spa. They laughed at the smell, but it was gloriously thick and creamy. She reciprocated, until his hands began to move over her breasts, and then with infinite delicacy, between her legs and over her buttocks. She closed her eyes and lolled her head back, exposing her throat.

'That feels … almost *too* good.'

He kissed her face and her throat, moving gradually to her lips and this time, she opened her mouth to his and her hands roamed his body, dispelling any idea that she was shy and retiring.

When she finally broke away from him, he just about had the foresight to turn off the water, then he enveloped her in a towel and carried her to the bed, where he began to dry her.

'No one's ever done this for me,' she said, searching his eyes.

'*Shush*. Lie down.'

The complimentary Manuka honey body butter and oil duo scored a lot more points perfume-wise than the weird soap. He oiled, rubbed, and stroked every inch of her, until she was glistening and the sweet honey stickiness was flowing in full. And when he finally moved into her, it was like finding the right slipstream after years of swimming against the tide. And it was all because of the essence of her, of *Kate*. When she climaxed, she took him with her, followed by a long moment of exquisite aftershock.

'Don't talk ... and don't move. I want to stay suspended in this moment,' she whispered, her eyes closed. 'Is that corny?'

'Yeah, but it's good corny.'

He hugged her to him, her leg slid across his, and they must have fallen into a fathomless sleep because when he opened his eyes it was dusk and his stomach was rumbling, but the thought of a big meal was nauseating because it somehow felt like breakfast time. Bloody jet lag on top of sex and champagne added its own, surreal spin.

Kate was making coffee. 'So it's not true,' she said, passing him a cup. 'That the water goes down the plug hole anti-clockwise.'

He struggled to sit upright. 'Maybe that's what wrong with me. Everything's upside down and back to front; including my guts.'

'Stop moaning. Can we go for a stroll on the waterfront?'

They went for a stroll on the waterfront, and he took her hand in his. When they passed the plate glass windows of the stores, he couldn't help noticing how much a couple they looked. They even stopped to look at the same things. That had never happened with Helen or Jo. When they found a bar on the harbour, instead of studying the menu, he stared stupidly at her as she glanced down the list of drinks, sunglasses on top of her head. She was wearing a blue linen dress with a chunky silver necklace and matching bangle, and the colour combination was perfect against her skin.

It fascinated him how grown-up she was and how incredibly vibrant she seemed to him, as if he'd looked for the wrong kind of woman all his life. He watched her talk to the waitress and order something, then they both stared at him expectantly. 'Uh ... the same,' he said, closing up the menu. When the waitress had gone, Kate unwrapped her cutlery.

'So, I ordered the sea food special with extra deep-fried whale belly.'

'Good,' he said, then caught the smirk. 'OK, very funny. I've a feeling I'm going to be lousy company till this will reading is out of the way.'

'I've no complaints about your company so far,' she said and touched her fingertips to his, then sighed. 'Tell me what's in your head?'

'Oh, you know, the usual stuff, chaos and mass destruction.'

Looking around, everything still seemed lost in the eighties. Jim Silver would have felt at home, which was a bittersweet irony. The local drawl sounded like an American Australian blend and he wondered if Ruby had spoken like that. More to the point, had any of these strangers known his mother?

Had she eaten here?

'Just seems an alien concept to think I was born here,' he said.

'Do you remember anything, as a boy?'

'No, nothing. I went through that scenario the last time I came here, but I still don't like the place, let alone feel any connection to it.'

She raised her brows at this, and in truth, he was slightly surprised at his own venomous admission. If he didn't keep his mouth shut, he had the feeling he was going to be forever apologising to Kate, so he drank the beer instead. Well, they called it beer but it was more like bottled lager.

'When's this appointment?'

'Can't remember, sometime tomorrow afternoon.'

She smiled and covered his hand with hers. 'Al, it'll be fine.'

The following day they did some tourist stuff and watched idiots jump off the Sky Tower, then unable to postpone the moment any longer, they walked the hot streets searching for B. Bennet & Sons. He couldn't wait to get Ruby's business all squared away and draw a line under it, then he could maybe look at the rest of the trip with a different agenda.

The office was located in an old, Colonial building and they were shown into a mercifully air-conditioned room, to wait. He'd got the day and the time wrong, of course, but no one seemed bothered. Brian Bennet pottered out of a secondary office to shake hands. He was easily into his seventies, skin like distressed leather and sporting a pair of bright shorts and a polo shirt.

'I'm very sorry for your loss, Mr Black.'

'Thanks. It's Al.'

'Brian,' he said, pumping his hand.

'And this is Kate.'

In another room, they pulled out chairs to sit at Brian's desk. They made small talk about the flight, the weather, the hotel, while Brian shuffled huge files of paper around. At his request, Al handed over his passports, bank details,

226

and birth certificate. *Father unknown.* Brian gave him a good look and scrutinised the documents. 'You're so like her, you know?'

'Look, I don't mean to be rude but can we just get on with this? I had no relationship with the woman. In fact, I don't even know what I'm doing here.'

He was aware of Kate staring at him, but then she took hold of his hand and nursed it in her lap. Brian passed his documents back across the desk, then looked over the top of his spectacles at him before he read the last will and testament of Ruby Martinez. The mumbo jumbo seemed to go on forever and Al zoned out, his heart hammering, his palms sweating. Through the window he could see the top platform of the Sky Tower, a line of people in safety harnesses, waiting to jump off.

'To my son, Alistair Black, I leave the sum of five hundred and fifty-three thousand dollars, my property at Rotowaro, and all the contents therein.'

To my son.

Brian opened a safety deposit box and slid a heavily-labelled bunch of keys across the desk to him. 'It's a bit of a drive, I'm afraid.'

'I know. I've been once before,' he said, and shoved the keys back across the desk. 'I don't want it, and I certainly don't want to search through all her stuff either.'

Kate put a restraining hand on his arm. 'Al, think about it. Let's at least take a look.'

Brian nodded and agreed, 'Kate's right. I can arrange a clearance and a sale for you in due course, but there might be some items you'd like …?'

Something buzzed and crackled on his desk.

'Ah, I'm sorry. I have another client waiting. Why don't we meet for dinner before you head back? We can have a better talk, off the record and all that.'

'Did you know her, Ruby?'

'A little, yes.'

He left it to Kate to pick up the bunch of keys and make arrangements with Brian. He just couldn't get his head past those three, powerful words; To My Son. When they got outside on the pavement, he'd walked half a mile or so in the wrong direction before Kate snatched at his sleeve and pulled him to a stop.

'She had to *die* before she could acknowledge I was her son?'

'I know, *I know,*' she said. 'Can we get a drink or something? It's too hot for this marching.'

She guided him back towards the harbour, where there was a breeze ruffling the water and they shared a bottle of Sauvignon Blanc from a local vineyard. Ironically, it was cheaper to buy the same label in the supermarket back home, but Kate pointed out that he didn't need to go looking too closely at the price any more.

'Five hundred thousand dollars is a fair wad, even in old money.'

'I don't want it. I'll give it all to Tom and Maisie. It means nothing to me.'

She sighed and filled his glass. 'Are you going to let me be the voice of reason here?'

'I'm being a jerk, aren't I?'

'I understand your feelings, I really do.'

'I just want to know *why?*'

'Guilt? I dunno, maybe she had an awful life herself, but she clearly wanted to make some sort of gesture, at the end.'

'What fucking use was that, *at the end?*' he said, hunting for his cigarettes. The temptation to light one was overpowering but he threw the packet down and drained the wine instead. He felt suddenly, inexplicably, close to tears. It made him feel stupid, a grown man crying in the street, all this emotion wasted on someone he'd never known. Kate got up and came round to his side of the table and cradled his head against her. 'Al –'

'Don't do that, I'll be a blubbery mess,' he said, so she went to sit down again and passed him a tissue.

'Where are you up to with the adventures of Jim Silver?'

'What's that got to do with anything?'

'Quite a lot, I think. You left me with an interesting piece of dialogue at the end of the last book. Jim said something about death being the ultimate beginning and that's why we are all born with our eyes closed and die with them wide open.'

'Did I honestly write that rubbish? It's not true. My eyes *are* open, possibly for the first time in my life, and I'm looking at you. And I'm still alive.'

She smiled a long, thoughtful smile.

They hired a car and drove south from the centre of Auckland to Ruby's house in the middle of nowhere. New Zealand was an odd country, too young to have any soul buried in its soil. The little townships they passed through were ex-mining communities from the last century, most of which resembled stage sets from the American Old West. The countryside in between was unremarkable, monotonous, and bone-dry brown. The only divisions running across the land were thousands of miles of identical wire fencing.

Kate read sections out of a tourist guide about the gold and silver mining industries but soon, even she lost interest in the scenery. 'I can't imagine anyone wanting to live out here, alone.'

'Maybe if you didn't want to be found?'

'Are you sure this is right road?'

'It's the *only* road.'

She fanned her face with the map and turned up the air-con. When the dirt track to Ruby's property came into view, his stomach turned over with the memory of his last shaming visit. Mostly wooden, like most of the houses in the country, the bungalow sat in a pleasant enough location, surrounded with some semblance of a parched garden.

When he killed the engine and the dust cloud settled, they sat for a moment contemplating the scene before them. It didn't look like the property of a movie star. Kate fumbled with the keys. Inside, it was just as he remembered some fifteen years ago. He sank onto the first available chair in the main living room and took a long draught of bottled water. The place was crammed with books, film posters, and memorabilia. It presented an opportunity for answers and information, but now that he was faced with all her belongings, the prospect of how to go about it seemed altogether too complicated and weighed down with a tangle of emotions.

Outside, the sky looked too vast for the scrubby land, and all he could really see was his mum and dad back at Chathill, the meandering stone walls, and the way the dirty, unwashed clouds draped across the mountains. New Zealand had no real identity, and it came to him that he didn't belong here. In a way, the sure knowledge of that was strangely comforting. This place, flooded as it was with uncompromising white light, seemed to strip back the very flesh from his bones.

'How do you want to do this?' Kate said, breaking into his daydream.

'I don't actually want to do it.'

'Right. I'll have a look around then, should I?'

He waited outside, turning a cigarette over and over, pathetically grateful to her. Presently, she emerged with a box and some rolled up posters. He took the items from her and placed them in the boot. The remnants of a life. It seemed wrong to just walk away with a box.

'Let's get out of here,' he said, kissing her hot, dusty face.

They reached the Coromandel around late afternoon,

stopping along the way at a friendly bar decorated with chainsaws, guns, and knives. It was all about hunting, fishing, survival. He wondered vaguely what Jo would make of it, when there were no choices. Along the way, billboards advertised the services of the local slaughter man; Homekill.

The drive along the peninsula of land climbed through acres of inaccessible bushland and forest, dropping eventually towards the coast alongside vineyards and long, deserted beaches. Given it was the tail-end of the Kiwi summer, the place seemed empty, but to Al the whole country felt empty. Maybe this added to his feelings of desolation. He stopped the car at Cooks Beach. It was the stuff of tropical postcards, bleached sand, infinite sky, and ocean, bordered by palms and kauri trees.

'Wow. This is where Captain Cook first sailed ashore in 1769. He thought it was part of Australia,' Kate said, reading from the guidebook, then she wound down the car window. 'Oh, but this place is just … *stunning*. Can we stay here a while?'

'Whatever you want.'

She dived out of the car and, shoes in hand, trotted across the swathe of warm sand. He went to join her and his spirits soared when she caught hold of his hand and kissed him. It was late afternoon and the light was softer, more diffused. Her lips were salty with sweat, but he loved the taste and scent of her. She was his home, his refuge in this alien place.

'This is so gorgeous,' she said, and a whisper of wind lifted the hair from her face. 'It's been tough for you, the will, the house, and everything, hasn't it?'

'Yeah, it's helped sort out a few things in my head, though. I mean, at least Ruby didn't have a fucking abortion. She gave me the chance of a better life, didn't she?'

She frowned at him, then walked on.

231

'Kate?'

'No, no you're right, she did. I think you're starting to forgive her, and that's pretty amazing.'

'You know I couldn't have got to this stage without you?' he said, drawing a line in the sand with his foot. 'This is where all the depressing, negative stuff ends, right now, on this beach. I want to take you somewhere where there's a beginning.'

'I like the sound of that.'

He pulled her across the line, then placed his hands around her face. 'I love you, Kate Roberts.'

Chapter Eighteen

Kate

They spent four days on the Coromandel coast, visiting the vineyards and exploring the few places to eat, staying at a basic motel offering bed and breakfast with no breakfast to speak of. It wasn't the most comfortable arrangement, mostly because they hadn't really forward planned with enough clothes, or shampoo. There was no air-conditioning, no Internet, and an unreliable mobile phone signal. The only shop sold mostly fishing tackle and the closest thing to a grocery store was a boat ride away, where there was also a rumoured Wi-Fi hotspot.

None of it mattered. It seemed of more importance to lie on the beach in the velvet blackness, holding hands and gazing at the stars. Kate had never seen a night sky quite like it, it seemed encrusted. The tension of the last few days was quickly lost as they relaxed into a rhythm that consisted of nothing much more taxing than making love, sampling wine, and lying in the sun. She knew they were lost in a time capsule, a dreamscape of sorts. The very location, that of being on the other side of the world, was in itself a barrier to all that had gone before or that continued to exist elsewhere.

Al was an easy companion for such a vacation. They had much conversation, mostly about food and wine, literature and people, although they'd managed to avoid discussing family and ex-partners. He noticed what she was wearing and had no interest in sport which felt overwhelmingly liberating. Sex was the best thing since sliced bread, after all. They even managed to make love outside, and afterwards ordered Sex on the Beach cocktails from the woodclad bar, giggling like schoolchildren. Most of all though, she relished the maleness of him and the fearless way he dealt with errant cicadas in the motel room.

'Makes a right racket,' he said and she agreed.

'Don't pick it up though, don't they pierce the skin?'

'Nah,' he said, casually snatching it off the wall, before flinging the poor creature over the balcony. '*Shit*, the fucking things bite!'

'Told you!'

They travelled back to the hotel in Auckland, and never had the luxuries of a city seemed quite so attractive. Kate carefully emptied the hire car before it was returned. Al was suspicious about the box she'd claimed in Ruby's bungalow. She sat on the bed and removed the lid.

'Don't you want to know what's in here?'

He wandered out of the shower, rubbing his damp hair. 'What?'

'Detailed journals, dozens of them. This is where you get your writing skills from.'

'I had to learn how to write, it's not inherited.'

'Do you mind if I read them?'

'Why should I mind? Kate, I trust you completely.'

'They look intensely personal.' He just shrugged, so she continued, 'It didn't feel right, leaving them for clearance people to find.'

'No, I guess not.'

'Are you really OK about meeting this guy for dinner, Brian Bennet?'

'It's just another line-drawing exercise, isn't it? And then I want to go home,' he said, resting his arms across her shoulders.

'I don't, I don't want to go home.'

'Why?'

'As Tia would say, it's a no-brainer. I'd rather stay here with you than go home to be embroiled into my sister's problems and my mother's dementia.'

'I'd like to meet Tia.'

'I know, and you … and you *will*, but for now, I want you to myself.'

He kissed her with intent, pulling her head back gently by her hair and almost bruising her lips.

'Wow,' she whispered.

'I can't tell you how much I love being with you.'

'Show me then. We've got fifteen minutes.'

She hardly recognised herself as she unknotted the bulging towel from around his waist.

They were almost late for their meeting and found themselves dashing hand in hand through the blistered streets looking for The Rialto. Breathless and flushed with the afterglow of fast, intense sex and the undiminished heat of the day, they arrived to find Brian already there, this time in dark, tailored shorts, briefcase under the table. He rose quickly to shake hands with them both before calling a waiter. 'Champagne?'

'Oh, well, that would be nice,' Kate said, wondering what they might be celebrating and if it was entirely appropriate. At Brian's instigation they toasted Ruby and although Al made all the right gestures, he did so with distinctly low-key enthusiasm.

'She was cremated, ashes scattered off Cape Regina,' Brian said, getting into his stride. 'Off the tip of Northland. Strange place, like some kind of global seam; where the Tasman Sea and the Pacific Ocean meet.'

He made a spectacular rolling motion with his hands, presumably illustrating the coming together of two masses of water. Kate nodded politely and exchanged a quick smile with Al, but his eyes remained on the menu. Once they'd ordered, they talked about selling Ruby's property, and Kate passed the bunch of keys across the table to

Brian.

'I'll get onto the agent first thing, and then I'll get back to you with all the details,' he said to Al. 'Are you still at the same address in the UK?'

'Er, maybe not for much longer.'

'Well, you can let me know in due course, these wheels usually move very slowly,' he drawled, draining his flute and offering the bottle around again, before bringing out an envelope. He shook out four antique dress rings onto the table, three diamonds and one ruby. They looked impressive, even to Kate's untrained eye, their dark glitter reminiscent of the Coromandel sky.

'I can include them in the general sale, if you'd rather?'

Al picked them off the checked cloth and held them in his long fingers, where they blinked in the candlelight.

'They're beautiful,' she said to Al. 'I think you should keep them.'

Brian tore into his garlic bread. 'Maybe pass them on to a daughter? You have a family, yes?'

'Tom and Maisie.'

'And grandchildren. Maisie's expecting, isn't she, Al?' Kate said, trying to lighten the atmosphere but he remained mostly monosyllabic and impassive.

The pasta arrived and it was sublime. Conversation trailed to a halt as they concentrated on lasagne and clam linguine for a while, and Al ordered two bottles of Mercury Bay wine. He made short work of a whole bottle of red, which was unusual, but she couldn't really blame him. It was a slightly surreal situation and even she wasn't quite sure what Brian was going to come out with next. They moved on to desserts and coffee.

'Is there *anything* you'd like to know, about Ruby?' Brian said, dabbing his mouth with a napkin.

'Nope,' Al said, and got to his feet. 'I think we're all done.'

'Don't be too hard on her, or yourself. She had a *real*

tough life, used and abused, you know? Bad health at the end, too.'

'How do you mean?'

'Stubborn old woman wouldn't go into the hospital until the last few weeks. She struggled for years with a heart condition, only got tested a year or so ago.'

'And then she died. I *get* it.'

He excused himself and went to the gents, swaying between the tables and apologising to other diners when he fell over their feet or handbags. Kate took a deep breath and began to make apologies, but Brian stopped her.

'Don't worry about it, he's just dealing with it like a regular bloke.'

She stirred the remains of her coffee. 'I suppose it makes me realise how much I've taken my parents for granted, the normality of it. The enduring, unconditional normality of it.'

Brian grunted in agreement and they talked about the visit to the bungalow. 'Did Al find anything he wanted to take?'

'No, but I did, on his behalf. The old film posters ... and the journals.'

'I'm *glad* you've got them! I would have removed them myself, don't want some old hack getting hold of them and blabbing about her private business.'

'I'm hoping Al might get some answers in time.'

'You know, you're a thoroughly decent woman, Kate,' he said, then leant back in his chair, where he seemed to quietly consider something before speaking again. 'I need your help.'

'Oh?'

'I think, maybe when you get home and things have settled down this would be better coming from you. I feel ... let's say, bound by a duty of decency to tell you, that Al's mother had a congenital heart disease.'

'Oh ... I'm not sure I understand?'

He leant forward across the table. 'There's a possibility that the faulty gene could be passed on, it's hereditary. Now, I don't want to alarm anyone, but it's advisable to get his daughter screened, Maisie, is it? You mentioned she was pregnant?'

Kate stared at the rings on the table, her heart hammering.

Daughter. Daughters.

Everything she'd tried to forget for a couple of weeks was about to rise up and be counted. She took a long draught of water and fanned her face with the pudding menu. When she cast around to see where Al was, she spotted him in the queue at the counter, waiting to pay.

'What is it called, exactly?'

'Ah, you've got me there.' Brian rummaged about for a slip of paper in his inside pocket, which he passed to her, along with Ruby's death certificate. She folded both pieces of paper and slipped them into her handbag. As Al walked back towards their table, Brian pushed all four rings onto Kate's third right finger and folded her hand in his. 'Good luck.'

Then he rose to shake hands with them both and she was relieved that Al still had the wherewithal to be polite. She'd never seen him drunk before but at least they managed to get out of the building with no major catastrophes, verbal or otherwise.

Back at the hotel, he said, 'Come here, gorgeous woman. Have you *any* idea what it feels like to have you in my life?'

'Shut up, you're plastered.'

'I know, but I *know* what I'm saying.'

She went in the shower room and he appeared in the mirror as she wiped a make-up wipe around her face.

'I still can't quite believe I've come away with a load of cash and no real sting in the tail.'

She tugged the rings from her fingers, so she didn't

have to look at him eye to eye. 'You need to put these somewhere safe.'

'I want you to have one.'

'I ... I couldn't.'

'Why the fuck not? Just choose one, will you?'

He disappeared from view and she heard him curse, stumbling over her discarded shoes. She leant her forehead against the cold glass of the mirror. What the hell was she meant to do with this information? It impacted directly on Tom and Maisie, Jo and Tia. She could, of course, run both bits of paper through the shredder at home and forget all about it; but she wasn't made like that.

Not so long ago she'd had no concerns whatsoever with the consequences of sleeping with Alastair Black; but that was before she'd fallen in love. So much for thinking she could have a holiday with sex. It might work for the twenty-somethings but it was a no-go for her. How long had it been since she'd felt like this? *In love.* Age was no barrier to feeling vulnerable under its spell, caught in the many layers of loyalty, trust, and truth.

When she peered round the door, Al looked to be almost asleep, spreadeagled across the bed. She touched his hair. 'Al, I'm just going to see if I can get online, tell Tia what time the flights are tomorrow.'

He grunted. Down in Reception, she logged on to the communal computer. There was an e-mail from George, just to say they were all OK, Fran was improving, and the sale was still going through. She dashed off a quick response, then fished through her bag for the correct name and spelling. She hated these medical sites, they were generally alarming and complicated and it was easy to get the wrong end of the stick. Annemarie was a classic case in point, punching in a list of symptoms and coming up with a life-threatening ailment in less than a minute. This was more specific though, it was even mentioned on the death certificate.

239

She read quickly at first, not quite taking it all in, her spirits sinking with every word.

Hypertrophic cardiomyopathy is a weakness of the heart muscle and symptoms are most often revealed when the heart is put under pressure, such as intense activity or pregnancy. In the majority of cases the condition is inherited, although it can miss a generation. Sudden death and collapse can occur, although rare.

No matter how many times she read it, the facts brought with them a black cloud of fear and apprehension. She sent an e-mail to Tia, then dragged herself back to the room on autopilot, where she crawled under the covers and curled herself around his back. He took hold of her hand and held it against his chest.

'Why are you shaking?'

'I'm cold, that's all.'

He turned to face her and pulled her into the wine-soaked warmth of his body, still completely loveable even when drunk. She stopped shaking eventually, but her eyes remained wide open.

The journey back was punishing. Al woke with a thunderous hangover and as soon as they boarded the flight for Singapore, he fell asleep, even with Morrissey blasting through his iPod. The connection from Singapore to Manchester was late, and by then it was already something of an endurance test, before they boarded another packed flight for some fifteen hours, this time with major turbulence and a head wind.

Kate began to feel ill and even Al waved away the airline food.

'Why are they bringing bloody Cajun chicken round in the middle of the night?'

'Can we please not talk about food?'

He put an arm around her shoulders and she rested her head against him, burying her face in the soft leather of his jacket, her fingers threaded through his. Ruby's diamond ring was jammed on her finger. It was too small but he'd told her to get it altered and cleaned and he'd pay for it. It meant he was coming to terms with the situation and she wondered how on earth she was going to deal with dropping the medical bombshell.

Tia was her other concern. Did she tell Tia the problem and let her work out how to get the information across to Jo, or was that unfair on her daughter? Really, it was Jo who was in the wrong by keeping the pregnancy a secret from Al. He had every right to know about it, and the way she'd broken his heart and continued to do so by letting him think she'd had an abortion was just despicable. On the other hand, she'd not even had the baby yet, so it could wait ... but then wouldn't that make her an accomplice?

As the flight droned on, the issues loomed bigger and became clouded with her fuzzy double thinking. By the time they landed at Manchester she was barely able to function, let alone think clearly, and she just wanted to lie down and close her eyes. Al found her somewhere to sit while he waited to get the luggage, then it was standing in queues again. Kate sank onto the top of her bag, feeling weak and nauseous, her head pounding.

'I'll come home with you, I'm not leaving you like this,' he said, 'I'll sleep on the sofa or something.'

'Why the sofa?'

She knew he'd said it because of the marital bed but Kate couldn't have cared less. As it happened, when they eventually reached the sanctuary of her bedroom, they both fell into the deepest sleep imaginable and she remembered nothing more till she woke, some sixteen hours later, not knowing what day it was.

Meanwhile, her symptoms had developed into the head cold from Hell, no doubt the result of being trapped in an airtight metal tube travelling at 550 miles per hour with hundreds of coughing and sneezing people. Al was the best nurse ever, surprising her with homemade lentil and tarragon soup, serving it to her bedside wearing not much more than an old flowery apron that used to be her mother's.

'You'll make someone a lovely wife one day,' she said.

'Been there and done that but I came away with less than a T-shirt.'

Through the window, she could see the tops of the trees, profuse with blossom and birds against a slate blue sky. He busied himself getting dressed and she decided she liked both bits of scenery very much. He spoilt it a little when he began to think out loud.

'Do you think I should gift Helen some of the inheritance?'

'What on earth for?'

'I still feel kind of guilty for messing up her life.'

'I refuse to feel guilty about anything or anybody *anymore*. Anyway, I thought you'd already given her the majority share?'

'Yeah,' he said, then after a moment, 'Do you think I should buy Chathill?'

'What, and live there by yourself?'

'No, for George and Fran, and Becca.'

'But it would just go back to how it was and get in a mess.' She put the mug of soup down and hitched herself up the bed, 'Actually, I think you should stay out of their way for a while. I had an e-mail from George to say they were doing OK.'

He sat on the edge of the bed and contemplated this and she couldn't help thinking how much more simple it had been on the beach. Now that they were back home their respective problems were not only poised to resurface but begged for attention.

'You don't know what to do with this money, or with yourself, do you?'

'I need to go and re-stock your fridge, that's the first

242

job,' he said. 'Then buy somewhere to live, I guess. My head's all over the place to be honest, the jet-lag doesn't help.'

'You can stay here while you decide.'

'Are you sure? I'll pick up some of my stuff from the farm, if that's OK?'

'I'm sure, yes,' she said, then began to cough. 'Sorry. Sore throat.'

'Can Marge and the puppy come? I'll leave Butter with Maisie.'

'Of course, I'd love that.'

He kissed the top of her head and promised ice-cream.

A couple of hours later, she managed to get dressed and reached the hall just as the landline rang. It was Tia, in curt mode. They hadn't spoken since the aborted Skype session, other than very short text messages, but presumably on receipt of the recent e-mail, she was curious to know if her secret was still safe.

'I hope you haven't said anything, have you?'

'Thank you, I had a lovely time.'

'Good. *Well?*'

'No, I haven't, but I intend to.'

'You promised!'

'I didn't promise, and anyway, it's become more complicated,' she said, then began to explain, but Tia lost patience when she came to the part about Ruby's will, and started to interrupt.

'What? I don't understand what you're going on about! Actually, I don't want to hear any of this!'

Kate raised her voice, determined to have her say. 'Basically, there are now *medical* reasons, *ethical* reasons, and the most important reason of all; I love Al and I'm not going to lie. I've asked him to move in.'

'Oh, for fuck's sake! Where does that leave me?'

'Tia, it's not about *you!* Look, Jo needs to know about

this medical condition. And she needs to tell Al.'

'It's *her* choice alone!'

'Not anymore.'

They disconnected and Kate stared at the handset for a moment, heart hammering and feeling slightly woozy from the exertion of shouting. When she heard the sound of something falling to the tiled floor in the kitchen, she moved as if in slow motion through the snug. The back door was open and Al stood there, his arms loaded with a haphazard array of grocery shopping, a bunch of flowers balanced on top. Her mouth possibly dropped open but her dry throat made only a croaking sound.

'Interesting conversation you were having there,' he said quietly and unceremoniously dumped the shopping onto the table. A box of eggs and three different flavours of Ben and Jerry's ice cream spilled out and rolled across the surface.

'Al ...'

'Talk.'

All the ingenious, more gentle ways of sharing the information, all the conversations she'd rehearsed in her mind over several days, were rendered useless. She was reduced to more or less blurting it out while he fired random questions at her. His physical reaction on hearing of Ruby's condition was like the coming together of the two seas Brian Bennet had described; a biblical-style tsunami of emotion. He didn't utter a single word as she stumbled through, trying to explain it all, and his eyes never left hers, but there was a palpable wave of tension in the small space, almost to the point of suffocation.

'Next question – next *two* questions, in fact. Why were you telling Tia instead of me? What's Jo got to do with it?'

'Good questions,' she barked, then began to cough, and he waited as she filled a glass with water and gulped some of it down, her eyes on the bottles of New Zealand Mercury Bay he'd slotted in the wooden rack on the worktop.

'*Kate?*'

In fits and starts, she managed to get it all out; Tia's job, Jo's continuing pregnancy. He was incredulous at this.

'How long have you known about Jo?'

'Not long, just before we flew out. It's just a crazy coincidence.'

'And you didn't think to mention it to me, this *crazy* coincidence?'

'Tia was worried about breaking a confidence, about losing her job.'

'Oh, she could lose her fucking *job?* Oh well, we can't have that, can we?' He raked a hand through his hair. 'Just give me the address, *now please.*'

She shuffled into the snug, fired up her laptop, and found the address, then he asked her to write down the medical term she'd used. 'I want to know exactly what it is.'

'Hypertrophic cardiomyopathy.'

'Hyper *what?* Show me!'

He paced about while she found the medical site and printed out the information. He snatched it from her and scanned it quickly, then just as she'd done herself, went back to the beginning, frowning.

'Al, can we just –'

'Have you any idea how serious this is? Hang on … Maisie had chest pains at Christmas!'

'She had indigestion, more likely. Don't jump to dangerous conclusions.'

'What, like my kids could drop down dead? Those kind of conclusions?'

He stuffed the printout in his back pocket, along with Jo's address then went upstairs, taking the steps two at a time. She heard him pacing to and fro, collecting things out of the bathroom and throwing them into a bag. He came down minutes later with all his gear stuffed into a holdall.

'I never thought you'd be capable of anything like this,' he said, grabbing his jacket off the bannister. 'I trusted you.'

'Al, you've got more skeletons than shirts in your wardrobe so don't throw any trust issues back at me.'

He ignored this, opened the front door, and slung the bag into his car. She followed him, momentarily stunned by the fresh wind.

'Where are you going?'

'Where do you *think?*'

So it was all over, was it? She had no idea because she was doubled over coughing every few minutes, her eyes streaming. He slammed the car door shut and she watched him reverse at a dangerous speed off the drive, a horrible clanking sound coming from the exhaust. Her first, her only thought, was that it was Greg all over again. The argument, the slam of a door, the accident. His death, her guilt.

Chapter Nineteen

Kate

It was a kind of death. Whether his or hers, it didn't matter because all she could do was crawl back to bed and sob but even that wasn't proper crying, it was more a miserable combination of heaving, coughing, and sneezing until it made her retch. The sheer frustration that she'd been unable to quantify any of it into words that made sense, or even simply to stay in control of the situation, came out as a torrent of tears, no use to anyone. The rest of her pain was plain old heartache, something she'd not had the pleasure of associating with since her teenage days.

What an insensitive hash she'd made of it. Would he ever forgive her? She should have told him right away and then helped him deal with it, but hindsight was always so obviously correct. Who could she talk to? Tia wasn't picking up her phone but then why should she warn her that Al was likely on his way? The cat was out of the bag now and it was Al's problem to deal with. His phone was switched off too, of course, but she left a pathetic message about driving carefully. She imagined him speeding along the motorway in his wreck of a car. At first he was jet-lagged, slumped at the wheel, then the exhaust was hanging off and the car was exploding into flames. She tried the phone again, but stopped herself in case he answered it while he was driving and veered off the road, down an embankment, the car rolling over and over …

When she heard a vehicle pull on to the drive, she ran to the window, but of course it wasn't him. For one thing the engine sounded quiet and powerful. It was Annemarie, wanting her waxing kit back.

'You look ... *shit*,' she said, when Kate finally answered the door. She followed her through to the snug. 'Thought you'd been on holiday?'

'Yes, well, the holiday is well and truly over.'

There was a split second of acknowledgement on both sides to this, then she burst into tears. She cried it all out, getting it off her chest in big, noisy sobs. Her sister sat mesmerised, passing tissues. Role reversal never came easily to Annemarie and she was mostly unsympathetic. Even when she asked questions, they were dumb ones.

'Where did you get that ring?'

'It belonged to his mother.'

'Which one?'

'Oh! What does it *matter?*'

'Just trying to show an interest! I don't get why you're so upset. From what you've just told me, all this stuff is his business not yours. Anyway, Tia says he had a thing with Auntie Fran, of all people! I mean, you turn your nose up at the blokes I go with and here's you, destroyed over some waster who dresses up as a clown.'

'Just go, will you? You're *not* helping.'

'Where's the waxing kit?'

'Bathroom.'

She went upstairs and clumped across the landing, then minutes later reappeared at the snug door. 'You know where you went wrong with him, don't you?'

'Oh, I know what your mantra is, I've lived with it for too long.'

'Then you should have learnt something. Falling in love is never an option.'

'You're a sad bitch.'

'Ha! You're the one with tears and snot running down your face.'

Kate sighed, blotted her face, and blew her nose. Was she right? In a way, it was still worth it to have had the peaks register on her life-ometer. It was the thought of flat-lining again which was thoroughly depressing. Although Annemarie might understand that aspect, her idea of a likely solution would always be to find another man.

'Anyway, now that you're not working anymore,' Annemarie said, winding the cable round the waxing kit, 'could you see your way to looking out for Mum again? I'm renting the house out and going down London for a bit.'

'*What?* When was all this decided?'

'Ages ago. Can't believe how much money you can get if you rent a four bed to a company. I'm sharing a flat with Carol, it'll be such a blast!' she went on, gyrating around the coffee table. 'Just imagine … *nothing* to clean or look after, no garden, and the centre of the fucking universe on the doorstep.'

'And what about Jake, and Robyn?'

'Robyn's going to college somewhere in Twickenham and living with her boyfriend and his mates.'

'She's much too young!'

Annemarie sneered at this. 'Rubbish! She's nearly seventeen. Jakey can go to school down there as well, can't he?'

Kate thought she might explode with despair. She didn't want to think about her sister's selfish mess.

'What are you running away from?'

'A *boring* life,' she said, sliding a set of keys onto the table. 'Keep an eye on the house for me, yeah?'

Trapped by her sister's hand again, that's what it felt like. She couldn't blame her mother but sadly, that's how it came out as they struggled round the supermarket. She felt washed out from a restless night, down to a mix of jet-lag and a stuffed up nose, but mostly due to a heart like lead. Every time she woke, she tried the phone, then finally switched it off in an angry fit. Sod him!

'Look at the price of those potatoes!' her mother said.

'Same as they've always been.'

'They go up every week. I bet they're foreign as well,' she said, squinting at the bags. 'Where are they from, can you see?'

'No idea and I don't care.'

'It hasn't done you any good, that trip. Don't know why you wanted to go gallivanting halfway round the world in the first place.'

I went for fun and sex, came back in love, lost the lot. *Sod him.*

The dairy aisle was painful. It was where she'd stood, not that long ago, talking to Al, her phone pressed to her ear as she thought up names for Marge's puppy.

'How about Flora?'

'It's a boy, a big one.'

'Lard?'

'Hey yeah … *Lardy*, I like that.'

They'd laughed and laughed, but today it all seemed childish. She pushed the trolley to the checkout and waited impatiently as her mother counted out coupons for five pence off bread, double store points on something else. Then the coupon didn't work because it was the wrong brand, so they held up the queue while a disinterested member of staff strolled back to the bakery to change the bread.

During this convoluted farce, she spotted Richard Jones from her school days, same age as herself, pushing his mother round in a wheelchair. He looked like an old man in brogues, shirt, and tie, and a comb over. A sudden vision popped into her head of Al, the way he'd looked at her through his fringe, the way he felt under her hands, and the masculine smell of his skin. The way he'd disturbed her sleeping body and woken her up inside, as if she'd been dormant for years, like Sleeping Beauty.

Good grief, she really must be in love.

250

The cashier broke into her daydream, leaning across the conveyor belt as if she were deaf. 'Sixty-nine pound and fifteen pence, love. Do you need help with your packing, sweetheart?'

'Do I look so decrepit that I can't put a few items in a bag? And I'm not your bloody sweetheart!'

'Well, *excuse* me!'

Her mother butted in, 'She's jet-lagged, that's what it is.'

Kate marched out of the store and across the car park. She threw the shopping into the boot, then revved the car impatiently when her mother stopped to talk to Richard Jones.

'His mother's got awful bad grout,' she said when she eventually flopped into the passenger seat.

'Gout, you mean *gout*.'

'That's what I said, grout.'

She slowed as she went past Annemarie's house and there was indeed a sign, Let By Redman Estates, with a red slash through it. She rammed the car into third gear and speeded up.

'She kept that quiet, didn't she?'

'Oh, don't ask me, I don't understand what she's doing.'

At Rhos House, they put the shopping away, then began sorting through the post. There were dozens of unpaid bills and the flat was grubby. Although Kate felt physically debilitated, she worked through cleaning and tidying, fuelled by a fermented mix of anger and frustration, highlighted every now and again with self-pity. Every so often she stopped and tried Al's mobile number but it remained set to voicemail.

'Who do you keep phoning?' her mother probed. 'I hope you're not chasing him, it never works you know.'

This made her laugh, but it came out as a hysterical choking noise, which made her cough and then her eyes

251

started streaming. Her mother patted her arm and put the kettle on, and the scenario was like going back forty years when she'd fallen out with her first boyfriend at primary school and she'd wanted to believe that her mother could make it better somehow.

'What's he like, this fella?'

How could she answer that? It was difficult to quantify Al in a sentence. The Charles and Diana mugs came out.

'Time you changed these. It all ended in disaster for them.'

'It's how it started that matters. And those boys. You can't wipe them out, it's already history.'

She wondered if Al had gone to speak to Helen. Her mother shuffled round the kitchen, going through the ritual, adding stale biscuits to a plate and then topping up the sugar bowl, even though neither of them took sugar. It was the placebo effect on full throttle. She was expecting to be exasperated by it, but found herself talking. No matter how hard she tried to be cynical, it all sounded like a complicated fairy tale, a bit like Charles and Diana.

'I was never sure of you and Greg, you know,' her mother said, eventually.

'What's Greg got to do with it? Have you not listened to anything I've said?'

'Everything. I've never seen you this upset. Not even at his funeral.'

At home, she kept herself busy and went through her mother's paperwork, paid all the bills, and discovered that her sister had withdrawn cash totalling around six thousand pounds. No great surprise. The other pertinent discovery was that of Al's phone. It was on the floor behind the laundry basket in the bedroom, suffocated with holiday washing. Again, no great surprise. Both things were beyond frustration, because there was little she could do about either of them.

She deleted her own message from Al's phone and noticed three missed calls from George, and a short, terse voicemail message. 'Where the bloody hell are you? There's a contract needs signing!'

Facebook revealed no clues, although she hadn't expected it to. Maisie had friend requested. She clicked "confirm" and saw lots of interactions with her friends about being pregnant, and a funny picture of Lard. She deliberated over messaging her, but what could she say? 'Oh, by the way, your dad might turn up with some devastating news'? No, she had to stay out of it, and anyway, it had only been a couple of days, although it felt like weeks, months even, of crawling face-down across a desert.

Later in the day, she answered the door to George. He looked pointedly at Al's sandy deck shoes in the porch, but his face gave nothing away. They exchanged the usual pleasantries and he asked all about the trip, which she answered in monosyllables between coughing and sneezing, and the conversation soon trailed to a halt.

'Fran's got a job,' he said.

'No! Really?'

'Maisie got her an assistant manager post at the animal sanctuary, the one by Gwydir Forest.'

'Oh! But that's just great.'

'Well, it's early days but I think it's good for her, being busy … back with the animals, you know? At least she can't bring anything back to the flat.'

'And Becca?'

'Oh, fine. Well, I think so, they never really talk, do they? Seems worn out most of the time, making new friends at the yard. Practically lives there.'

'And yourself? Enjoying retirement?'

'Learning to cook, someone has to.'

They both smiled and nodded.

Hypothetically, they twiddled their thumbs until George

set his cup and saucer down. 'Right, let's cut to the chase, Kate. Where is he? I've been phoning him for two days, I've got the bloody agent on my back.'

'I don't know. Look, we had a row. He left his phone here.'

'Typical! So, what was in this will?'

'Money … there was just cash, and property.'

'So what's his big problem? Don't tell me he feels fucking rejected again!'

'No, no it's more complicated than that.'

'*What* then?'

'I've already said too much. Please, don't pressure me.'

A huge sigh. '*If* you speak to him, please tell him that these bloody buyers won't wait forever, and there's still stuff to shift from the farm. They want it totally clearing.'

'Right, yes, I will.'

'I want this business wrapping up!'

'Yes, I get it.'

He grunted and made to go. She sympathised with George in a way, but being in the dark was not his sole prerogative. Yes, she felt unbearably hurt by Al's reaction to the situation, but there was clearly something bigger beneath the surface, and if Al decided to forgive her then he'd have to accept that forgiveness and honesty was a two-way street. He needed to come clean about his marriage, and about everything that had gone on with Fran, and his brother.

Tia called as she was in the bank the following day with her mother, sorting out the mess Annemarie had made.

'I can't really talk now,' she said, cupping the phone under her chin as sheets of paper were passed over for her to sign.

'Al's been. Thought you might want to know. Boy, was he mad.'

She scrambled to her feet and went to face the window,

her mouth dry with trepidation. 'Where is he now?'

'Out with Jo again, *talking*.'

'Did you get any blame?'

'No, he said he overheard you speaking to me. Anyway, Jo was cool about it. I mean she was OK with *me*. I don't know what's going to happen with *them* though, so I guess I don't know where that leaves *you*.'

Tia was typically blunt, and did nothing to spare her feelings.

'I mean, Jo was all over him, she went to bits in the end.'

Her heartache demanded more than a shred of attention over this. At least none of it had backfired on Tia. It was a silver lining of sorts but any complacency was quickly followed by a sharp stab of jealousy; he was with the young and pretty Jo, and she was pregnant with his child.

She looked back at the desk and the new bank manager shot her a patient look, so she rung off and apologised, then concentrated on the matter in hand. In the face of Annemarie's deceit over the deposit account, her mother had finally admitted that her youngest daughter was not to be trusted.

'She must have been desperate.'

'If you say so.'

Business completed, including the setting up of numerous direct debits and the cancelation of Annemarie's authority, Kate took a small detour to hand in Annemarie's house keys to the Redman Estates office in Conwy, while her mother sat in the car with *The Archers* on full volume. There was a moment of complete satisfaction when she told them to charge Mrs Annemarie Dixon the full management fee or whatever they called it, as no one in the family would be available to do it.

'I can't be running round there every time the tenant has a problem or they want to know how to work the washing machine.'

'No, I quite understand.'

'So please, cross my contact details off your file. My sister should have asked me first.'

'We'll write to her and explain.'

'Good, thank you.'

She couldn't remember the last time she'd stood up to her sister in this way. Annemarie had always got in first and somehow had her cooperating, usually because it was the simplest solution. It was surprisingly guilt-free, the refusal to toe the line. The final item on her agenda was the suggestion of a daily home help at Rhos House.

'You can easily afford it.'

'I might not want one,' her mother said. 'Can't you do it? It's only a bit of shopping.'

'No, Mum, not all the time. I'll have to look for another job.'

'I don't want strangers coming in.'

'They won't be a stranger after a couple of weeks, will they?'

'They'll see all me drawers.'

'I'm sure they've seen underwear in all its many forms.'

As she was restocking the little fridge with one slice of corned beef, a ready-cooked sausage, and two pickled eggs, she tried to remember the grateful feelings she'd expressed to Brian Bennet about her parents. She partially opened the bottle of mayonnaise and took the seal from around a tub of butter, otherwise her mother couldn't open them, and blinked away a couple of errant tears. When she looked at the back of her mother's white head, nodding forwards onto her shrivelled chest in the pose of an afternoon nap, an irrational fear flitted across her subconscious.

What was that about? Fear of growing old or fear of loneliness? A niggling feeling that love may have passed her by? Had she blown her second chance, her amazing second chance, with one mistake?

She found out much sooner than she'd anticipated. The following lunchtime he bounced noisily onto the drive in a cloud of black smoke, and the second he stepped from the car, her resolve to at least defend her actions buckled like cheap tin. It was easy with Mother and Annemarie, but Al was a different prospect altogether.

The desire to throw her arms around him was severely tempered by his grim expression. It was his turn to look wretched. His clothes looked like he'd slept in them, but his bleary eyes said otherwise.

'Hi …' she faltered. 'I was worried.'

'Did I leave my phone here?'

'Yes, yes you did.'

'Can I come in?'

She stepped back from the door and he went silently into the snug, where they moved awkwardly around each other in the small space. She handed over his mobile then waited patiently as he switched it on and listened to several messages, the most prominent of which was George's, shouting something about the contract of sale. After a minute or so of this, she began to feel like a spare part in her own home.

'Tia called me,' she prompted. 'I hope you got something sorted with Jo. Did you? Al?'

He glanced up briefly from scrolling through the rest of his messages.

'I did, yeah.'

She folded her arms, irked by his attitude. 'Can we talk about this? All right, look, I'm *sorry* you had to hear it all secondhand but … are you going to look at me or not? It's like talking to Tia!'

He held up a hand, which felt horribly like a snub, and dialled a number, while her blood pounded noisily through her ears, and she paced about like Stilton held in a tight circle, champing at the bit. Eventually, someone answered his call and he ran a hand through his hair.

'It's me ... stop yelling! Yes, I've pulled out ... *Yes*, there's a good reason. Meet me at the farm, alone ... in about an hour? I've got something I need to tell you. It's important.'

Finally, he slid the phone into his jacket and passed a hand over his face. 'I've had a hellish three days, can't think straight.'

'It's not been great for me either. You could have called me, somehow!'

'Look, when I overheard you on the phone to Tia, I panicked. I'm still panicking. You've had me running all over the country like an idiot, scaring the living daylights out of Tom and Maisie.'

She sighed at this. 'Obviously, I didn't mean for it to happen like that.'

'Ruby knows how to throw a good curveball, doesn't she?'

'You can't blame *her.*'

'I wonder how long you'd have kept it a secret?'

'A secret? That's a bit rich! Coming from you, owner of a fine family skeleton. Don't you *dare* judge me over any of this unless you are prepared to open your own wardrobe door.'

'My past has got nothing to do with what's just happened.'

'It's got everything to do with us, though.'

She hadn't even raised her voice but he looked crushed, as if her words had cut off his fragile life supply, and he slumped down heavily onto the sofa. Time didn't seem to pass and there was a moment of tense suspension, a crossroads of tangled emotions.

'What do you want to know?' he said quietly.

'The truth. About you and Fran. And about this ... this *feud* with George.'

His eyes locked on to hers and she was thrown by what she saw there, almost to the point where she forgot what she was saying or asking. Everything she'd learnt about love, about herself, seemed mirrored. The abstract part of her psyche, those unexplainable aspects of herself which made her Kate, seemed to belong there.

'I slept with Fran,' he said.

It shot out and pierced her heart like a blunt arrow.

There was an edge of belligerence or self-loathing in his voice, as if he were maybe throwing out a challenge. She didn't flinch, at least not outwardly, because deep down she'd already known.

'Did you have an affair?'

He closed his eyes and shook his head. 'No. A one-off, both drunk.'

'Go on.'

'Nothing much to tell. I was in a bad place after my so-called mother couldn't bring herself to look at me. Helen had thrown me out and Fran was ... well, she was just there, miserable with George about something. It was despicable, there's no excuse, and I *hate* it ever happened. And I pay for it *every* fucking day.'

So, now she had the truth. Al had slept with his brother's wife, and yet, she felt some crazy relief that it had been a one-night stand and not a full-blown affair. An affair meant love, meant deception and plotting. A one-night stand meant drunken sex, it was a different animal altogether, wasn't it?

He'd slept with Fran

'What happened after that?'

He slid a cigarette between his lips, then his gaze dropped to the floor.

'Al?'

'You know the rest, years of animosity and regret.'

'I get the feeling there's more.'

He looked up at her with a lazy squint and shrugged,

but she was clean out of ideas along this route. 'All right, what's going on with the farm? Why have you pulled out of the sale?'

'It's my home,' he said simply. 'I'm not selling it.'

'George will kill you.'

'Huh, he could make life very complicated if he did that. I can easily buy him out when the money comes through. I'm going over there now, talk to him face to face,' he said, then wearily got to his feet. She was surprised when he caught hold of her hands. 'I can't run any more, Kate. I know some more about who I am. I'm kind of sick of dodging about and feeling guilty. I'm not that person anymore.'

A beat. 'And what about us?'

'If you've any sense, you'll start running in the opposite direction.'

'What if I don't want to?'

'Now, why would an intelligent woman like you want to be with me after everything I've told you and everything I've done? I think you wanted a piece of me ... but maybe not the whole, permanent package? You said something once, about risks bringing out the best and the worst in human nature. Can't have one without the other, that's what you said.'

Why would nothing come out of her mouth? He'd crossed an unforgivable line.

He'd slept with Fran.

Resignation crossed his face. He dropped her hands and made for the door, closing it quietly behind him this time, and she crossed to the window. His car backed slowly off the drive, the front bumper just clipping the kerb and making a horrible scraping noise. The gears clunked out of reverse and he sped away, a billow of toxic smoke following, eyes front.

Presently, she went to her car and brushed off the sweet, damp cherry and apple blossom from the windscreen. Was his past infidelity a problem, or was it a question of pride? How many chances of love did one come across in a single lifetime?

She drove slowly along the valley road with the windows partly open. The sharp air helped her to crystallise all those thoughts, suspicions and buried emotions which had possessed her since the day she'd met Alastair Black. He might have unearthed a new direction for himself, but could she honestly take that leap with him, or was he just too much of a gamble?

When she pulled up outside Chathill, George's vehicle was there, parked at an odd angle, and so was Al's wreck of a car. The farmhouse looked stripped bare, like a shell of its former self and she couldn't help drawing a parallel with Al. The front door was wide open and a single red kite hovered silently above the roofline, which was less reassuring.

Taking a deep breath, she walked slowly, purposefully, into the hallway; then as she heard voices, froze.

Chapter Twenty

Al

He managed to drive around the corner from Kate's house, then stopped the car by the park and watched people walking their dogs, kids riding bicycles, normal family stuff.

He felt like his guts had been kicked to the moon.

At first he told himself it was just tiredness and stress, but he knew what it really was. It was like being on a perpetual rollercoaster, set at such a speed that you couldn't really contemplate jumping off. The first drop had been Ruby's death and finding out about the heart condition, and then a mix of small loops with Jo and the baby, and then all those highs with Kate.

Kate. She hadn't mentioned the L word all the time they'd been away and he had a horrible feeling he'd been some kind of experiment for a woman who'd wanted to taste some excitement. He'd fallen so very hard for her, but then he'd needed, felt compelled almost, to give her a chance to walk away. Like all the other women in his life.

It wasn't pity that had him wiping his eyes, although sometimes he did feel cursed. Maybe it was some sort of Maori spell, but no, he was done with guilt and self-pity. And he *was* tired, spaced out with all the driving, the meetings, and explanations. If he rested his head on the steering wheel he could easily fall asleep, but there was one more conversation he had to have. He turned the key in the ignition.

The verdant green tunnel of trees along the valley was his real homecoming, and he knew for certain that his decision about Chathill was the right one, at the right time. In his mind's eye, his children and his grandchildren were running about the paddocks and clambering over the walls, and right now it was the only vision he had of his future, the only motivation spurring him on. He had Ruby to thank for this of course, but hers was a double-sided legacy, one side safe and smooth and the other a jagged blade of uncertainty. Seesawing between good and bad was not an uncommon position as of late.

When he'd set eyes on Jo and his gaze had travelled down her body to the swelling location of their child, she'd broken down. There wasn't much to talk about because he knew he didn't love her, *she* knew he didn't love her, but they were both overwhelmed by the strange solidarity it created in providing something positive for their unexpected offspring.

She was seeing someone else, but Al felt removed from any sense of injustice. He'd not even been especially angry with her, more dismayed and betrayed.

'I'm just so glad you didn't have an abortion, but I'm so *fucking* mad you kept it from me! *Why?*'

'I just … changed my mind. Some of the stuff you said, it got to me.'

She'd cried torrents of over-emotional tears, totally out of character, but that was maybe hormonal. Anyway, none of it mattered. She'd dealt with the medical news in her usual calm, practical way and the whole visit had been easier than he'd been expecting, although his complacency soon flew out of the window, replaced by the dread of telling his children they needed to get tested for something possibly life-threatening.

He'd bottled out with Tom, calling him by phone rather than be faced with the wrath of Bernice and the bubbly excitement of the boys. Maisie had allowed him to book an instant appointment at a private clinic for an ECG and some other tests. Maisie's fiancé, Simon, had looked into it all and researched it more thoroughly, his medical brain quickly assimilating the facts and understanding what it meant.

'Al, I know it's scary, but it's doubtful Tom and Maisie are affected. It tends to show up in teenage years. And given how active they've both been, I don't think we need to panic.'

'But it can jump generations. What about Barney and Rupe?'

'They can get tested, the treatment's simple enough.'

Personally, he felt this was over-simplifying but he tried not to dwell on it too much as the tension became unbearable. And now he was home. He pulled up outside the farm and clambered out of the car, then stood for a moment, drinking it all in, inhaling the scented earth and willing the serenity of it to somehow get under his skin. He knew it would in time, but right now he needed some kind of intravenous drip. If he stopped to think about everything, he felt physically sick.

He slipped a cigarette between his dry lips and looked across to the house. All the doors and windows were wide open and his old bedroom curtains were billowing out, flapping in the breeze. It looked better for the clear-out if he was honest, and he felt a faint stir of enthusiasm at the thought of breathing some life into it, something fresh and untarnished.

First though, he needed to have a conversation. George was in there somewhere. He walked through the hall and into the study – straight into the business end of his father's old rifle. He jerked his head back an inch. It had the lingering smell of cordite about it, or was that his imagination?

'Go on then, pull the trigger. Fire another blank.'

George looked down the sights and followed him around the room, until Al knocked the barrel away.

'You've done this before, when I beat you at

orienteering, and again when Clare Edwards said she didn't want to go out with you.'

'Lucky for you, it's not loaded.'

'Load it then, go on. The bullets are right there. I'm not even a moving target.'

He walked around the small space. Everything was piled into the middle of the room, all the stuff they didn't know what to do with; boxes of old school books and reports, china pigs, and dried-up fountain pens. The old gun cabinet was off the wall, exposing a square of old-fashioned wallpaper and some childish scribbles.

'Do you remember Dad teaching us how to shoot with this?' George said, running his hand along the smooth beechwood stock. He lifted it to his shoulder and followed the path of a lone blackbird flitting past the window. 'The old rimfire eh? Point twenty-two bolt action. *Boom!*'

He made a poor imitation of the gun being fired, then lowered it and sneered. 'You were always better at hitting a moving target than I was. Better at everything, in fact.'

Al heaved a deep sigh. 'Can we get past this, move it on a bit?'

'To now, you mean? To why you want to keep Chathill and rub my nose in it, huh? Dangle it in front of Fran? For it to be a constant fucking reminder of what you did?'

He couldn't believe George was still trotting out the old argument, as if he'd committed the act single-handed. 'Fran was there as a willing accomplice, you know?'

'Leave Fran out of this.'

'Why? You pushed her to the brink of desperation!'

'Rubbish!'

'You promised children, knowing you were virtually sterile, just like Dad. You put her through *all* of that, *all* the tests, and then you refused to adopt. She was heartbroken, you selfish bastard!'

George pushed his face up close. 'Oh, so you stepped in and saved her, did you? Got her up the duff for me? It's a good job Becca looks like Fran and not you.'

'Consider this. If it hadn't happened, Becca wouldn't be here now and Fran would likely have gone off and met someone else.'

'Oh, so you did me a *favour?*'

'It's one way of looking at it.'

'So long as you come up smelling of roses, eh?'

'I kept your grubby secret from Fran for years!'

'Maybe, but then you went and told Helen, didn't you? The three of us had a pact and you broke it!'

'I did, yes.'

Al went to the dirty window and looked across the greening paddocks to the outline of Snowdon's foothills, disappearing to a distant haze beneath a sharp blue sky. Closer to home, the broken concrete yard was full of weeds, but they were flowering and it managed to soften all the edges of neglect. Elderflower was especially profuse, foaming over the walls and fences, highlighted with long tendrils of wild honeysuckle and old roses.

There was a pile of rubbish too, a towering bonfire of hacked-up beds, old rickety furniture, and animal pens. He wondered if it would be cathartic to set fire to it. Some of the memories would do well going up into smoke.

'I'll talk to Helen, but to be honest, we might have to tell Becca anyway.'

'*What?* Over my dead body!'

'It might not be down to you.'

'She's *my* daughter!'

'Totally. I've never disputed it and I never will,' he said, then ran out of steam, tired of all the angst. He turned to face his brother and dropped his voice. They both needed to be calm. 'Sit down, will you? There's something you need to know.'

Al knew he was about to stick the knife back in, but there was a bigger issue at stake. He had to reopen the wound, and if it dripped with tainted blood, then so be it.

He took the crumpled sheet of paper from his back pocket and studied the words again, as if they might miraculously change.

'What shit are you going to sling at me now, huh?' George scowled.

'You need to read this.'

'What is it?'

'Ruby left me an unusual condition in her will.'

His brother sank onto a packing case with the rifle across his legs, his fat finger still curled through the trigger, as if it made him feel the bigger man. He took the sheet of paper, taking a moment to glare warily at Al before he began to read. As George studied the medical printout, all he could think about was the way Becca had complained about feeling ill on Boxing Day after the exertions of the hunt. She'd been so white-faced, too. That wasn't normal for a teenager, not after a day in the fresh air, surely? Simon might have a valid point about Tom and Maisie, but he had a horrible feeling of inevitability about Becca.

He watched his brother's expression as some of the repercussions sank in.

'The problem is,' Al began, 'The problem is, she'll want to know *why*. If we suggest all these tests … won't she? And then if Maisie or Tom or the boys get diagnosed with the same, she's going to ask more questions, isn't she? I mean, she knows we're not blood-related.'

George seemed to be panting, he was breathing so heavily. He shook his head and pursed his lips, going over and over the information. Then he dropped the sheet of paper and staggered slightly as he got to his feet. With no warning then, he rushed towards Al like a charging bull, pinning him to the wall with the rifle hard across his chest, his fist still balled clumsily around the mid-section of the rifle.

The element of surprise was fully engaged. It was like

they were teenagers again, only George was a lot bigger and heavier, and he was incandescent with years of pent-up anger. Al no longer had the energy to retaliate but since it was under his nose, he could see the rotating bolt of the rifle chamber, clearly pushed forward. From what he remembered, that could mean there was a bullet in there and the rifle was ready to fire.

'Put the fucking thing down!'

'Scared, eh?'

'Only of your stupidity.'

A touch of insanity crept across his brother's face which Al had never seen before, and then he heard a noise outside the room, like a soft foot shuffle. There was someone in the hallway, he could sense it. Maybe George heard something too, because his attention wandered for a split second.

He shoved him backwards then, using the length of the rifle for leverage – when it suddenly fired. Within the small confines of the stone-walled room, the ear-splitting noise was like an exploding bomb, followed by an inconsequential puff of acrid smoke.

George dropped the weapon as if it were neat explosive. For a long, startled moment he stood motionless, every breath sucked from his body. Al could see his mouth moving but his ears were ringing from the blast and he could only make out random words.

'I *swear* I didn't know it was loaded, I swear I didn't know, Al.'

He spotted her hair first. A red flare crept into the far left of his vision. When he finally drew his eyes from his brother's gaping mouth, when he dared to incline his head, it was to see Kate slumped over in the doorway.

'It was an accident,' George kept saying, over and over.

The fear was indescribable. He was petrified, everything seemed set in stone as he eyeballed his brother, one hand across his mouth as the taste of cordite hit the back of his throat.

It was possibly the longest thirty seconds of his life as he contemplated the fact that his brother may have shot the woman he loved. One of them must have shifted their weight because breaking through the roaring silence, the bullet rolled across the uneven floorboards, and came to rest in a film of sunlit dust.

His legs moved, finally, and he crawled to where she was sat in a tangled heap on the floor. She was dazed, or unconscious. He picked up her warm, limp hand and rubbed it carefully. 'Kate?'

There was a rip across her boot at calf level, but of more concern was the bloodied bash at the back of her head. It looked like she'd collided with the doorjamb where it met a ragged edge of stone. He lifted her hair from her beautiful face and noticed her eyelids flickering, caught a whisper of her perfume.

'Kate … come on, wake up, love.'

All the time he knelt next to her, George was hovering, blabbering in his ear. 'I mean, you know how Dad was, at the end? He used to leave it loaded all over the show, didn't he? Remember when he shot himself in the foot? He was hopping mad, wasn't he, Al?'

'Will you *shut up* and go and call an ambulance?'

He watched his brother slope outside to get a mobile signal, then turned his attention back to Kate. What the hell had they done? How long had she been there, and why? She was in an awkward position but he didn't dare move her. A trickle of blood crept down the side of her face and he rubbed it away with his thumb, then carefully snaked an arm around her shoulders and kissed her hair.

Her eyes opened but she looked unfocused and deathly white. By the time the ambulance trailed to a stop outside, full-on siren, lights flashing, the works, she was more or less fully conscious but shaking with shock. The small room filled with strangers and medical equipment, blankets and blood pressure cuffs, and Al had to stand aside.

'What the hell?' Kate mumbled, then winced when one of the paramedics carefully moved her leg and began to inspect the damage on the back of her head.

'What happened then?' number two medic said, looking pointedly at the rifle, clipboard and pen at the ready. George began a convoluted explanation, then tempered it and looked to Al for confirmation. 'We were clearing up, didn't know it was even loaded. It … it fired, just went off! She got caught in the leg and must have fallen. Isn't that right, Al?'

'Yeah. And tomorrow, he's taking that rifle to the police and handing it in personally. Isn't that right, George?'

'That's right, yes.'

In the face of this brotherly collusion, George looked like he'd experienced some sort of epiphany and kept trying to catch his eye. Medic number one gently lifted away the flap of singed material from Kate's shin.

'Nasty flesh wound that, but I'm more concerned about the bang on the head. She's going to have one hell of a headache,' he said, slipping an oxygen mask over her face. Kate looked out over the top, and her eyes seemed full of pain and shock. It was quite possibly the worst moment of his life.

He was allowed to travel in the ambulance but she didn't want any contact with him. George followed behind. Throughout the journey to Bangor they asked a lot of questions, most of which were directed at Kate and designed, he suspected, to keep her lucid and awake. Most of the time, he stared at the floor. What more could he put this woman through?

At the hospital they were made to sit in a waiting room, presumably while they cut off the remains of her boot, then cleaned and dressed the wounds.

'Tell her I'm so *very,* very sorry, will you?' George said

to the staff nurse.

'Can't I sit with her?' Al whined.

'I'm sorry, she's indicated very clearly that you are *both* to wait out here.'

'They must think we're a liability,' George said, after she'd gone, then punched a fist into his hand. 'Shit!'

'Agreed. Sit down, can't you?'

They both sat and folded their arms, staring at the pile of dog-eared magazines on the plastic table, until George got to his feet and began to pace, jingling his keys and loose change.

'Do you think Kate heard anything, I mean, what we were discussing?'

Al shrugged. 'You know what? I don't give a fuck anymore. Bottom of the scare list right now.'

George grunted. 'Agreed. I mean, she's not the sort to be indiscreet, is she? I'll tell you something,' he said, stabbing his finger in Al's direction, 'she's too bloody good for you.'

'Agreed. I've totally messed up there.'

'You think?'

'It's called a self-fulfilling prophecy.'

'It's called being a twat. I know this, because I've got the same badge.'

Al shot him a look of acknowledgement. Another minute of intense quiet, then George said, 'I'm sorry, but I can't stop thinking about this … this *condition*. What are we going to do about Becca?'

'Depends if you're ready to listen to reason.'

His brother took a seat on the opposite side of the room, drumming on the wooden chair arms with his fingers. 'She's been feeling tired, looks pale all the time. Have you noticed? When I read that list of symptoms …'

Al's stomach tightened. 'Right. Doctor's first, then. Just a check-up, nothing too scary.'

'That's what I thought. Should I tell Fran? I mean, she's

doing really well at the moment.'

'No need, is there? Not till we know.'

'That's agreed then.'

There was an unspoken, united strength in this, and Al hoped it was some kind of turning point. Maybe their relationship needed to get to rock bottom before it could be rebuilt, but it was a sad indication of how messed up they were, that it had taken a near fatality to reach something approaching a genuine truce.

'Anyway, what about yourself?' George said. 'Did you get checked out?'

A beat. 'Me?'

'You haven't, have you? *Idiot!*'

'Didn't know you cared.'

'Well, I do.'

Another epiphany. Two in the same day had to be some sort of record. Despite this, the afternoon dragged on and George eventually left to collect Becca from school. Al hunted through his pockets for some cigarettes but found only Freddie's orange wig. He pulled it on and looked at his crazy reflection in the vending machine. A leather-jacketed man with bags the size of potato sacks under his eyes, and bright orange hair.

'Idiot,' he said, and studied the row of chocolate bars, held in a wire rack before they fell to their death in the tray below. Who knew what the hand of fate would choose; B3 or B4? It was all a lottery.

An hour, half a family size pack of Jelly Bears and two chocolate bars later, he was allowed to see her. It was only an overnight stay because of the head injury, but he couldn't get much information out of the staff nurse because she was mostly transfixed by his hair and looked at him as if he were about to run amok with a deadly weapon, or laugh himself into a straitjacket.

'The police will want a word, we have to report bullet wounds.'

'Oh, it's all sorted out, amnesty day's tomorrow.'

'A day too late. And it depends on whether this poor lady wants to file charges.'

He began to protest his innocence, but knowing he was probably punch drunk with tiredness and quite possibly borderline irrational – down to the astonishing amount of E numbers in Jelly Bears – he decided to postpone all communications with officials and take the easy route.

'You're absolutely right. I agree.'

The nurse shot him a warning look, then turned to go, heels clacking down the ward. The woman in the next cubicle yanked the dividing curtain across.

Finally, he sank onto the edge of Kate's bed and kissed her cheek. She had a huge dressing covering the back of her head and a swathe of her beautiful hair had been shaved off. On the point of closing her eyes, she gave him the onceover and he bitterly regretted not removing the wig, but it seemed too late now.

'How do you feel?' he asked gently.

'Sore! And my best boots have been shredded.'

'Can I get you anything?'

'Some peace and quiet.'

'Kate, I'm so, so sorry. George is as well, he's mortified. He should have left the bloody gun locked up. I don't know what he was thinking.'

'I do! Someone could have been –'

'I know, I *know* ...'

He picked up her grazed hand and kissed her fingertips. 'It should be me lying there instead of you. I wish it was, I really do. I don't know what to say, what you must think.'

'I know I've had a knock on the head but just tell me, did I hear right? Rebecca is your child, but all three of you pretend she's not? And you told Helen all of this, thinking it might save your marriage?'

'Everything I've ever done since, all the secrecy and subterfuge, was to protect Becca.'

'So why can't you understand I was trying to protect you?'

'I just flipped out, with all the complications.'

She exhaled shakily and continued more slowly. 'At least I've got the full story. Everything makes perfect sense now. I can't believe how badly you've all behaved, and yet you gave *me* the cold shoulder.'

'It's because I'm an idiot.'

He dropped his eyes from hers, not knowing where all of this left him. Above all, he felt crushingly ashamed. Face to face with her , he felt compelled now to accept his fate.

'Why did you follow me to the farm, anyway?'

'I felt we had too much unfinished business, and I was right.' She paused to take a sip of water, and when she spoke again it was with a different tone all together, and there was a catch in her throat. 'And, I wanted to say I loved you, I *so* wanted to say it truthfully. I wanted to say I loved every part of you, regardless of what had gone on with Fran. And then you go and throw another curveball with Becca, and shoot me in the foot! Have you *any* idea what it took to swallow your adultery? For goodness sake, Al, stuff just keeps on coming with you!'

Adultery. All of this jerked him to a stop. He'd spent several days travelling along at the speed of light, strap-hanging on a zip wire, braced before he finally plummeted to his demise. Until she said those words. Her words of love may have stopped his fall, but now he had the feeling he was swinging by his balls, hanging over a pool of man-eating crocodiles.

I wanted to say I loved you.

'I *swear* there's nothing else … just things like the heart tests, and the police interview to get through. Helen might get nasty, not gone there yet.'

'Al, just *go away*,' she said, then turned over to face the wall.

Having nowhere to go away to, he placed the remainder of the Jelly Bears on the bedside table and settled himself into the winged-back chair by the bed.

Chapter Twenty-one

Al

The days following the accident were a lesson in patience. George collected them both from the hospital and they travelled back to Kate's house with little conversation.

She limped up the drive in her stockinged feet, refusing any help.

'I just want to have a shower and some downtime,' she said, turning the key in the lock. Al followed her inside, carrying a fifty-head bouquet of cream roses, purchased by his brother. He wished he'd thought of something like that. George waited on the drive with the engine ticking over, the rifle stowed in the boot, wrapped in a beach towel.

'How are you going to manage?' he said to Kate.

'I'll be fine, there's even a district nurse or whatever they call them, coming in every day to change the dressings.'

'I mean, with shopping and driving. Please let me help.'

'I don't need to go anywhere and I can get groceries delivered.'

She threw her keys down onto the work surface in the kitchen and went to fill the kettle. He felt like an unwashed, unshaven spare part. A passing glance in the gents at the hospital had confirmed his suspicions; he looked like a tramp. He just wanted to hug her and look after her but it was probably pointless pursuing any of this given his grubby presentation.

She turned to face him. 'George is waiting for you. Go and get rid of that gun.'

'I'll call you later, is that all right?'

'I might be asleep.'

'Well, will you call me, then? I'll get the landline phone connected again at the farm, and the Internet.'

'You're going to the farm?'

'Where else can I go?'

'But the place is empty, where are you going to sleep?'

'I can put the sofa cushions on the floor. I'll recreate Snowdon Base Camp,' he said, with a lot more enthusiasm than he felt. 'It's a game George and I used to play. Funny, the stuff you remember.'

'I'm glad you're both acting like adults.'

He wasn't sure if she was making a point about their brotherly love or just being sarcastic about base camp, so he made for the door. 'Call me if you need anything?'

A cool, imperceptible nod.

The police station was next. It was easier than he'd imagined because somewhere along the line, Kate had waived any accusation. He let George do all the talking and form-filling, and then they handed the rifle over, and that was that.

'Did you take Becca to the doctor's?' he asked George as they headed back down the valley.

'Give us chance. It's tonight, after school. Fran's at work till five or maybe later; there's a glut of abandoned hedgehogs.'

'Right. Let me know as soon as you know anything.'

'They'll likely do a blood test and then we'll have to wait a fortnight for any results. I can't hurry it up without blowing our cover, can I?'

'No, I guess not.'

Back at Chathill and alone, time passed as if the hands on his watch were rotating anti-clockwise. Sleeping on the floor in the sitting room was just about passable but only because he was exhausted. At least the phone got sorted out quickly and it was altogether a better prospect, having a reliable link to the world. He called Kate, pretending he was testing the line but she saw right through him.

'How are you? Do you need anything?'

'I'm fine. No thanks.'

'Phone sounds good. I've turned the ringtone up as loud as it will go, so I can hear it outside. Unless I'm at the back of the paddocks, can't hear it then.'

'Al … I just want some space, is that all right?'

The second he put the receiver down it rang again. Maisie had been trying to track him down. She blurted out her news first.

'I told you it was only indigestion!'

A tsunami of relief, he slid down the wall and sat on the floor. There was a small blood stain on the door frame. Kate. The time he'd spent with her in New Zealand seemed a lifetime away, and the current cavernous void was especially acute at times like this. He wanted to call her again, he wanted to share something good with her, but she'd withdrawn from him big style.

He couldn't really blame her, she was a Capricorn, after all. What would a sensible goat want with a bloody scorpion? She was standing, aloof and surefooted on a cliff face and he was running about in circles on the beach below, snapping his claws, then having to crawl into his shell.

Maisie cut into his thoughts. '*Dad?* Are you still there?'

He told her about his plans for Chathill, what had happened with Jo, and all sorts of stuff she wasn't really interested in, aware that he was talking gibberish half the time. He arranged to collect his dogs, including Fran's collie, Fig.

'Good,' she said. 'Four dogs in here is a bit nuts '

'Nuts feature a lot for me lately, both meanings. Saturated in the sweet stuff one minute then dipped into neat cocoa,' he went on, thinking he should write that down for Jim Silver. 'So, has Tom had any news?'

'Er, yeah, but he wants to tell you himself. Don't worry, it's kind of bittersweet.'

Galvanised into positive action by Maisie's news, the day passed in a more normal timescale. He set fire to the mountain of rubbish out the back. It went up like a tinder box, probably down to all the dry wood. He threw Freddie's pants and wig on there as well and the hair melted to a red blob along with the plastic ring out of the trousers and a few other bits and pieces.

At the back of the cattle shed in an old lean-to, he unearthed his father's toolbox and was wondering about dismantling the kitchen when Tom's BMW swung onto the drive. This could only mean bad news Tom had to have an official pass from Bernice to visit at random. If it was good news about the tests he'd just call, wouldn't he? And why wasn't he at work? Tom was always at work.

He waited impatiently on the doorstep while his son grabbed a huge holdall from the boot and a six-pack of beer.

'What is it ... is it the boys?' Al yelled, unable to contain himself.

As Tom walked towards him, he looked drawn, positively grim. 'No, me and the boys are mostly fine, tests came back mostly as a negative.'

'Mostly? Tom, come on!'

His face dropped. 'OK, they think Rupert's got a bit of a murmur.'

'Oh, shit, so there *was* something?'

'Still looking into it, you know what's it like. They're not even sure if it's related to the thing that Ruby had, but good that we got in early.'

'*Anything* you need for him, I'll pay.'

'Dad, I know. It's all under control. Can I come in?'

They went into the sitting room. Al was desperate to ask a lot more questions but Tom wasn't like Maisie, and since Bernice had come to office, so much had changed with his son. At least he'd stopped calling him 'Father'.

Tom looked around at the bare rooms and the makeshift bed on the floor with borderline despair. Cans swinging from his fingertips, he dropped the holdall to the floor and ran a hand through his hair.

'It won't be like this for long,' Al said. 'When the money comes through from Ruby, I can kit it all out. The boys can have bunk beds, whatever they want.'

'Do you think you could put that axe down?'

'I was just going to smash up the kitchen.'

'Can it wait?'

They sat face to face on the shell of the sofa frame and the one remaining chair, the lager and the axe sitting like cryptic clues in the middle of the floor.

'Thing is, Dad, I've left her. I've left Bernie. I was wondering if you could put me up for a bit?'

He tried very, very hard not to grin.

'It's just, well, I just can't *stand* living with her another minute.'

Al flipped open a can of lager and passed it to Tom, who swigged it straight from the can – something he'd not done in years, so far as Al knew.

'I mean, she was always a *bit* domineering, but when our sex life is reduced to me being tied-up at the office –'

'Come again?'

Tom flapped his hand at this and continued ticking off a long list of faults, with detailed scenarios of conversations as back-up evidence.

'And now she's started on the garden. I'm not even allowed sole residency of the shed anymore, it's *intolerable* …'

Al knew Tom had to get it all out of his system but he was simply repeating what he and Maisie had always imagined, laughed about. He could fully imagine Bernice with a whip and a pair of secateurs. No, no, he couldn't.

Kate had surprised him. The way she'd initiated them

sharing a room in Auckland had been the first hint that there were many layers to Kate's personality, most of them not on public show. The first time they'd made love had been quietly intense. It remained etched in his mind, and not for the reasons sex usually haunted him with.

It had him in mind of spring flowers and autumn fruits. How madly romantic was that? Wild white flowers growing into ripe purple berries had always struck a chord of sensuality in himself. On reflection, it probably had lots to do with her fragility, the way she'd trusted him with her failing – as she saw it – femininity. Trust *was* a big issue, more than a magazine for the homeless.

Once Helen had lost her trust in him, it had sounded the death toll, but it came to him that he'd maybe, subconsciously, used his confession of adultery to get closure on an already failing relationship. Looking at Tom prompted a sudden heartfelt regret for the passing of his marriage, but he was so completely in love with Kate that it obliterated most of what was happening under his nose, because the memory of being with her was eclipsed by the pain of being without her. The desire to drive to her house and plead for his stupidity grew more urgent on a daily basis.

In comparison, his son was beginning to sound increasingly upbeat, as if he'd had an early prison release. Al knew he'd crash and burn, probably when the alcohol wore off. Tom waved a third can of lager in front of him, like a hypnotist's pendant.

'Hey! Should there be flames outside like that?'

'Huh?' It took him a moment to come back to earth, then Al turned to see leaping flames outside the window. '*Fucking* fuck. The bonfire!'

Tom leapt to his feet and made a run for the hosepipe while Al just slung buckets of water at it until it was reduced to a sodden, smouldering heap of timber decorated with bright pools of plastic. The surrounding area was a mass of blackened grass and foliage, even the window frames were singed.

'Honestly, Dad, even at your age you're not safe with a box of matches! Why did you set fire to it so close to the house? Why have you chucked metal and plastic on it?' Tom said angrily, back to scolding him.

Al had no answer, other than it had felt good at the time. They were both wet and filthy. Tom wiped his face on an arm, his smart tailored shirt looking distinctly grubby. 'I remember burying Granddad's dog somewhere here. Me and Maisie made a daisy chain to put round her neck, do you remember that?'

'Audrey, yeah.'

'What are you going to do with all this space out here, anyway?'

'Make it into an amazing garden. Grow things in it, you know?'

'Seriously?' he said, sniffing. He poked at the remains of the fire with a stick. 'Is that Freddie's stuff there?'

'Yeah ... the flowers were dead and the pants were getting too tight, I think I put it through the wrong wash.'

'But the kids *loved* it.'

'Bernice hated it.'

'She hates everything!'

At this point, he had actual tears streaking down his grimy face, and there was a catch in his throat. It was maybe nonsensical but this was the one thing Tom had said since his arrival that held any conviction. He realised, of course, that this outburst of emotion had nothing much to do with Freddie and everything to do with leaving Bernice, the effect it would have on the boys, and the diagnosis of Rupert.

He put an arm across his son's shoulders and Tom seemed to sag against him, wiping his face with a sooty hand. Even though he was nearly thirty, it made little difference to the way it made Al feel.

'I'm *gutted* about Rupert and Barney,' Tom said, as if he had to explain. 'What will they think of me? They already think I'm a rubbish dad, thanks to Bernie. She tells them on a regular basis.'

Al was quietly incensed by this. He made a mental note to buy some more pants, bigger, louder, and brighter ones. 'When the boys come here, they'll see that we're the best dads in the world.'

Tom nodded sagely, but a little half-heartedly.

The back porch and the kitchen door were both open and the partially dismantled kitchen was likely filled with smoke as well. Coupled with the outside scene, the effect was not so much quiet rural escape, but more along the lines of *Apocalypse Now*.

For a while, it was like a permanent lad's night out. Takeaway cartons and cans littered the floor, a huge television bolted to the wall, courtesy of Tom. Encouraged by his son's return to normal behaviour and fuelled by copious amounts of beer, Al told Tom about his love-child with Jo and his complicated love affair with Kate. When it was all strung together, following on from his separation and subsequent divorce from Helen, it sounded more and more like the life and times of Jim Silver. They laughed about their current predicaments in a laddish way, but he sensed Tom's real opinion hovered between admiration, and disbelief. And this was discounting the loss of Kate's job, the accident with the rifle, and the family skeleton's day out. When it was all laid on the line, he could fully understand Kate's reticence to take up with him again.

In the meantime, the dogs came home. Lard was enormous. Marge was worn out by him and frequently crawled into the airing cupboard. Butter and Fig had formed an alliance of sorts, which created a snarling atmosphere of jealousy. It was a canine love triangle.

In between supervising dog fights and moaning about

women, Tom ripped out the old kitchen cupboards with a manic energy and Al somehow finished the last Jim Silver book. What he really needed at this point though, was Kate's input and opinion. Logging onto Facebook for the first time in weeks he saw that she and Maisie were friends. There was a request from Tia. He accepted it and a message popped up more or less straight away.

'Hi, have you spoken to Mum? She's blanking everyone, she's being proper childish lol.'

He asked Tom for advice about this. Tom puffed out his cheeks. 'No idea. I cancelled my account on there because everything I said seemed to upset someone, *somewhere*, you know? I'm amazed you even bother with it.'

He explained then about the Jim Silver books and there was a spark of interest, but nothing like the genuine connection he had with Kate over this character he'd created, his escapades, and most importantly, the accuracy and understanding of the decade it was set in.

Talking to Kate was the sexiest thing ever.

He decided to take the bull by the horns and responded to Tia thus, 'Hi. No, I'm in the dog house lol.'

A row of smiley faces came back.

A couple of days later two items of post arrived. Full of curiosity, he opened the box first, to find the fully deflated Chinese swimming pool folded into a neat square, with a compliment slip from the hotel in Auckland. He slung the whole lot onto the second humongous bonfire they'd made out of the kitchen and the back porch, confirming that his life was mostly rubbish.

The second item was a formal invitation to dinner, from George.

'What's this about?' Al said, over the phone. 'It's a bit Victorian, isn't it? Why didn't you text me?'

'It's a proper dinner invite. Kate's had one too, so it will be just the four of us. *Formal* mind, no denims or stupid hats. I've got a small announcement to make.'

'What about? Have you spoken to Kate?'

'Briefly, just to enquire how she is.'

'Well? *And?*'

'She's fine. I told her about Tom and Maisie, but she already knew.'

'Oh, leave me out of all the loops why don't you? Did she say anything about me?'

He laughed, sounding like The Count from *Sesame Street*. 'She's really got you all sewn up, hasn't she? Kate must be the first woman ever to give you a bit of a knock-back and here you are, desperate.'

'Tell me what you know.'

'I don't know anything! See you Friday.'

'Hang on! Any news about these blood tests for Becca?'

'I'll tell you on *Friday*. I'm cooking, so don't be late.'

The phone went down. He deliberated over calling Kate to make sure she was going to attend. It was only ten days since the accidental shooting but it felt so much longer. The prospect of seeing and talking to her had him in a lather of anticipation. *If she turned up.*

To save himself from going mad, but mostly on impulse, he emailed the completed book to her, with an explanation as to why he'd written three possible conclusions. Option one had him killed off, murdered by a single silver bullet. Option two was the most understated ending and had Jim walking down a lonely suburban street with his suitcase. Option three had him reacquainted with a woman from his past, his soulmate, from book three.

'I want you to choose the ultimate ending,' he typed. 'Whichever option you think is the most appropriate for Jim. Then you can tell me. Friday night?'

She replied in the affirmative on both counts, but it was a single, solitary sentence with no clues to anything else. By direct contrast, Jo called him and they had a grown-up discussion about him going down to London again and talking about access and money, maybe seeing a scan. This was pleasing, to the extent he booked train tickets.

When Friday evening rolled around, an authoritative rap on the door had Tom and himself exchange a look. No one knocked on a door like Bernice. Tom scuttled to the window and keeping flat against the wall, looked furtively through a chink in the curtains.

'It's her. Tell her I'm not here.'

'I'm not lying,' Al said. 'Anyway, your car's out there.' He was in his boxer shorts, ironing his best shirt, and his Abercrombie denims were flung over the back of the sofa.

'She's walking round the back! What now?'

'You could go hide in the airing cupboard? Ah … problem. Back door is unlocked.'

'Dad, *please*.'

Keeping below window level and crawling along the hall in his underwear, the dogs leaping all over him, was something Jim Silver would have taken in his stride. He reached the back door and stealthily dropped the latch, seconds before it was tried. Mission accomplished. The only problem was that Bernice clearly intended to wait, and paced around on the drive, looking up at the windows for a further twenty minutes.

'Tom, I have to go *out*.'

'You can't, just wait till she's gone.'

Consequently, not only was he running late but he sensed a vague impression of an iron stamped on the back of his shirt between his shoulder blades. Other than that, he felt full of anticipation for the night ahead. He brushed off his black felt fedora and shrugged on his leather jacket. As a last thought, he snatched a splash of his son's Givenchy Gentleman.

'What do you think?' he said to Tom. 'How do I look?'

'Like an older guy on the pull?'

Finally, Bernice decided to call it a day and as the acceleration of her powerful vehicle faded into the distance, he called up Fig and ran to his car. It made a single groaning noise and refused to start. If he got the bonnet up he could probably suss it out, but he'd get covered in oil so he kicked the front tyre instead and went back inside, the dog on his heels questioning his every frantic move.

'Tom, help me out here.'

The keys to the BMW came his way but Tom followed him outside and hovered nervously as he flicked switches, adjusted mirrors and moved the seat back. 'Look, just be careful, will you?'

'I'm only going five miles in it.'

'Irrelevant, as far as you're concerned.'

Fig leapt into the passenger seat and Tom fussed about her claws on the leather seats while Al connected his iPod and Morrissey's velvet tones flooded the interior. Nice. He jammed his hat down at a jaunty angle and rested his arm on the open window.

'How do I look?'

'Like a *desperate* older guy on the pull?'

Al rolled his eyes as the window slid back into place.

As he sped across the engorged river, the sun was sinking, infusing the water with a cool metallic sheen and it seemed like every colour was reflected there. Love did that, it found the romance in everything, changed a void of grey into a rainbow of opportunity.

He was around forty minutes late, not too bad, and when he parked outside George and Fran's flat, it was immensely gratifying to see Kate's car. Fran answered the door and there was a moment of madness as she and Fig were reunited. She looked so much better, like the old Fran.

'Oh, thank you for bringing her! I've missed her so much,' she said, hunkering down so the dog could lick her.

'How are you, really?'

'So much better. I *love* my new job.'

'That's good. Where's Becca?'

'Sleepover.'

A beat. 'Fran ... Kate *knows*.'

She looked up and caught hold of his hand briefly. 'I know, and we've talked. And so have me and George, I mean properly. Tonight is a fresh start. He's let go of a lot of hate, Al. Give him a chance, for me?'

He followed her up the narrow stairs, Fig bounding alongside.

Upstairs in the flat, there was a trestle table in the middle of the sitting room covered with a white cloth; flowers, Champagne on ice, candles, the works. George grumbled about Al's attire and insisted he remove the hat, but filled his glass generously with a cold, fragrant Chablis.

'You're late as well.'

'Sorry, sorry, long story,' he said, staring at Kate. She was in dark blue, something with a cowl neckline and her breasts formed the most exquisite cleavage, a chunky silver heart pendant nestling in the swell. He went to her first and kissed her cheek, unable to draw his eyes from hers as he made his way back round to the only available chair opposite. It seemed too far away. He couldn't even hold her hand under the table.

'How are you?'

'I'm fine, much better, thanks. You?'

He could have echoed her words and kept it simple but found himself talking too much, and it was all about the fire, crawling around in his underwear and the return of the Chinese swimming pool. Fran laughed, and it was good to see her so relaxed. Kate just smiled enigmatically. Although her eyes shone with amusement there was a coolness there that had him anxious.

During all of this, George fussed and flapped in the

kitchen, then emerged with four small plates on a tray, cursing at the dog under his feet. 'To start, we have seafood on a bed of samphire with a balsamic reduction of something.'

Al frowned at the lopsided tower of scallops placed in front of him. 'What's all this in aid of then? I hope you've not overcooked them.'

'Certainly not.'

'I hope you've not undercooked them either. Last time you tried anything like this we were all ill.'

'They are *perfect*.'

'He's been to cookery school,' Fran said, grabbing Fig by her collar and making her lie down.

'I'm not eating anything till you tell me about Becca.'

'She's just anaemic,' Fran said. 'I could have told you both if you'd asked.'

George grinned. 'Good news, eh?'

'Why couldn't you tell me this before? I've been worried for fucking days!'

'Keep your hair on!'

'He wanted tonight to be full of good news,' Fran said, warningly.

Some of the tension in his guts dispersed, because it *was* good news, and with the arrival of the main course – roast lamb – the conversation moved on to the New Zealand trip.

'I've been reading Ruby's memoirs,' Kate said, helping herself to glazed parsnips. 'I think you should read them, Al.'

'Maybe.'

'Why not publish them?' George said, refilling everyone's glass, this time with a dark Merlot. 'Get in before someone else does.'

'I think they're meant to be private,' Kate went on. 'Personally, I hate the way everything is plastered over the Internet. The sharing of someone's inner thoughts is a privilege, not a right. I'd hate her story to be ripped to shreds when she's not even here to defend it.'

George raised his brows and he and Fran busied themselves clearing the plates. Al let his eyes rest on hers, still unsure how he felt about Ruby's inner thoughts, but Kate's calm logic made it feel more comfortable somehow. He wanted her to expand on this, but it wasn't the right time or place.

'Did you get to read anything else?'

'Uh-huh.' She sipped some of her wine through beautifully outlined lips and he tried not to fixate on them, or her breasts. Or the fact that she was about to announce the concluding scene for Jim Silver.

'It was option one for me. A clear winner.'

'What, kill him off?'

'Yes, it was far better written, held more impact too. Had a ring of truth about it.'

'So … not option three then?'

'Well, it's not a romance, is it?'

Pudding arrived, a cherry tart with the pastry base suspended in the middle of the filling. He managed a small portion, but the longer he considered it the more it had him in mind of that old cliché, a second bite of the cherry, and how much it applied, hopefully, to him and Kate. He pushed the food around his plate and she smiled. 'You don't agree, do you?'

'I'm stuffed,' George said, patting his belly.

'It was absolutely delicious,' Kate and Fran said, and elected to make coffee. When they were all settled back in the lounge, with the table shoved out of the way, George popped the cork on the champagne.

'I'd like to make a toast. Well, more than one, actually.'

'Just get on with it,' Al said moodily.

'Fran and I have decided to renew our wedding vows and we'd like you both to be there as witnesses.'

'Oh, that's wonderful news,' Kate said and rose to kiss

them both, offering congratulations. Al did what was expected of him, but he felt fed up. He wanted to make a happy announcement as well but there was nothing to say and there were no kisses coming his way, no reunion of hearts and minds with the woman he wanted to spend the rest of his life with.

'And,' George went on, 'a second toast for good health. I think it goes without saying that little Rupert will have our love and support. Oh, and best wishes to Kate, in her new job.'

'What job?' Al said crossly.

'I have an interview with the council, that's all. I applied a few months ago.'

'The council?' he said, unable to hide his disgust, and she glared back.

The party broke up and they were all in high spirits, apart from Al. The way the evening had gone, he felt left in the dark, toyed with like a cherry tart. Like they'd all discussed everything before he got there. Like everyone's life had moved on except for his, because he was waiting for Kate.

She'd even killed Jim Silver. A bullet for a bullet.

He carried some of the plates through to the kitchen and managed a tiny smile at the sight of an old glass fish tank on the work surface. Devoid of water, and fitted instead with a heat lamp, it was occupied by a row of sleeping baby hedgehogs. Fran wrapped up the lamb bone for Fig.

'When we get sorted out with money, we're going to buy a little cottage with a garden, and I can have her back. Just the one dog, mind.'

He flopped an arm across her shoulders. 'You're both OK with me living at Chathill?'

'More than OK. It needs to stay in the family.'

He thought about these precious words as they said their goodbyes. When he followed Kate down the stairs, he was pleased to see she was no longer limping but the dressing on the shaved patch of her head made him feel weak with love. Out on the pavement, he placed the wrapped lamb bone on the car roof and leant with his back against the door.

'Nice car,' she said.

'It's Tom's.'

'Al, have you had this heart test yet?'

'No, there's no point without you,' he said, and reached to take both her hands in his. Before he could say anything else, she moved closer and touched her lips to his and it felt so good he manoeuvred her fully into his arms. The joy of having her so close was like a molten shot of adrenaline; it flushed through his body like the golden, silvered river, swollen with the spring tide.

He didn't know if he could quantify how he felt about her in a single kiss, but every nerve and muscle in his body seemed up for trying. She tasted of heat and champagne, and as her mouth opened to his the connection was undeniable, real and raw. The possibilities seemed endless, the future seemed like a safe, sun blessed place when she was in his arms. She broke away and there was a mistiness in her eyes that had her search out a tissue in her bag.

'When you kiss me like that I feel like you've woken me from a long sleep.'

'Sleeping Beauty?'

She laughed, but then it was awkward. 'I've had so much stuff going on in my life since Greg died, I've barely had time to find out who I am without him.'

'Hell, Kate, this sounds like there's a brush-off coming.'

She looked away and something deep in his subconscious snapped. Maybe it was something he'd known since the start. 'Here's an idea. I'm going to London on Monday. I need to see Jo again. You could come along, meet her new bloke and maybe I could meet

293

Tia? We could go shopping for new boots and fun pants, maybe pick up a show in the West End? *The Muppets* are on …' He trailed to a stop and she frowned.

'That's the strangest list.'

'Meet me at noon at the station. If you're not there, I'll consider myself dumped.'

She folded her arms and sighed. 'So theatrical. Your mother's son.'

There was no clue in her face, nothing to give him a shred of hope. He left her on the pavement outside the newsagents, her blue dress fluttering in the cool air.

There was a tiny morsel of positive thought in giving her an ultimatum. He told no one. Two days to get through and then he'd know if she wanted to be with him, despite the appalling trail of baggage that not only haunted his past, but seemed set to cling to his future as well.

Not having a better idea, he threw himself into clearing up the mess outside, and unpacking some of the boxes inside. He stayed up most of Sunday night, worried about killing Jim Silver, then woke late on Monday morning feeling sick for no good reason. When he looked through the sitting room window he saw that not only was it raining but Tom had gone to work, leaving his wreck of a car as the only means of transport.

The old address book was in one of the packing cases and he flicked through it looking for taxi firms, distracted by old phone numbers written in his mother's neat hand. Always ready to extract a possible drama, and with impeccable timing, Helen popped round for an argument to see if she could convince him that she was entitled to some of his inheritance.

'You've had the majority share of the house!' he said, watching the hands of the clock fast forward to eleven fifteen.

'I worked all my life for that house, you earned nothing. It isn't fair.'

'Fair? If I was a woman who'd been an organic, free-range, stay-at-home mother and brought up her children like it was the most important job in the world, and you were a bloke, moaning about the commute, we wouldn't be having this conversation.'

He moved to the fireplace and concentrated on his reflection in the gloomy mirror as he slid the train tickets and some cash into his inside pocket. When he glanced up, it was to see Helen's face snarling at him through the glass, and it made him wonder what on earth he'd seen in her for so many years. When did she get to be so mercenary and uncaring?

'I could make life very uncomfortable for you,' she said, almost sweetly.

'Are you trying to blackmail me over Becca?'

He turned to face her then and she had the decency to look away, a twist of the mouth, downcast eyes.

'You'd put a kid through that, would you?' he said quietly, then grabbed his jacket. 'Look, I have to go out.'

'Where are you going?'

'To see *The Muppets*. Drop me at the station, will you?'

A filthy look shot his way, but he didn't care. He cared about nothing except Kate. His bluff paid off and he followed her outside, his heart rate soaring.

Helen drove like a tourist, braking on every bend and slowing to a virtual standstill for every concealed driveway, or so it seemed. When she pulled in to the drop-off area at Llandudno Junction, he did a quick scan for Kate's car. It wasn't there, and his feet were like lead as they shuffled up the first flight of dirty concrete steps, across the covered bridge stinking of nicotine, and down the second flight of concrete steps.

The platform was virtually deserted even though the express service to Euston was due in four minutes. He couldn't keep watching the entrance, so he fixated on the weed-strewn rails instead, until the sound of the approaching train scorched along the track. If this was Kate's idea of some sort of dramatic denouement, he had to hand it to her, she knew how to tighten the screw to within a hair's breadth.

He lifted his eyes and exhaled as the train thundered in, the ground vibrating beneath his feet. It was over, he was finished …

He spotted her hair first.

THE END

Jan Ruth writes contemporary fiction about the darker side of the family dynamic with a generous helping of humour, horses and dogs. Her books blend the serenities of rural life with the headaches of city business, exploring the endless complexities of relationships.

For more about Jan Ruth and her books:
visit www.janruth.com

WILD WATER

BY

JAN RUTH

*Jack Redman, estate agent to the Cheshire set. An unlikely
hero, or someone to break all the rules?*

Wild water is the story of forty-something estate agent, Jack,
who is stressed out not only by work, bills and the approach
of Christmas but by the feeling that he and his wife Patsy
are growing apart. His misgivings prove founded when he
discovers Patsy is having an affair, and is pregnant.

At the same time as his marriage begins to collapse around
him, he becomes reacquainted with his childhood sweetheart,
Anna, whom he left for Patsy twenty- five years before. He
finds his feelings towards Anna reawaken, but will life and
family conflicts conspire to keep them apart again?

CIDNIGHT SKY

BY

JAN RUTH

Opposites attract? Laura Brown, interior designer and James Morgan-Jones, horse whisperer - and Midnight Sky, a beautiful but damaged steeplechaser.

Laura seems to have it all, glamorous job, charming boyfriend. Her sister, Maggie, struggles with money, difficult children and an unresponsive husband. She envies her sister's life, but are things as idyllic as they seem?

She might be a farmer's daughter, but Laura is doing her best to deny her roots, even deny her true feelings. Until she meets James, but James is very married, and very much in love, to a wife who died two years ago. They both have issues to face from their past, but will it bring them together, or push them apart?

WHITE HORIZON

BY

JAN RUTH

Three couples in crisis,
multiple friendships under pressure.

On-off-on lovers Daniel and Tina return to their childhood town near Snowdonia. After twenty-five years together, they marry in typically chaotic fashion, witnessed by old friends, Victoria and Linda who become entangled in the drama, their own lives changing beyond recognition.

However, as all their marriages begin to splinter, and damaged Victoria begins an affair with Daniel, the secret illness that Tina has been hiding emerges. Victoria's crazed and violent ex-husband attempts to kill Daniel and nearly succeeds, in a fire that devastates the community. On the eve of their first wedding anniversary, Tina returns to face her husband - but is it to say goodbye forever, or to stay?

Made in the USA
Charleston, SC
29 September 2016

CAS Paper 31

Priorities for a new century – agriculture, food and rural policies in the European Union

Proceedings of a conference organised by the Centre for Agricultural Strategy, held at Chatham House, 10 St James's Square, London SW1Y 4LE on 24 November 1994

Edited by B J Marshall & F A Miller

Centre for Agricultural Strategy
University of Reading
1 Earley Gate
Reading RG6 2AT

April 1995

ISBN 0 7049 0647 3

ISSN 0141 1330

Printed by TA Printers, 43-45 Milford Road, Reading RG1 8LG